The detonation rocked Kamahl back. The light was bright enough that he could see through his eyelids as the edge of the energy brushed him. The crowd was stunned into silence. The magic ignited the spore cloud and the explosion sped back to the mole, devouring it as the molds detonated in sympathy with Kamahl's attack. The dementia caster rolled on the ground, unable to stand. She had been flung back several yards, and the sand stripped most of her clothes off as well as much of her skin. Her teeth bared and bloody, she stood, gathering herself to summon more monstrosities.

W9-DDP-374

Experience the Magic

MAGIC: The Gathering®

ODYSSEY™

ODYSSEY CYCLE • BOOK 1

Vance Moore

CONNIE E. W. REGISTER
105 ELIZABETH STREET
RICHLANDS, NC 28574

Odyssey
©2001 Wizards of the Coast, Inc.

All characters in this book are fictitious. Any resemblance to actual persons, living or dead, is purely coincidental.

This book is protected under the copyright laws of the United States of America. Any reproduction or unauthorized use of the material or artwork contained herein is prohibited without the express written permission of Wizards of the Coast, Inc.

Distributed in the United States by Holtzbrinck Publishing. Distributed in Canada by Fenn Ltd.

Distributed to the hobby, toy, and comic trade in the United States and Canada by regional distributors.

Distributed worldwide by Wizards of the Coast, Inc. and regional distributors.

MAGIC: THE GATHERING and the Wizards of the Coast logo are registered trademarks owned by Wizards of the Coast, Inc., a subsidiary of Hasbro, Inc. Odyssey is a trademark owned by Wizards of the Coast, Inc.

All Wizards of the Coast characters, character names, and the distinctive likenesses thereof are trademarks owned by Wizards of the Coast, Inc.

Made in the U.S.A.

The sale of this book without its cover has not been authorized by the publisher. If you purchased this book without a cover, you should be aware that neither the author nor the publisher has received payment for this "stripped book."

Cover art by: Kev Walker and Donato Giancola
Internal art by: Matt Wilson, Arnie Swekel, Darrell Riche, Glen Angus
First Printing: September 2001
Library of Congress Catalog Card Number: 2001090123

9 8 7 6 5 4 3 2 1

UK ISBN: 0-7869-2675-9
US ISBN: 0-7869-1900-0
620-T21900

U.S., CANADA,
ASIA, PACIFIC, & LATIN AMERICA
Wizards of the Coast, Inc.
P.O. Box 707
Renton, WA 98057-0707
+1-800-324-6496

EUROPEAN HEADQUARTERS
Wizards of the Coast, Belgium
P.B. 2031
2600 Berchem
Belgium
+32-70-23-32-77

Visit our web site at **www.wizards.com/magic**

OTARIA

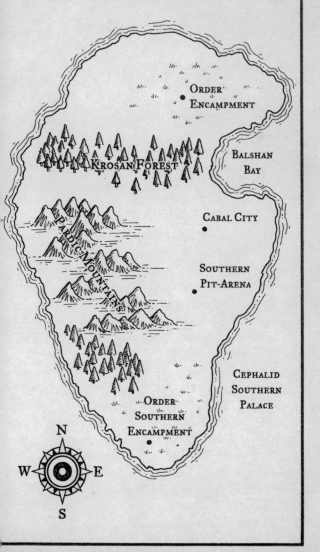

Order
Encampment

Balshan
Bay

Krosan Forest

Pardic Mountains

Cabal City

Southern
Pit-Arena

Cephalid
Southern
Palace

Order
Southern
Encampment

N
W   E
S

CHAPTER 1

The sun lay sullen to the west. Hovering on the horizon, its rays cast the hills in shadows. The pits lay ahead. Finally he was drawing near after months of travel. Kamahl looked at the heart of the games and saw only a gaping hole of darkness. The twilight prevented him from seeing the city that lay in the hollow. Even as he watched, torches were lit, the dull red light illuminating the site of Kamahl's future triumphs. From mountain obscurity he traveled toward his destiny.

Cabal City was the largest in the continent's interior, but only a few signs of its size were visible from Kamahl's vantage point. He could see just the roofs of a few buildings and

1

the residential quarters' laundry hanging in the still air. The city was held in a huge rocky crater, its sides uneven but highest on the western outskirts. The glow of torches and the streetlights near the great dome of the arena began to color the walls of the buildings as Kamahl moved closer. The flare of both ordinary fire and magic lit the streets, but the dark shadow cast by the crater walls shrouded most of the city in darkness.

The barbarian started down the shallow incline at a slow run. He breathed easily, even with the armor in his pack and the great sword strapped to his back. Skin the color of brass showed no flush of exertion. His smooth beardless features were calm. No sweat dampened his inky hair, and his violet eyes were clear. Living in the mountains had given him good night vision, and he looked through the increasingly dim light to the town's gate. The road began to rise and he breathed harder as he neared the city limits. The crater walls were notched, and the entrance reminded the barbarian of a pass through mountains, though far smaller in scale than the peaks of his childhood home. Drovers hurried a string of camels into the city, their whips snapping as they moved the animals through the high gate. Merchants from across the continent come to satisfy the tourney crowds, the warrior thought.

Kamahl breathed deeply, the prospect of the games exciting his blood more than the run. Years mastering the fighting arts lay behind him, and now he rushed to show his skills before the wider world. Veteran of many a duel in his home mountains, he wanted more than the championship of an alpine valley. The best fighters on the continent converged on this tourney, and he belonged here.

His stride lengthened as he left the hills, his boots

ounding into the road's surface. The guards waved the
merchants through, uttering only a few threats to increase
the bribes offered. They turned their attention on the jog-
ing figure. His light throwing axes softly rubbed against
Kamahl's wallet. He had run for days approaching the con-
est and lost what little fat he might have had. The strict
egime of exercise had refined him down to his essence. He
pulled up to the gate without any sign of exertion except his
eep breaths.

"Another jack," muttered a guard as he took a firmer
old of his halberd and moved out from the gate. Kamahl
rowned, for the soldier used the term for an arena fighter
s if it were an insult. He was a champion, and only the
bvious inferiority of the speaker prevented a demand for
atisfaction. The man looked nervously at a stack of orders.
he rest of the troops had withdrawn inside to the guard-
ouse. Two stout men-at-arms slowly lugged a crossbeam to
race the gate when it closed for the night. The road lead
irectly into town with only a portcullis to bar the way.
he wall was only twelve feet high and the guards served
nore to collect tolls than defend the city.

"Why have you come to the pits of the Cabal?"
ntoned a guard who drew away from the gate as if to
uck behind the wall.

"I have come into my own," Kamahl said absently, look-
ng to the city beyond. The guard was confused and
nconsciously gave way as the massive barbarian came
loser. The fighter drew his attention to the minor servant
efore him. "I will compete in the tourney. Where would
find the Master of the Games?"

The guard blinked at the bald statement but regarding
he warrior seemed uncertain how to respond. Shouting

broke out on the road behind him, and he turned from th barbarian to the commotion. There were several wagon backed up the causeway leading down to the pit. Kamah could see soldiers gathered in a clump in front of the wait ing vehicles.

"As you can see, the road is backed up due to a wreck. The guard said, drawing a little confidence from the sigh of his fellows so far away. "The elevator cable snapped an killed a mule." Kamahl just strode forward, ignoring th guard's outstretched arm.

"No profit from crazy men anyway," the soldier mutter as he stepped away from the barbarian.

The road's decline prevented horses hauling fully loade wagons into the city. An elevator dropped cargo from th staging area just inside the guardhouse to the bottom of th depression. Once relieved of their loads, merchants coul then safely take the horses down the slope. Traffic heade into the city rode the brakes all the way to the flat at th bottom, using the animals just to steer. The elevator ha just broken, however, and the snapped cable had behead a mule, overturning a wagon and blocking the causeway.

Kamahl drew a dagger, holding its blade against his arr He used the hilt to prod people out of the way, ignoring angr words. The decapitated beast lay tangled in its traces, i blood pouring down the steep roadway. Kamahl gathered whisper of power and wrapped it around the dagger's blad He shoved aside the owner and guardsmen and skimmed hi blade along the beast's side with a single stroke. Harnes leather and chains parted like air before the blade, singing a tension released. Kamahl shoved the corpse hard with hi boot. The barbarian's physical power became plain to th angry guardsmen. The donkey shot down the ramp lubricate

its own blood. The animal hit the railing, wood coming
art in a spray of rotten timbers. The remains of the beast
d fence fell to the ground below with a heavy thud.
mahl withdrew power from the blade and continued down
e road, walking just along the bloodied skidway.

"The Cabal pit masters bought that carcass!" bellowed
meone. Kamahl's ears picked up the conversation even as
continued away.

"Leave it alone," he heard someone else hiss. "Jacks are
crazy; just consider the meat tenderized."

* * * * *

Fighters from throughout the continent moved in the
eets. Kamahl saw races of all descriptions—faerie,
man, dwarf, centaur, and others that he could not
me. They came to the pits to compete for their own
ory and the prizes offered. Everywhere in the land the
ntest between warriors played out every day, but it was
the pits that jacks of known mettle found opponents
rth the sweat of battle. Kamahl came for worthy adver-
ries and to prove his mastery. Most of his opponents
re there for more.

The Cabal had opened up its vaults to supply the
izes. Booty from centuries of collecting and a thousand
ttlefields was available. Sages and historians were
arly as prevalent as fighters in the city. All converged
see the treasures drawn from the rock deep below the
ts. With the fighters and the learned men, an influx of
mblers and enthusiasts filled the avenues. Moving among
e throngs worked pickpockets, whores, and sellers of the
rbidden. The barbarian sauntered over the cobblestones,

seeing unfamiliar sights. Tents stood with ragged a
dirty men calling for custom. Though from the spars
settled mountains, Kamahl was completely civilized in h
cynicism. False wonders filled the streets as the hope
went from stall to stall, determined to find the lucky pr
that surely must be hidden in all the chaff.

Torches flared and some burned brightly with mag
enhanced lights. Kamahl took a second to feel the warm
of the energy with his mystic senses. Stretching forth h
mind and spirit he felt the beat of power and dissonance
contesting magics fractured against each other. It cou
only be the pits that called to him, and he hurried throu
the collected throngs to take his place.

* * * * *

The crowd roared its approval as two men moved in
the arena, the masses calling encouragement. Kamahl ha
bought entrance with a small nugget of gold from a moun
tain stream. He imagined the Master of the Games woul
be in the arena, and the barbarian was determined to fin
him. The building was huge, seating thousands. The wal
leaned inward overhead, evoking the feeling of an unde
ground cavern. Huge torches flared continuously behir
reflectors, directing the magic light onto the floor of th
stadium. Red and black sand covered the circular fightir
area. Inside the wide ring were obstacles and a few obvio
trap doors. Despite himself, Kamahl was impressed. For th
first time he was in a building that made him feel closed
even though it was several spear-casts across.

The two men on the sand moved together, and Kama
shook his head. The opponents were hesitant, and th

arbarian wondered how any could find such a match
nteresting. A young man standing close by noticed
.amahl's mild contempt and spoke.

"Do not give up hope just yet, sir," he said, shuffling near.

His clothing was dark and loose, the tailoring and rich-
ess of the fabric suggesting a person of means, yet he was
oung and had no attendants. Kamahl thought him likely
) be a lord's servant though he saw no obvious crest or
tandard to announce his affiliation.

"The name is Chainer," the man said, moving closer.
The pair are partners against Lieutenant Kirtar, a cham-
ion from the Northern Order."

"Kamahl," the barbarian said, glancing briefly at the
outh and then to the stands, "here to win the tourney.
Vhere do I announce myself?"

Chainer's eyebrows raised slightly at the boast, and he
miled. Kamahl turned more of his attention to the young
nan.

The youth still had a trace of innocence in his face, but
lready the fighter could see some of the hardness and
ynicism that characterized city toughs. The boy's hair was
n tight corn-rolls that grew down over his eyes. His only
isible weapon was a large, ornamental dagger that he
vore at his side. As Kamahl considered him, Chainer's fin-
ertips lightly brushed the hilt in an apparently uncon-
cious gesture.

"You'll want to speak to the Master of the Games then,"
Chainer said. He pointed across the enclosure to the box
eats across the arena. "There's the master now, talking to
he Mer ambassador."

The other side of the building held a host of individual
oxes, most of which were empty now, these being only t

early elimination rounds. Kamahl could see separate floa
ing pods hovering over the boxes, clustered around doo
and a narrow platform high on the arena wall.

"Those are only used by high officials and wealth
patrons of the games." Chainer said as he followed Kamahl
eyes. "Usually the Master of the Games oversees from ther
but with so much work still to be done, he is holding cou
where messengers can easily be received and sent."

At the mention of a court, Kamahl turned his ey
down and looked at the official's box. There sat the arena
ruler, rotund and covered in drapes of expensive lookir
cloth. However, it was his companions that fixed the ba
barian's attention. Two figures stood out against the bacl
drop of aides, guards, and servants. Kamahl's teet
clenched as he considered the Mer seated at the rigl
hand of the Cabal official.

The ambassador looked remarkably human. Kamal
could see two small silver-capped horns against the blu
skin. The different skin tone was barely worth mentior
ing. The barbarian had learned something of the greate
world during his years in the mountains. Those born o
and allied with the sea were well known for their mor
strous and bizarre appearance. The only oddity excep
for the blue skin was the ambassador's clothes. Th
wraps of cloth lay plastered against his azure flesl
While Kamahl looked on, a servant slowly poured liqui
over the limbs of his master. The ambassador absentl
presented a leg for additional treatment, never turnir
from his conversation.

The massive figure off to the side fitted Kamahl's idea o
Mer citizen should look like. A sideboard piled hig
ay open to the box patrons, but only one perso

ook advantage. The barbarian could think of two reasons
or the single eater.

First was the dangerous look of the diner. Kamahl was
eminded of a giant frog. The hulking figure would have
overtopped the barbarian by at least a foot, but until
Kamahl compared him with the other patrons of the box,
he thought the frog quite short. The amphibian was a mass
of muscle, so wide that the mind made the creature shorter
han it was. The creature's brilliant blue and yellow skin
was dotted with short growths that reminded the barbarian
of spikes on a mace. The mouth gaped wide as the frog swallowed an entire leg of lamb with a single gulp.

The second reason that others might forego the repast
was the thick slime dripping from the frog creature's webbed
hands. The excretions covered the food as the amphibian
grabbed up more to eat.

"The ambassador's champion, Turg," Chainer offered, a
hint of distaste in his voice. "He competes for the prizes and
the ambassador's glory. It is said his race is one of complete
savagery. The frog is a testament to the money and time the
ambassador has spent training him."

Kamahl looked to the arena floor where the two
novices shifted uncertainly. If such as these can compete,
he thought, then I should have no trouble. The city man
saw his look of dismissal.

"They may not look like much, but those willing to risk
certain death are sometimes in short supply." He pointed
toward the posted standards and gates. "Whether or not
quarter may be offered is posted by where the standards
hang and which gates the opponents use. Kirtar always
passes through the gate of no quarter. The Master of th
Games must be flexible in scheduling opponents for

lieutenant in the opening bouts. Experienced fighters ar
usually closer to the final round before they chose deatl
matches. The arena also tries to save death matches for th
final days of competition lest a capable fighter be killed of
too early. You could find a death match easy enough, but t
be considered a serious competitor you must be known o
impress the officials with your power."

The growing murmurs of the restive crowd drev
Kamahl's and Chainer's attentions back to the arena floor
The team of mountain mages was looking more confiden
now as cries of "forfeit" began to rise from the stands
Their opponent still had not appeared, and Chaine
snorted in disgust at the lack of a champion to oppose th
pair. The chants stopped as a near naked figure move
onto the field.

"He shows his contempt for the games," Chainer mut
tered as catcalls rose from the stands. "Trust a member o
the Order to belittle the honor of the tourney."

Kamahl was no worshipper of pageantry, so Kirtar's fail
ure to obey the forms did not upset him, but the arroganc
that the figure showed as he walked nonchalantly towar
the opposing pair put his teeth on edge. An aspirant to th
victory circle, Kamahl ached to show Kirtar that he shoul
show respect for the other fighters if not the venue. As th
barbarian took in the warrior's pale skin, he became mor
irritated. Kirtar was a bird warrior.

Centuries before, a race of three peoples had fled from
other planes to Dominaria. All were descended from
ancestors who could fly, though most had lost their wings
The furthest from their winged forebears were the elen
iant humanoids stood nine to ten feet tall with
s of near solid bone. Slow and ponderous, the

provided the muscle for the society, though in war they served only as massed troops with little status.

The raypen lay at the other end of the size spectrum. Dwarf-sized creatures with withered legs ending in prehensile feet, they could still fly with their innate magic. Magical feathers covered their long distorted arms giving them, for short periods of time, the freedom their ancestors had known.

Kirtar's milky skin and massive hands identified him as aven. The warrior caste of a militant people, they had joined the Northern Order en masse. Though not prolific, they rose to many positions of power in the north and many a party riding into the western mountains was led by bird warriors. Mountain societies respected strength, but that respect must be individually earned and honor conferred on the basis of personal achievement. The Order advocated the submission of all to the movement's leaders. Kamahl—by birth, training, and inclination—bowed only to those more powerful. His whole life was dedicated to proving that, now in his prime, no one could order him about with impunity. To give up your will to others, all of whom lacked the power to beat you or claim your respect with their own deeds, grated. Kamahl regarded the bird warrior narrowly as his possible opponent in the tourney walked into battle.

The two mountain mages attacked simultaneously. They separated in a fast shuffle, their movements slowed as they called upon their magic. Neophytes, thought Kamahl.

The one on the left appeared to be a shaman. Furs and small amulets fluttered as he scuttled to one side. The boy's dark skin contrasted with his blond hair. The spell that followed was slow to form. Eventually it congealed into reality as the universe created a creature in response to youth's wishes. With a roar, a slavering troll stalked toward the bird warrior.

The emaciated monster approached warily, showing a degree of cunning unusual in the breed. The head darted from side to side, pausing to take in great gulps of air. Seemingly satisfied that nothing threatened, it jumped at Kirtar. Kamahl realized the bird warrior had not even bothered to raise power until the monster actually leaped. Golden energy erupted from his skin, coating his head and upper torso. It solidified into armor even as the mouth of the troll opened wide, the teeth and jaws of the monster seeming to leap out of the massive mouth. The beast stooped down to devour the warrior, but the bird warrior's armor did not give at all. Vainly its jaws clenched, and its claws scratched. Like a dog worrying at a pole, the beast tried to throw Kirtar to the side or gnaw through.

Now the other young caster entered the fray. Clad in piecemeal armor, he was shorter than his companion. As if he were his partner's negative, his dark hair contrasted with his pale skin. Spiral tattoos traced out magic sigils on his face and upper arms. He gripped a war hammer with both hands, but he did not use it to assail the bird warrior. Rather, he directed his summoned minions, who entered existence at a run. Dwarf warriors charged Kirtar and the troll.

Pick-axes and hammers rose and then fell. Kirtar rolled to the side; one blow driving through the armor that now encased the warrior's lower legs. The troll howled in delight at the fresh blood, and Kamahl believed the aven would pay the ultimate price for his arrogance. The bird warrior did freeze, and he reinforced the power of the magic encas limbs. Then the lieutenant struck with his bare

The huge fists were encased in energy, and Kamahl could ar the troll's jaws being pulverized. Teeth sprayed across e ground, digging furrows as they buried themselves. The ast screamed with pain, striking out blindly and falling on a dwarf. The diminutive warrior's sturdy metal armor oved unequal to troll claws. Chunks of flesh and blood l to the sand as the dwarf was eviscerated. The audience oed loudly as the shaman tried to redirect his beast.

"The pair has lost the crowd," Chainer said, shaking his ad sadly. "For allied creatures to fall upon each other is a unforgivable amateur mistake."

Kirtar was on his feet, weaving from side to side as the st of the dwarf troop tried to take advantage of his reduced obility. At first, his movements seemed forced, almost ambling as he retreated. Kamahl watched as the bird war- or grew stronger. The barbarian realized that what wounds e lieutenant received healed even as he fought. The en's opponents could heal too, and the troll stood up, re from his mistaken victim covering its face and chest, e dwarf's blood mingling with the flow of foulness from e beast's own wound. The wound diminished as the troll entered the fray. The deformed jaws moved back into osition, and Kamahl could see new teeth glinting in the rchlight.

Kirtar attacked the surrounding dwarves, killing and aiming as the troll reached for him. The lieutenant's fists ere swollen balloons of power as golden energy armored e bird warrior's flesh. Heads collapsed under the aven's ows. Shields and weapons shattered as the dwarves strug- ed to bring the bird warrior down. Kirtar leaped, whether ving or merely by enhanced muscles, Kamahl did not 1ow. He soared through the air toward the dark-hair

mountain mage. Kirtar's bent legs absorbed much of th
energy of the landing, but the armored youth still fell—
bag of broken bones. The barbarian thought the ma
might survive with proper care, then Kirtar batted th
man's head with a slap. The new corpse was not decap
tated, but the mage's head lolled off one shoulder, leavin
no doubt of the man's death.

The troll ran at Kirtar, a high cry of bestial rage soun
ing as the few remaining dwarves vanished at the death
their master. The shaman coaxed fire from the air, and a fe
small balls of flame hurtled toward the bird warrior. Most
the spell wasted itself upon the open ground of the aren
The aroma of cooking meat carried everywhere as the fall
mountain mage was devoured by the ill-aimed magic. Bur
ing flesh and charred leather fought with the odors of th
food vendors making their rounds of the stands.

A flock of birds soared from the lieutenant's hands. Th
small castings were brilliant, and Kamahl forced himself
look at them directly. Slightly translucent they rose u
into the air, drawing near the upper booths. Patrons fe
silent as the small energy spirits turned. The flock dive
toward the floor of the arena, converging on everythir
still alive. Like ghosts, they slipped into bodies as all stoc
still. Bursts of light shone forth from eyes and ope
mouths. The troll's rays cast a giant shadow of the bi
warrior against the far wall of the arena. The last mou
tain mage was a fallen star, shafts of light erupting from h
skin. All except Kirtar collapsed. There was a moment
silence, and then thunderous applause filled the arena.

* * * * *

Odyssey

So you think you can compete in the games, do you, my
?" the Master of the Games said.

Kamahl restrained his irritation with difficulty. The man
 fat and festooned in bolts of garish cloth, like some
nstrous jester taking his ease at a party instead of entering. All of the Cabal members that he had seen were
dued in color and outward demeanor, but the Master of
 Games showed a flamboyance of color and style that
ulted the barbarian's eyes.

You might be powerful enough to compete in the
hes, but you will have to satisfy me." The official stood
h some difficulty and walked toward a room off to the
 of the box.

Guards drew themselves to attention only to be patted
iliarly by the figure strolling by. Kamahl followed,
ked by another set of guards. Kamahl appeared
ponless. His great sword and axes lay in the entry
mber "as a matter of security." Only his mild amuse-
nt at the guards thinking him disarmed prevented him
m laying waste to the Cabal's servants. His amusement
 passing, and the effrontery of the official made him
hink his participation in the tourney. To allow someone
such low character to stand in judgement of him was
h unbearable. Kamahl came for the glory of combat
inst equals. How equal could his opponents be if one
h as the official controlled their entry into the games?
mahl became more and more convinced that he would
hdraw beyond the city and challenge the winner of the
rney, that is if the barbarian did not return to the dis-
t mountains instead.

Only one who is worthy should have a chance at
se," the master said, slightly out of breath as he move

15

to the side of the doorway and gestured over the trove
treasures.

Kamahl heard nothing but the pounding of his o
heart for several seconds. A mound of gold, a few jewe
and numerous artifacts filled the center of the roo
Mechanical limbs of ancient war machines lay next
charred books. Open scrolls showed letters that the ec
cated barbarian could not even identify much less re
Leaking bags of coin lay against a massive breastpl
worn by some forgotten giant. The room contain
wealth, history, and shards of power from past wars, bu
was a dull metal orb that locked Kamahl's gaze. It lay p
tially concealed by a fine sword blade, which Kama
ached to throw away that he might better see this tre
ure. The rest of the room was filled with dross to the w
rior's mind. The orb appeared to be no larger than his f
yet he was mesmerized by it. His interest grew greater
he thought it responded to him. The light reflected by
seemed to grow brighter. The metal surface hinted
restrained power rather than the dull glint of comm
metal. Kamahl's line of sight was broken as the Master
the Games entered his field of vision.

"Speechless, eh." The fat man chuckled. "A shy barb
ian. An uncommon sight, but one which is still not spec
enough to have in the ranks of the tourney."

Kamahl's jaws ached as he restrained himself. This c
pulent fool was nothing, but now Kamahl burned to en
and win. The metal sphere called to him still. The barb
ian thought briefly of just taking the item, but he was a w
        not a common thief. The official drew breath
        aunt, but Kamahl had heard enough. His ha
        o his pouch at his belt. He could feel the gua

16

awing closer. Chainer, who had stayed far back during the
ntire conversation, came forward. Out of the corner of his
e he could see the young man's concerned face drawing
earer, perhaps to defuse the situation.

Kamahl drew out a single copper coin, worn thin with
ge and clipped by the truly desperate. The official's
ready florid face grew darker at the perceived insult of
e pitiful bribe, but the barbarian had no intention of
ying to buy his way into the tournament with any cur-
ncy other than his own power. Kamahl's muscles relaxed
he channeled force to his hand. The copper brightened
the patina of age and wear sloughed away from the
etal. The coin grew brighter as the guards moved in,
eir spear points poised to open up Kamahl's back. Like a
urist casting into a wishing well, the barbarian tossed the
pper over his shoulder. The stone wall proved no barrier.
ke a hot knife through butter, the red-hot coin melted its
ay through. Shouts of surprise sounded as it exited
rough the box wall as well. The sound of the cooling slug
tting the arena floor was lost in the confusion of the
ards and the white face of the Master of the Games.
ooking at the deflated official, the barbarian knew he
ould have no problems entering the tourney.

CHAPTER 2

"I assure you, my lord, that no such displays of arrogance would be permitted in the palaces of the emperor. Such a boor would be summarily executed, especially one who lacked a suitable patron."

The merman tried to sound sympathetic and outraged, but it was hard to feel much empathy for the fool who sat in front of him. The Master of the Games came to the fete in high dudgeon and had released a spew of bile, detailing the attack on his honor and dignity. Ambassador Laquatus thought nig had no dignity. Moreover, a man of true power or waited to act. The pointless railing grated on lor's nerves.

The merman might be mistaken for human with the
exception of his coloring and the small horns that lay half
hidden by his hair. Of course, under the sea, his ancestry
was much more obvious. At a mental command, his legs
transmuted to a great fish's tail. The long couches he
favored recalled the decadence of lost civilizations but also
allowed him to recline when transformed. Long gilded nail
extensions flashed in the subdued light as he spoke and
gestured.

"I assure you, Laquatus, that your sympathy and hospitality at the end of this difficult day will not be forgotten."
The Cabal official almost gushed as he relaxed and turned
to consider the temporary court that the ambassador had
established. The merman offered only a nod before looking
back upon the revel before him.

The embassy to the Cabal had procured a house that
butted up against the bluffs surrounding the city. A huge
cavern had been dug out and expanded. In the middle of
the excavation, a huge pool was filled with salt water and
sea plants carefully transplanted. The ambassador could feel
the waves of energy that moved through the water, warm-
ing it and sending gouts of mist into the air.

The life in the pool relied on constant infusions of power
from the ambassador's mages to live and even flourish. Brilliant coral and anemones lay in the waist deep water, their
color and motion suggesting beds of flowers. The soporific
compounds they released acted as invisible poisons to the
minds of those not rendered immune, yet the revelers in the
pool showed no signs of ill health.

The large lagoon was full. Competitors moved in the
water, dangerous but temporarily safe to all. Like carni-
vores after a full meal, they appeared logy. One fighter

saluted his host as Laquatus's gazes swept over him. Bur
and covered with scars, he waved a prosthetic arm i
greeting. The metal arm ended in serrated pincers tha
rasped together softly as the athlete picked another gobl
from the circling waiters. His companion for the evenir
only cooed appreciatively as the arm gathered her in. Fo
the amount of money the ambassador paid for the escort
he expected nothing less.

The mechanical limb of the fighter was nothing unusua
Laquatus could see many other examples of grafted liml
and skin. Pit fighting was dangerous, and those lucky ar
powerful enough to survive often left the floor of the arer
with less than they entered. Mechanical parts salvaged fror
ancient war machines were used along with limbs and hic
from exotic beast and fallen warriors.

A few Cabal sponsored fighters circulated as wel
Laquatus curbed his pout of distaste. Many of the loca
champions sported limbs from zombies and the dead. Th
rotting stench was almost completely covered by the pe
fumes filling the air, but nothing could curb the disgu
many of the guests showed. The Cabal fighters relied on
steady supply of shattered bodies and dismembered fighte
to supply them with new parts as the ones they reclaime
eventually failed.

The pit frog Turg lurked in the shadows, crouche
behind a miniature reef with only his bulbous eyes showin
above the water. The ambassador's champion had stuffe
himself to the point of immobility, and Laquatus cursed h
personal failure to curb the creature's insane appetite. It wa
so easy to be lost in Turg's simple pleasures of the flesh. Th
official noticed Laquatus's lack of attention and cleared h
throat loudly.

The merman's manners and style automatically equated
n with the nobility in the eyes of his guests. His background
fact was not distinguished, and the human good looks were
trike against him in the Mer kingdom. The emperor and
e empress resembled the octopus on their house flag.
eir malleable bodies and eight limbs were the standard
the court, and he was far from the current definition of
auty. He was banished to the land like a malformed child
lden from sight. He felt the injustice of his exile and con-
npt for the land-locked with which he must interact.

Laquatus speared a small fish that swam past. His long
ger extensions were often filled with poison at the under-
court, and it amused him to use such deadly devices for
rpooning snacks. The small blood slick lightened his
od, and he regarded the boor next to him.

"How terrible you say," Laquatus drawled. "The barbar-
destroyed the wall of the vault."

He had of course already received a full report from his
es. Kamahl's casual display hinted that another powerful
ampion had entered the contest. Perhaps new alliances
re in order.

"I am terribly sorry, but I do see Caster Fulla over in the
ner alone." He interrupted the official who had contin-
d to drone on like an inconsequential insect. "I would be
oor host indeed if I did not look after all my guests. Why
n't you join me in extending greetings?"

"No, no," the official said hurriedly, rising and moving
ay quickly enough to leave a wake of disturbed water. "I
ve things that must be done," he tossed over his shoulder.

Laquatus was not surprised at the swift withdrawal. He
nsformed back to his legged form, his fins absorbed
k into his body, and his tail splitting to form the limbs

he must use away from the sea. Small fish swirled arou
his submerged limbs as scales and destroyed flesh te
porarily fouled the water. He rose with initial care a
waded across the pool.

Turg rose from concealment in response to a men
command and moved toward the ambassador's back. De
ing with dementia casters was often dangerous. Their g
on reality could become quite tenuous as they grew m
powerful. Caster Fulla was very powerful indeed.

"Hello, my dear," the ambassador exclaimed. "I am
glad that you accepted my invitation."

The caster turned, and he waited for her eyes to fo
back on the present.

Caster Fulla "Braids" appeared a weathered thirty yea
Her dark skin and clothing seemed in perpetual shadow, a
Laquatus felt a faint increase in tension as she looked on h
fully. Her right arm brushed the short sword at her si
before extending toward the ambassador. Kissing a woma
hand was a ridiculous piece of theatre most of the time, a
it was particularly ridiculous now. Fulla's right arm was m
shapen with scars and chunks of missing flesh. Leather a
iron bracing showed conspicuously as he lowered his head
the misshapen claw that she must call a hand. He brush
his lips against the tainted flesh and slowly straightened. I
her profession, Fulla was really quite comely.

Dementia casters, like many mages, called forth monst
to fight for them and serve their purposes, but even the d
magic of their Cabal brethren was twisted in bizarre wa
The trances that dementia casters fell into seemed to op
the dark recesses of the mind, bringing forth hideous mo
sters. Many only existed in insane dreams before the pow
called them. Some used drugs to alter their thoughts a

22

ceptions to bring forth ever greater horrors until they
what remained of their sanity. Then instead of using
gs to free their minds, they engaged in a pharmacologi-
war to retain some connection to reality. Laquatus
ed that such a fragile grip on existence would offer the
dhold he needed to twist her into his service.

"It was something to do," Fulla said in a dead tone. The
ds woven into her hair clinked together softly as she
ved. "But it is only the same party. I've been here a hun-
d times before and since." Boredom filled her voice, and
eyes were focusing back into her internal world to the
bassador's irritation.

"Surely something must interest you." Laquatus
mmed, a low thrum began to pick at his ears as the
rman fed instructions to the magic plants and springs
ding the grotto.

The corals released bursts of drugs into the water. The
bassador felt a curious mixture of energy and languor
n though he and his personal servants regularly dosed
mselves with antidotes. The party seemed to grow quiet
he guests succumbed to the chemicals in the water.

"I think that we should work together." The ambassador
l, crowding closer. "The bouts offer us a chance to realize
mendous profits if we could just cooperate." The merman
his hand on her maimed arm, controlling his expression
he touch of the gnarled flesh.

"I hope we might become something more than partners."
Laquatus breathed more heavily as he tried to suggest
uction. He had less than no interest in the women above
sea, but he had set this hook before. Fulla showed only
tation and broke his grip easily.

"You're boring," she said flatly. "Everything is boring

23

now. I am going back to the Casters' Quarter. At least it never boring."

Fulla started wading toward the steps leading into t pool. She moved surely and with purpose, showing no si of being affected by the water. Laquatus realized that, a dementia caster, she dealt with shifting reality often. T Casters' Quarter that she was headed for was notorious the monsters and dark passions that gripped its inhabitan Fulla's being was far too vicious a battlefield for the gen persuasion of the grotto's waters. Turg, feeling his mast irritation, cut through the partygoers to grab Fulla's arm

Braids swung around, curling inside the pit frog's a and breaking his grip. Her sword was in her hand, a Laquatus felt a burst of pain as her blade slapped along t frog's side. The ambassador could feel the bestial rage of champion surging to dramatic levels, and he tried to fo the beast to calm.

Laquatus and the frog were tied together on many lev feeding off of each other's emotions. The frog supplie dramatic amount of muscle the ambassador used to cow enemies, while the merman supplied the intelligence a drive to make Turg more than a savage animal. The p and snub eroded his control and Turg acted to hold caster.

"At *last!*" Fulla exalted. "Something interesting in t sewer."

Laquatus paused in his attempts to restrain his champi A sewer! He was sick of insults from these land-bound si pletons. Turg attacked as the ambassador's pique weaker his hold. The frog skin grew mottled as the amphib forced more foulness into the water. Turg leaped to the s plowing into a crowd and sending a spray across the p

24

e ambassador could feel the fresh chemical assault
inst his senses. Colors seemed to strobe as the mind-
ering chemicals fought his will for control of his vision.
lla's eyes seemed to gleam as she went into a trance. The
eams of the other guests began to waver as well as Turg's
direct attack merged with the suggestive chemicals of the
ol. Laquatus could see an escort flailing at hallucinations.
'Close the doors!" he screamed to the servants at the gate.
The guards slammed the decorative doors shut as one pit
hter ran for the exit. A huge minotaur, it lowered its
ad and charged. The expensive façade cracked over the
nor beneath as the giant humanoid went down, blood
wing from its nose and ears. Other guests began to stum-
out of the pool.

Turg erupted from the water beside Fulla. His skin was
very, and he was almost impossible to see. Like the octo-
s and cuttlefish of the ocean, the frog could blend against
ny backgrounds. Fulla was a veteran of the pits, and her
ewed mind edited out the madness surrounding her. The
g's attack met a summoned creature that threw the com-
tants apart as if a bomb had exploded.

The eel that wrapped itself around the frog showed
nes and frayed flesh. Turg spun to throw it off, but its
eping skin seemed to glue the creature to the frog. The
phibian's wild gyrations threw gobs of rotting meat
ross the chamber, which rained down on the guests and
uggling servants. The ambassador could see blackjacks
ed freely by his mercenaries as they struggled to contain
e growing riot. Only their fight with imaginary demons
evented a total bloodbath as pit fighters went down
der the swinging sacks of lead shot. Laquatus felt Turg's
in as the eel struck again and again, pumping venom

into the humanoid's frame. The frog tore off portions of own hide but hurled the writhing eel away into a group musicians the ambassador had hired for the evening.

"Enough!" Laquatus snarled.

A bolt of energy erupted from his hands, and a ribbon power connected the merman to the eel. Flesh boiled un the attack, and the popping of exploding bones could heard over the cacophony of screams and curses filling t chamber. The hired servants trembled, and their bor cracked as the overflow of energy created a circle of dea Laquatus ignored them as he destroyed the last of the e Their cooked bodies fell beneath the waters as the amb sador cut off the stream of power.

Fulla gaily laughed from the side of the grotto, I knees drawn up like a little girl's. "A wonderful party!" s yelled as she toed a drifting corpse away. "You must inv me again." Laquatus heard his teeth grinding as restrained himself and the amphibian warrior who cre behind her, his fists raised high.

* * * * *

"I will send over a supply of the oysters you so enjoyed Laquatus said, his eyes locked with the confused me chant's. "I am sure a regular shipment can be arrang within the month." The eyes slowly cleared, and the ma looked down at himself. He was dressed in waves of s silk, the draped cloth more appropriate on a young maid than a stocky man of fifty.

"Thank you for the loan," he mumbled. "I can't belie that I fell in the punchbowl and ruined my clothes. I pro ise to pay for any damage."

His eyes were clearing, and he looked at the outside of
e embassy gate. The ambassador could see him trying to
member what exactly he had done. The merman sent
other tendril of deceit into the man's mind, reinforcing
ages of drunken debauchery.

"Keep the cloth as my gift. I only regret that I ran out of
othes for the other guests." Laquatus forced out an indulgent
uckle. "A party without a little damage is hardly worth
ing to. I am sure everything will be shipshape by morning."

His jaw clenched as he shook the man's hand and sent
m on his way with an escort. His mind drifted back to the
otto. The decomposing eel had killed off the coral and
led the cavern with an indescribably foul odor. The dead
ere packed into sealed barrels which must be disposed of
mediately. Worse, the entire cavern must be rebuilt into
completely new environment. Laquatus was sure the false
emories he implanted in the survivors would withstand
ost reminders of the violent episode, but it made no sense
tempt fate. The expense would be tremendous, but he
uld afford no flashbacks by guests at future affairs. His face
ew forbidding as the last guest left his sight.

He started back to the cavern, but near the entrance he
ifted off to the side. The pulse of energy he directed at the
pestry activated the quiescent spell, and he drifted
rough the wall. He could feel the defensive spells slam-
ing back into place as he stepped into the small room.

Laquatus was alone with his thoughts, his ties to Turg
t. The amphibian was sleeping off the exertions of the
ght and the pain Laquatus had inflicted on him to prevent
e amphibian from killing the dementia caster. Fulla had
oved entirely resistant to the merman's attempt to change
r memories. Only the full attention of the Cabal—should

such a powerful figure die—had prevented Laquatus fro
ordering a full scale attack to kill her. She was complete
insane, but she showed no agitation and seemed in go
spirits when she left. However, she was a chink in Laquatu
armor of deceit and must be dealt with in the near futur
Perhaps the pits would prove particularly dangerous in tl
next few weeks.

The room was crudely mined and showed none of tl
fine workmanship that formed the rest of the embassy. I
construction had been long and laborious as Laquatus pr
cured a stream of disposable workmen. He was forced
install the winch and thick trapdoor in the center of tl
room himself, with only Turg providing the muscle to sh
the equipment. The merman cranked the heavy cover u
the rust falling like red snow. The remnants of some lor
destroyed fortress gate, its metal shielded the swirling po
of energy beneath. Without a double system of safeguard
magic users throughout the city might sense the power
the portal. It was vital that he keep his true strengt
hidden as long as possible. Laquatus removed his amba
sadorial robes; glad to strip himself of the rags that land
men expected him to wear. He dived into the pool.

The shock of hitting the icy water surprised him as alwa
and his entire frame shivered for a few seconds before he cou
take stock of his new surroundings. The darkness of the env
ronment glistened with the bioluminescence of various cre
tures. Many of them came from the depths of the ocean ar
had been transferred to the deepwater caves underlying muc
of the continent. The shimmering pool of light that he dive
into was replicated as a glowing vertical portal. The mag
bridged a gap of nearly a thousand feet. Here, unknown to tl
city above, an army gathered to sally forth in the name of th

er Empire. Laquatus floated blissfully for a moment, relish-
g the fact that only the emperor carried more rank than the
nbassador in these caves. Above he played the exiled noble,
t here he was the state.

"My lord," a quiet voice seemed to whisper behind him,
e tones swirling through the water. "You were not
pected for some time."

Laquatus turned in the water, careful to show no surprise.
small humanoid moved from the darkness of an over-
ng. Long whiskers twitched, searching the waters for
ent and movement. Its body was small and its limbs
indly. For a moment, it appeared harmless as it moved
to the light. Then the ambassador again saw the cruel
aws on its hands and feet. Their sheer size always startled
m, but it was the head that was most disquieting. Huge
d stuffed with glassy spearlike teeth, the mouth beckoned
s gaze. There in the center danced a tongue, endlessly
ndulating and shifting color. Blank eyes without pupils
oked blindly at him as the creature swam closer. Laquatus
re his eyes away and looked to the side. The tresias and
s people were common in the underwater caves and
rmed a substantial portion of the ambassador's guard.
aptain Satas was a loyal officer, perfect for command of
e subterranean force, but his appearance was a constant
urce of revulsion to those who swam the sunlit seas.

"Events on the surface may require action sooner than
nticipated," the ambassador answered. "We will need
ore soldiers stationed for assault on command." The
esias's tongue shifted faster though there was no other
gn of agitation.

"My people are slow to trust and slower to travel; we will
eed soldiers from the empire." Satas signaled to an aide.

The warrior who swam over resembled a giant octopus caught in the process of becoming a man. The tentacles and its great bag of a head floated and moved freely in the water, but signs of an underlying structure of bone and horn peaked through. "You will carry the ambassador's words to the emperor."

The soldier left in a jet of water, his body sliding through a narrow crevice in the side of the cave. The ambassador hoped that more cephalids and other soft-body troops would be available. With malleable bodies, they could move easily through the caves and take the shortest routes. The advantages of such a heritage and its beauty made him jealous as he watched the trailing tentacles disappear. That the emperor should be blessed with such a form while the ambassador should look so . . . human.

"How have the tunneling crews fared?" he asked Satas, focusing on the unsightly captain to occupy his thoughts.

The engineers of the empire were continually opening new routes in the natural caves that underlay the entire continent. Connecting the largest underground rivers would allow for the rapid movement of the large bodies of troops and the giant warriors from the open seas, but the secret ways were twisted and full of dead ends. The mapping and connection of suitable caverns was a meticulous and slow process.

"Weeks before the way clears," Satas said, drifting back to the wall. "However, two more mages have mastered the door spell." The tresias moved suddenly, his whiskers whipping as he struck at a blind crayfish swimming out of a small crevice. "When more soldiers arrive we can open enough portals to flood the city with troops," he whispered and devoured the tender morsel alive.

CHAPTER 3

"I will need the winnings before the matches end tonight." Kamahl said seriously, maneuvering through the crowds around the arena. Chainer crowded closer, raising his voice to be heard.

"Why not tomorrow?" the young man asked, slapping a youth whose fingers reached for his purse. The gesture was casual, but the boy fell down under the feet of the crowd. Kamahl could hear slurred cursing growing fainter they moved toward the preparation rooms.

"The price of my lodging is due tonight and I dislike guments about money," the barbarian responded.

His massive metal gauntlet nudged a too eager fighter ho tried to enter ahead of the pair. A cool stare by Kamahl

31

forced the warrior back into the milling crowd as the entered the fetid air of the common preparation hall.

The barbarian entered the city with enough money f normal times, but the tourney had inflated the prices food and lodging far above what he expected. The last the fighter's funds were totally expended in placing a bet c the matches today.

"What will you do if you lose?" Chainer asked with co cern. The young Cabal employee had warned Kamahl the dire straits that the destitute could be forced into. Th pits devoured a steady supply of the indigent to perfor jobs too disgusting and dangerous for workers with ar means. There were darker rumors that Kamahl heard him of, but Chainer had not commented on them. "You are i a multiple party match. The other fighters could combir against you."

"I never considered losing," Kamahl said. He smile and motioned the Cabal employee to leave and place th bet they discussed. "I also failed to consider a Phyrexia invasion destroying the city."

The barbarian chuckled slightly as he moved to pr pare. Losing in the preliminaries, before the champior even entered the lists? He laughed at the implausibility it as he moved toward the entrance of the arena.

The screaming and cheering crowd was a continuou background noise, overridden as the last competitor staggered in and were carried from the field. One lizar man lay on a stretcher, laid open like a butchered anima His hands grasped the wooden poles with desperat strength, and Kamahl could see the life ebbing from th grip in time with the pulses of blood. The fighter expire as he was ferried past.

"A shame to die so badly," a deep voice commented. amahl turned and could see only a wall of fur.

He stepped back, his eyes rising to look at the speaker's isage. A centaur looked down on him, smiling with his lips losed in apparent friendliness.

He was huge, towering over the other competitors wait- ng for their matches. He stood at least half again as high as ne barbarian. His features were simian with glimpses of ings showing as he breathed through his mouth. The lower ody was catlike though in sheer size it reminded Kamahl f a dray house. The fur over the body looked short and oarse. The barbarian could see the play of huge muscles nder its hide as the creature shifted. The gigantic club in he centaur's hands was a mass of wood and banded iron. A mall granite boulder capped the end, and the warrior owered it to the floor as he offered a hand in greeting.

"I am Seton, from the Krosan Forest."

The barbarian gripped the massive hand, showing no esitation or fear even as he felt the power in that grasp.

"Kamahl is my name," he answered. The barbarian ges- ured to the dead competitor being carried out. "Death omes to all. The lizard man lost and defeat often exacts the ltimate price." The centaur squeezed hard but seeing no esponse released Kamahl's hand.

"Defeat is often terrible, but the lizard man was the victor f the round."

The centaur held his weapon tightly, twisting his hands as ne watched Cabal servants clearing the arena of corpses and aking in fresh sand. The smell of old blood and rot wafted n through the lower entrances to the fighting area. Kamahl lropped his pack to a bench along the wall. Other fighters, ome almost green with fear and dreadful anticipation, made

room. The barbarian undid his cloak and put it in his pack.
A massive armored belt went around his waist as he moved
his purse and nonessential items into the pack.

"A victory that leaves you dead is no victory," the barbarian opinioned, moving his massive sword from his back.
The sword was a remnant of a massive artifact from the
invasion. The fighter he had defeated swore it was part of
Urza's staff, but Kamahl had his doubts. Still, the double-
edged great sword channeled power exceptionally well. Its
only flaw was the lack of a good stabbing point. "Better yet
is to leave even your enemy alive to grant you homage and
spread word of his defeat. Dead bodies feed only crows."

"Dead bodies do much more in the hands of the Cabal."
Seton spat to the side, the spittle running down the wall
and across the Cabal symbols on this side of the doors.
"Unless you have made special arrangements, the necromancers will raise your corpse or feed it to their monsters."

"If you fall, I will make sure that you don't end up depending on their tender mercies," Kamahl answered, his confidence such that he felt compelled to relieve the other's mind.

"Why do you care what happens to me?" the centaur
demanded, anger displacing the worry in his tone. "Do you
make some claim for me?"

Kamahl was calm as he sealed his pack and kicked it
under a bench. The Cabal servant overseeing the room
caught the barbarian's eye, and he pointed to his gear with
a forbidding expression. Power flowed from Kamahl's hand
and danced over the wire interwoven with the cloth of the
pack. The centaur was almost snarling as Kamahl finally
turned his attention back to Seton.

"I came to fight the best," Kamahl replied, checking
the fit of his armor. "I want to beat the best. Victory

ould be less pure if my opponents worried about what ould happen to them after they lost."

The centaur swelled at the sheer arrogance and effron-ry of the barbarian and then exploding in laughter.

"You are confident, hero," Seton laughed. "If you fight e tenth as well as you boast you will walk away with every ize."

Kamahl only smiled slightly then straightened. The gate-eeper posted three tiles. One of them was the crossed axe d sword that Kamahl was assigned upon entering the mes. Another was the Cabal house tile, stating that the abal would have a representative in the fight. The last tile owed a branch gripped by a hand. The barbarian watched eton move toward the arena and knew the forest warrior as now his opponent. The centaur pushed through the in screen of fighters in front of the door.

"Both against the Cabal fighter first, Kamahl," the entaur called to him. "After the undead are dispatched, u and I can discuss who should be the winner."

Seton spun his massive club like a light baton, send-g others scrambling away as the small boulder seemed whistle through the air. The barbarian smiled and odded, moving up to stand by the mighty forest dweller. e showed no concern as the club began to spin even ore wildly as they were directed into the arena. The owd noise heightened, and Seton put on a show for the owd. Kamahl attracted little notice, as he preferred to ve his energy for the fight. The Cabal opponent tered from the opposite side, heading for a platform. A rk and tattered pennant drooped limply from a metal agstaff.

The barbarian remembered Chainer's recitation of

arena practice and how it echoed the ceremonial fightin
practiced in the mountains. The Cabal fighter was fa
game during combat, but the simple act of taking the fla
would expel the house fighter from the match. The rul
allowed overmatched house fighters to retreat and lose
flag rather than their lives. Several matches Kamahl sa
earlier in the week involved the Cabal fighter losing to
stolen flag as they were overwhelmed and forced to prc
tect themselves first and foremost. One novice Caba
fighter pulled the flag himself as he was overwhelmed. Th
fighter lived, but the shame of his cowardly act woul
undoubtedly make his life a living hell. The contestant
not with the Cabal had no flag to lose. Only total defea
or humiliating surrender awaited them should a Caba
fighter prove superior. The barbarian heard many com
plain that the Cabal lost flags more often than lives, bu
he planned to win, so not having an alternate way to b
defeated did not bother him.

Kamahl ignored the Master of the Games' speech. The ligh
from the flaring torches along the rim of the arena made i
almost impossible to see the crowd. The viewing pods floate
down from high above the wall as a few of the important gam
patrons watched the bout. Kamahl could see the ambassadc
from the Mer Empire and his champion taking their ease. Th
ambassador gave him a languid wave, and the barbarian grit
ted his teeth, feeling his color darken. The Order champior
Kirtar was in the box as well and laughed at Kamahl's discom
fiture. The lights brightened as Cabal mages fed more power t
the torches, and the crowds and boxes were washed away i
the flood of light. The barbarian focused, ignoring the soun
of the crowds, blocking out superfluous noise until it seemed a
quiet as the highlands of his youth.

The Cabal fighter was a woman, her hair braided with beads and bones. She looked disinterested even as Seton bellowed a challenge, waiting for the fight to commence. Whatever the signal to commence the bout had been, Kamahl missed it in the charge of the centaur. His club spinning, the giant advanced in great bounds, hoping to close before the dementia caster could react, but his charge proved too slow as groups of fighters congealed in front of the Cabal fighter and her flag. Though humanoid, the creatures showed buglike qualities. Their dark exoskeletons rasped, and Kamahl could hear their pincers and mandibles working as he closed at a run.

Seton arrived first, the club falling like an avalanche on an evoked fighter. The armor broke with a wet crunch that reminded Kamahl of a lobster he saw devoured at an inn. Seton was tearing through the defenders, his club squashing them like the bugs they resembled. More and more flickered into being even as their unnatural ichor discolored the sand.

Kamahl arrived, and his massive sword cut out a great half-circle among the defenders. The barbarian did not even call forth energy to feed the blade, husbanding his power until more worthy adversaries appeared.

The Cabal magic user began to appear more interested, her eyes growing brighter as Kamahl and Seton approached, coming closer together as they neared the stand. The centaur swung his club less wildly, though the creatures still exploded at every strike. Kamahl cleared the caster's minions from his path with the same amount of energy and speed, his smooth swings showing no signs of slowing. The caster motioned, and the creatures tried to close on the pair of fighters from behind. Her tactics

proved futile as the centaur roused himself and with grea
leaps and bounds prevented any from closing with him.

The barbarian responded to the new attack with wide
swings and footwork. His mind and spirit cleared, and he
appeared almost to dance inside the lethal circle of steel
The creatures drew closer but died before they could close
The barbarian worried more about tripping over a smashe
or dismembered corpse than one of the monsters breakin
through his defense. Seton was proving faster as his grea
leaps took him around the fighters, who then closed on
Kamahl. The centaur's breath could be seen as great gout
of vapor blew out through the giant's nostrils.

Now the Cabal fighter smiled slightly, and new horror
issued from her mind. Kamahl could see a delicate an
beautiful face coming into being. The eyes opened as th
rest of the summoning took shape. The eyes were slit lik
a snake's, and from the torso down, that was what the mon
ster appeared to be. As more of the creatures flickered int
existence, the first attacked. The upper arms appeare
normal, but from the elbows down, her arms were grea
blades of bone. The leader attacked, and Kamahl dodge
one strike and blocked another. Though his sword cu
through the insectile drones like a knife through butter
this new creature's arm rang like fine steel. The scrape o
the edge along the bone made Kamahl's teeth ache. Hi
return strike left only a small cut that began to ooze an oil
liquid even as Seton joined the attack.

The centaur seemed to swell beyond his already prodi
gious size, muscles writhing under his fur. The club whistled
through the air, the head a blur as it struck at the monste
in front of him. Bone cleavers, raised to intercept the blow
were amputated as the forest giant literally disarmed the

mmoning. Seton turned to another enemy, but the first
vas not yet done. Pulses of blood jetted out of the form,
overing the centaur's chest and head. Seton's manic energy
eaked out of him as he screamed in pain.

The barbarian ran to intercept the caster's minions
alling upon his temporary ally. His sword ran with power,
he metal glowing as Kamahl fed it more energy. He struck
t the creatures' backs, the enchanted blade once again
hearing through his enemies. The limbs that fell did not
elease streams of corrosive blood, for the fire of his blade
urned its way through the creatures' bodies. The corpses
iled up; streams of fire burning through the skin as they
aced through the veins and arteries.

Seton slowly rose as the barbarian protected him. The
cream that he gave was deep and filled with pain, but the
entaur could move. The club rose and fell weakly, but it
reed Kamahl to act more aggressively. He chopped his way
hrough three of the demons and came back to protect
Seton's flank.

The centaur wove like a drunken horse, the fur on his
hest slowly growing back through bloody strips of skin. But
t took too much time, and Kamahl realized that centaur
vas a liability. The fight needed to end soon or the centaur
night yet fall to the Cabal warrior. Kamahl looked to the
platform. The flag flapped loosely as a new creature came
nto being.

It was the smell that hit the barbarian first. His nostrils
urled, and he breathed through his mouth. The creature
vas enormous, taller at the shoulder than the great buffalo
hat roamed the plains. In appearance, it reminded Kamahl
f a great mole. Its sharp snout quested in the air even as
t moved toward Seton and the barbarian. Kamahl ascribed

the hesitation to its lack of eyes. Empty sockets set i
rotted flesh and exposed bone left the monster without
means to see. Whether it had ever had fur Kamahl coul
not tell, but it had none now. Its skin seemed gone, leav
ing only rotting meat and a thick layer of mold. Each ste
of the creature left a mark of foulness.

Seton performed his own summoning. The whine o
insects could be dimly heard though cries of the crowd an
the movement of the Cabal castings. A cloud formed, grow
ing thick as insects came into being. One landed on th
barbarian's arm, and he flicked it away before it could d
any harm. The green locusts fell upon the dark minion
The barbarian absently killed the few creatures still in reac
as he considered the centaur and the Cabal mage. Th
bodies of the fallen were covered in a moving carpet tha
flattened as the insects devoured the flesh. Bone peeked ou
briefly, but the enchanted mandibles of the insect swarr
ground down even that.

Seton raised his arms, his giant club held loosely in on
hand. The cloud of locusts rose together, then fell upon th
giant mole. The centaur moved toward the platform, read
to kill. Kamahl came as well, walking around the locust
that orbited the main mound.

The attack on Seton was unexpected by the two allie
The insect-covered mole lurched into action, leaving
trail of twitching bugs. The creature humped itself up, i
spine breaking through the layer of dead flesh and dyin
locusts. The huge animal left the ground in a prodigiou
leap that equaled anything Seton had shown so far. Th
shock of the bodies meeting sprayed the remains of th
insect swarm across the arena. A thick cloud hung aroun
the pair as the centaur tried to grapple. The claws of th

mole carved hunks of flesh from the shoulders and flanks of the forest dweller. Showing unexpected flexibility, Seton ducked under the attack, scrambling clear. But only a few yards away he fell, his features slack with astonishment.

The mole twitched, each shake spraying spores into the arena. The remaining locusts cascaded from the air with each gust of the agents of decay. The spores came from the thick ropes of purple on the mole's back. The locusts' attack had served only to unmask a more deadly response. The mole swung its head from side to side as it made for the fallen centaur.

Kamahl stamped his foot loudly, sending an irregular rhythm into the sand. The monster paused, its head swinging and its feet shifting. The Cabal caster took her ease, and the barbarian could see her discounting the centaur and focusing on him. A smile lit her face as Kamahl drove his sword deep into the sand. The shock of the tip striking into the rock of the arena floor was a signal to the creature. It charged, each lunge releasing another cloud of death. It passed the platform as the barbarian stamped his feet. The Cabal fighter ignored the spores as her summoning closed. Kamahl's hands blurred as he moved—but not for the sword stuck into the ground.

The barbarian plucked a throwing axe from his belt and cocked it back to his ear. Like a great sigh, power poured into the steel and leather-wrapped handle. The head flashed brilliantly, and then, as a comet, it flew toward the mole. The metal glanced off the massive skull, and Kamahl saw the Cabal warrior becoming still, summoning additional creatures. The barbarian closed his eyes as the axe reached the apex of its deflected flight.

The detonation rocked Kamahl back. The light was

bright enough that he could see through his eyelids as th
edge of the energy brushed him. The crowd was stunned int
silence. The magic ignited the spore cloud, and the explosic
sped back to the mole, devouring it as the molds detonate
in sympathy with Kamahl's attack. The dementia caste
rolled on the ground, unable to stand. She had been flun
back several yards, and the sand stripped most of her cloth
off as well as much of her skin. Her teeth bared and blood
she stood, gathering herself to summon more monstrositie

Kamahl did not take his newly gained advantage, thoug
his other axe was in his hand. He pointed to the platforn
with the metal head. Scraps of the flag still fluttered to th
ground, signaling the Cabal fighter's defeat.

* * * * *

"You won more than five hundred!" Chainer said excit
edly. The young man gripped the bag of coins tightly, pro
claiming to all in sight that he held riches in his hanc
Kamahl only smiled thinly as he waited with the other vic
torious fighters in the winners' box. The arena attendant
seated those victors needing no medical attention. The win
ning fighters watched the remaining fights and wer
observed in turn by the crowd. A steady stream of visitor
and dignitaries cycled in and out, some of them obviousl
trying to steal some of the fighters' glory. Chainer had com
from the bet-monger with Kamahl's winnings. The barba
ian held out his hand and was surprised by the weight of th
purse. It felt much greater than the victory that had won i

"The bettors know you now," Chainer said. "You will ge
much lower odds now that you have won."

A voice interrupted the pair.

"That is because the servants of the Cabal mistake luck for skill," taunted Kirtar. The lieutenant strode arrogantly through the other fighters, pushing some out of the way. Kamahl noticed how the others took it and realized that the Order champion must be even more powerful than the barbarian thought. Perhaps the lieutenant's lop-sided victory had prevented Kamahl from seeing the bird warrior at his best.

"Most of the fighters here don't realize how lucky they are to be competing with their better," Kirtar continued. His pale skin flushed as he drank more deeply from the goblet of wine in his hand.

"I am surprised that you fight at all in these contests," Kamahl said slowly. "Surely you must realize how unequal you are to those who fight here."

Kirtar nodded his head and then realizing that the comment was more easily read as an insult advanced angrily. A massive webbed hand deflected his path. Turg patted the champion on the back as he led him over to the food, the ambassador smiling at Kamahl and Chainer.

"You must excuse our friend," Laquatus said. "He fights out of duty. The Order considers it their task to rid the world of the symbols of past evil. Many of the prizes that he wins will be destroyed at the Order's headquarters."

"He is not my friend," Kamahl said flatly. Chainer nodded slightly, a grim look on his face. "And when he faces me in the arena, he will discover that I don't need luck to win."

Laquatus, still smiling, bowed his head, but his eyes were serious, not merry. Kamahl turned as he felt a threat directed at him. Across the room Turg looked at him even as he shepherded Kirtar toward a bar. The amphibian's eyes held the same look of deadly concentration as the ambassador's.

CHAPTER 4

"Hail the conquering hero!" Seton bellowed, ignoring the catcalls that quickly followed. Kamahl only nodded, as if accepting his due. The centaur snorted as he saw the shadow of a smile on the barbarian's face. The other patients in the hospital could not read the mountain fighter and their catcalls continued.

Seton had been taken to the hospital to recover from his wounds. Though the druids of the forest were known for their healing skills, the punishment they endured to access those energies reserved them for life-threatening injuries

44

ly. Though the poison mold laid the centaur low, Cabal
rvitors administered an antidote within minutes of the
ght's end. Those who survived the games were taken to
.e healing halls behind the waiting chambers. Kamahl was
ld to return the next day.

The centaur lay in a shallow pit, his side against a move-
le board that allowed him to lie as if on a hillside. Other
.an a tendency to turn one's head to match up with the
.tient's orientation, it allowed for ease of access for the
.rsing staff. It also made conversation more convenient.

The barbarian's eyes swung over some of the patients,
.d his worries for his friend continued. Amputations
.ere common and many fighters lay as if dead, their
.umps leaking blood around the seams of their new
.mbs. Metal seemed the most common substitute, though
.ismatched furred limbs suggested other sources. Mold
.vered the wounds of some. Kamahl watched a caregiver
.reading thick mud over the weeping sores of a dwarf
.hose eyes wandered with pain. The barbarian hoped the
.abal was trying to help instead of preparing a fresh
.und of victims for rumored rituals. He renewed his vow
. avoid injury or at least care for himself.

Seton looked well. His coat was clean, and the patch-
.ork of new fur covered the worst of the stitches. The forest
.weller still made few movements, and Kamahl realized the
.ant was in pain despite his apparent high spirits.

"I am surprised that you have not already escaped," the
.arbarian quipped awkwardly. He wondered how the cen-
.ur stood the enclosed environment.

"I will leave here as soon as her 'majesty' says that I
.ay," the forest dweller said, rolling his eyes. The bar-
.arian turned, seeing an approaching healer. She stood

wrapped in armor, and her haughty stare curled his li
She went past, her robe clinking softly with the sound
chain mail.

"I am surprised to see a representative of the Order here
Kamahl said, turning his eyes away from the martial ma
back to his acquaintance.

"As healers, some of the Order's party feel compelle
to offer their services here," the centaur replied. "Thoug
we pay a stiff price for their services, being constrained
listen to them rail against the pit fights." The centau
spoke with some amusement, but Kamahl remembere
the snubs offered by the lieutenant and now one of h
retinue.

"Rather self-serving to urge competitors of their cham
pion to withdraw," the barbarian observed. "I am surprise
that you do not tell them so." Kamahl came to win hon
and respect. That other fighters would belittle the co
tests was extremely irritating.

"We all come for our own reasons," the centaur said. H
rolled further against the support board. He tripped a leve
and the clink of the mechanism sounded as he brought h
side down. "The Order fights to destroy the prizes. I fig
so I can meet the Masters of the Games." Seton lowere
his voice.

"I am not here on a lark," he said darkly. "What driv
me is serious." Seton looked to see if any were listening

"The forests are violated and their inhabitants stolen
feed the pits." He said softly. "Creatures vanish from und
the trees and nothing is done to stop them." The centau
shifted to bring his head closer to Kamahl.

"The forest will not suffer these raids forever. I kno
that one day the pit system will have to change, or

fall. The wild will not allow itself to be bled dry."

"I respect your convictions," Kamahl said, keeping his
ce even. "But I am not here to become part of your cru-
e. The pit provides the opponents I need to test myself."
turned and gestured to the crowds of injured.

"I have no wish to be hurt, but it is a risk I take to win
lace in this world." The barbarian lowered his hands
hooked his thumbs in his belt. His eyes looked
ard as he paused. "The mountains became too small.
nning a duel meant that a village or a family gave you
r due. Victory is sweet, but the portions were too
all." Kamahl shook his head sadly as he thought of his
ny victories.

"And you think the repast will be so much better in the
s?" Seton said crossly. "You think that the crowd will
member you for longer than your next fight?" The cen-
r's voice grew louder and other recuperating fighters
ked toward the pair.

"I think that it is better we each do as we think best,"
mahl said, his voice growing tight. He did not believe his
tory meaningless.

"I apologize, Kamahl," Seton answered. "I should not
my current injuries make me rude." The centaur
ved his hand and only lightly groaned at the pain of
movement. "I have you to thank for the all this." He
ghed. "But truly, I owe you my life," Seton said seri-
ly. "I was paralyzed and sure I would die when you
troyed the mole. My debt to you is more than gold or
rds can pay."

Kamahl nodded, accepting the gratitude with same equa-
nity he had accepted the crowd's adulation.

"I fought for myself, but whatever debt you owe to me

can be repaid by your friendship." The barbari[an]
extended his hand, and the two gripped arms, united
they were in the arena.

*   *   *   *   *

"Over here, Kamahl," Chainer called.

The barbarian looked to the front of the champions' b[ox]
He had returned to the arena to see the Mer champi[on]
fight. There was no posted opponent, and the barbari[an]
wondered who would battle the dangerous-looking amphi[b]-
ian.

"The match hasn't started?" he asked, taking a seat ne[xt]
to the Cabal minion. Chainer was eating olives a[nd]
cheese as he sipped from a cup. The barbarian nodded [to]
a servant who supplied him with a small loaf of bread a[nd]
a goblet of wine. Kamahl drank, noticing a sour taste a[nd]
looking toward the servant. Chainer noticed his look.

"Someone delivered lower-quality food to the kitche[n]
stocking the boxes," the young man explained. "They'[re]
scrambling to find decent food for the important patron[s.]"
He snorted and gestured around as if to comment that t[he]
actual pit fighters were obviously low on the list of the pow[-]
erful. Kamahl drank the wine without further commen[t,]
though deep inside the slight rankled.

"It's all maneuvering to embarrass the current Master [of]
the Games." Chainer said, sounding conspiratorial. "Som[e-]
one is trying to displace him and his connections."

The barbarian listened with little interest.

The crowd stirred excitedly as the fighters' gate opene[d.]
Turg strode forth, the massive Mer champion glistening [as]
if his skin had been freshly moistened. The placards nami[ng]

e opponents were not posted, and Chainer straightened
the frog stalked the empty pit. A concealed gate opened,
from the crowd. With a wild bray, an ass ran into the pit,
hooves flying with wild kicks as it tore around the sides
the arena.

The crowd exploded in laughter as Turg swelled up, his
nds closed up in fists. The amphibian shook with rage as
e audience continued to laugh. Many of the Cabal ser-
nts appeared stunned. The frog ran to intercept the
nkey.

"I can't believe someone would try to disrupt the
mes!" Chainer exclaimed as the Mer champion raced to
s ridiculous opponent. "This prank will offend the
nbassador and the Master of the Games."

The frog reached the donkey, and it spun and let fly. The
arp hooves laid open the skin, and the laughter
creased. Kamahl smiled slightly, though the other fight-
s' grins showed half-moons of teeth.

Turg darted in and grabbed the ass's skull. He turned,
rowing the donkey in a circle. The animal's neck
apped, its body falling limp to the ground. A light
hattering of contemptuous applause greeted the
nphibian. He kept his grip on the head, and his muscles
inched, rotating the skull and tearing it free. Blood
oured onto the sand, splashing up against Turg's legs.
e cocked back his arms and hurled his opponent's head
o into the crowd. The spells that protected the seats
ared, and the lights dimmed as power flowed to inter-
pt the bloody projectile. The skull rotted away, dimin-
hed by the forces of accelerated decay until it fell over
e seats in a spray of foulness. The sound of retching
mpeted with nervous laughter. The ambassador was

standing in his box, outrage visible on his aristocrat
features. The Master of the Games gestured wildly to th
gatekeepers down in the pit.

"He's sending out another beast," Chainer said, settlin
back into the seat. "He'll try to write it off as a mistake, bi
the patriarch will have a head before the end of the day."

A six-legged reptile rushed into the arena, soldiers dri
ing it forth with jabs from tridents. Its legs churned, and
froze in the center, its head turning in quick jerks.

"A Krosan dragonette," Chainer said, clucking h
tongue. "A decent fighting animal but not one wit
stature enough to balance the insult of the ass."

The dragonette saw the amphibian but did not charg

"They need to be driven to battle," Chainer sai
sadly as the Master of the Games went into a new spa
of shouting and arm waving. The gates opened agair
and more animals spilled into the arena. Great houn
milled, their foamy jaws hinting at madness as they b
at each other before the sight of the dragonette and th
frog set them running.

The six-legged beast tore into the pack as they cam
close. The reptile jaws snapped at the leg of a dog se
eral times, leaving it a bloody mass. The rest of the pac
piled on, but the beast thrashed. Howls of pain echoe
in the arena as the dragonette's rough hide stripped f
and flesh away. The amphibian closed, and half th
pack turned on him. There was a wave of magic, an
the frog seemed to fade. Around each of the hounds th
outline of the mer champion appeared, his legs draggin
as if hamstrung. The pack fell on each other as the spe
turned their instincts against them. A biting, dyin
circle spun between the frog and the reptile.

The dragonette bled from multiple bites, the blood
sing down its hide. Its long whip of a tail rose and then
ned into the dogs. A high yelp sounded as the reptile
ck again and again. Each strike left an animal with
ttered bones. The cripples were killed in an instant as
other ensorcelled animals fell upon them. Soon only
dragonette, frog, and a single bleeding hound
nained. Turg snapped into focus and struck the last
, his heavy fist destroying the skull. The dragonette
ned its tail, but the amphibian leaped to the side, once
re fading as multiple images moved away from its land-
place. The dragonette roared in bestial fury, its cry
oing up over the arena walls. Its tongue flickering
ely, it stalked one image exclusively, ignoring the
ers even as several versions of Turg made short rushes
inst it.

The illusions faded as the mer warrior realized the beast's
se of smell made the illusions useless. Catcalls rose from
benches at the turn of events. The frog crouched, its
s spread wide. Power crackled along its arms, and small
amers of lightning trailed from the tips of the frog's
ws. The two monsters leaped at each other, the crowd
ng to its feet. The reptile caught the skin of Turg's thigh
d lacerated it as hands closed over the beast's eyes. Both
frog and dragonette screamed now, but the cries of the
an warrior's opponent were full of pain and despair. The
ls grew shriller as the six-legged beast tried to escape, its
lows becoming more plaintive and fearful.

Kamahl's magical senses could detect Turg's power form-
a circuit between the reptile and the amphibian's own
sh. The frog's own magic made its flesh shake, but the
ge of energy increased as the frog cooked its enemy from

the inside out. The Mer champion shouted its triumph a
fed off its own pain. The ambassador across the arena sho
in sympathy as his champion bellowed in a self-inflict
orgy of pain.

Some of the crowd threw down tokens of appreciatic
the valuables reaching the sand floor as the Cabal servar
curbed the defensive spells protecting the stands. Tu
ripped a hunk of steaming flesh free and swallowed t
meat, reaching for another handful as the applause slac
ened. The mutter of the crowd asking for the next figh
was heard as Cabal minions posted new placards. Ther
cry was heard.

Kamahl stood, and the bellow repeated. The echoi
call was filled with rage and came over the arena wall. T
sound beat against the barbarian's skull as it grew loud
He looked to Chainer, but the youth seemed as confus
as any. The barbarian made his way for the exit, pushi
his way through the other fighters, the cries continui
unabated. Kamahl slowed as he recognized the soun
Though louder and far deeper, they were much like tho
Turg's dead opponent gave forth. Though the dragone
lay dismembered, a response to its dying cries filled t
arena and perhaps the rest of the city.

CHAPTER 5

"Something is breaking into the city!" screamed a
ice in the ambassador's ear. Laquatus struggled from
e depths of his trance, his senses assaulted by the trou-
ed noises of the crowd. The merman shook his head,
ll confused. On the sands below, Turg bellowed and
d into a feeding frenzy, losing any sign of civilized
straint. Again a cry filled the air. The rage and despair
its tone gave the ambassador's spirit a little burst of
y. Something was in great pain, and Laquatus could
ways smile at the pain of others. The erstwhile town

53

crier moved on and shouts continued down the line of box

"See what the noise is about," the ambassador said to guard standing nearby. The mercenary nodded and left a run. The merman stood, shaking the stiffness from muscles. The amphibian continued to eat voraciously a Laquatus saw the difficulty in reining Turg in. Better to the amphibian feed. Usually, the ambassador lost himself the frog's sensations when the opportunity presented its However, the tumult outside continued as crowds drif out of the pits.

"See about getting the arena gates open," he directe Cabal servant who came into the box, looking for a way please the ambassador. "Tell the Master of the Games th while I blame him for nothing, I want my jack allowed leave the field." Laquatus paused for a second.

"Right now," he said emphatically as the servant sto there stupidly. The servant left at a run, his sandals lou drumming on the stone floor.

"I wonder if the fools think I will forgive the insu offered me?" Laquatus asked himself pensively. The assa on his dignity burned, lying like a bed of temporar banked coals, ready to flare up at any moment. Whoev drove the ass out onto the field would pay a hideous pri As would the person that gave the order, their househol and any with close connections. Laquatus idly wondere the city should be razed to assuage his honor?

Perhaps not, after all he had plans for the Cabal and t pits. But the image of burning buildings and corpses seem very attractive. Turg's savage appetite bled into his co sciousness. Perhaps a minute passed before new even broke his reverie. Messengers returned with news, the o sent to the Master of the Games speaking first.

"The official is gone, and all the Cabal servants are called away," he explained, bowing in humiliation. "There is no one with authority to order the gates opened on the arena floor." Laquatus smiled slightly and walked to the refreshments laid to the side. A variety of seafood imported at great expense lay cooling in shaved ice. Laquatus reached for metal tongs used to crack claws. He grabbed the man's hand and grasped a finger quickly. The muscles beneath his aristocratic facade showed themselves as he broke the finger like a twig. The servant went white as the ambassador stepped back to the table. Laquatus picked up a lobster claw and some bread to feed the echo of his jack's hunger.

"I sent you to get Turg out," he said merrily, cracking the chitin to get to the meat. The servant turned even paler at the sound. "I have confidence that you will get my frog free before I run out of fingers." The man swayed, and Laquatus's personal retainer gave him a wide berth, waiting for him to go down.

"Now, now, now," Laquatus clucked, lightly rapping the man's cheek with the metal tongs. "You don't want me breaking more bones to wake you up."

The servant shook his head rapidly, bowing and backing away as he stumbled to the door. The ambassador smiled and motioned to the retainer. The man smiled as nastily as his master, his bald head flushed with excitement at the cruelty.

"Follow along, and if he collapses make sure he receives medical attention." At the disappointed look Laquatus chuckled and waved the man away. How could he punish someone for failure if he died from shock? These landsmen were such unthinking brutes. They had no sense of style. He invited the other messenger forward with a wave of his hand.

"And what is the commotion outside?" the merma asked. "A riot? A revolution? Come, come," he said, as t Cabal servant gathered his composure. "Use your tongue, I'll have it out."

"A monstrous beast has broken through the city wall a is making its way through the town," gushed the man. T ambassador briefly considered using the crushing ton again, but business before pleasure.

"Why the excitement?" Laquatus asked. "The are teems with monsters every day. Surely one more should n provoke such disarray."

"The beast, my lord," the servant said quickly, "is hug It overtops buildings and can be clearly seen from outsi the arena."

The ambassador nodded, intrigued enough that h decided to see the monster for himself.

The runner screwed up his will enough to speak on more before making for the exit. "It also resembles th beast your champion just killed." Then his nerve brok and he left at a run.

The guards made as if to block him, but the ambassad stopped them with a barely perceptible motion. The me senger was of no importance though his words were intrig ing. He waved to a skybox, calling it down. The pil promptly complied, and the merman soon stepped into th small floating craft with a single guard. He looked to th rest of his household. "Go back to the embassy," Laquat said and dismissed them from his mind.

The skybox was one of the smaller ones but an affording such luxury were rich and important. Th seats were of the finest leather. Though it had no buffe there was a collection of rare liquors stowed against th

de. The mage directing the craft was clad in black
egalia while the obvious patron of the box wore an
nderstated tunic and trousers of deep purple and black.

"I am so glad I could give aid," the owner said, moving
o the side to grant the merman more room. "I am Toustos,
n importer of animals for the games."

"I thank you for your courtesy," Laquatus smiled back,
ondering if he should send the two over the side. "I am
e ambassador from the Mer Empire. In the excitement
ere seems to have been a mistake. My jack, Turg, has been
bandoned on the field of victory." He shook his head sadly.
f you could direct this box to pick him up, I would be very
ppreciative." The importer nodded and, with a look,
irected the box down.

"There is a chance," he said, "that the protective field
ver the fighting area may be quiescent. If not, your fighter
 trapped until the guards let him out." The ambassador
odded in agreement but thought that Turg could escape if
e must. The box slowed suddenly as it neared the field.

"Warning spell," said the importer unnecessarily. The
erman could detect the roused energies waiting to destroy
nything that trespassed their vigilant watch. The amphib-
n below tore more flesh from the dragonette, and some of
e six limbs lay amputated. The frog had eaten itself nearly
nmobile, and Laquatus cursed the indulgence of appetite.

"There's no way we can get through the stand defenses,
our Excellency. Is there some other service I might
rovide?"

Laquatus curbed his temper. "There," he said, point-
g to the open air above. "Lift us up that I might see
his beast that draws the rabble so far from their posts."
he box began to rise toward the opening. The curving

galleries and conduits of power loomed over the fiel
and the conveyance drifted further to the side. The ra
of ascent slowed as they neared the limits of the aren
Finally they peeked over the wall and saw the madne
outside.

The merman enhanced his senses, his suddenly sha
eyes and ears bringing the scene into crystal focus.

"Krosan dragon," whispered the importer at the amba
sador's side.

Laquatus slapped the patron, his burning gaze demandir
absolute silence.

The dragon was Turg's opponent grown one hundre
fold. The six-legged beast looked down on the buildings
passed. The city guardsmen ran screaming before it, breal
ing down doors to hide inside. Its head ducked, and th
monster gulped down a flagging sergeant as a snack. Th
other guardsmen put on another burst of speed. The
slowed immediately, exhausted from their crazed run fro
the city walls. Laquatus could see soldiers converging fro
other parts of the city, but he doubted that many wou
arrive in time. The dragon's huge tail lashed behind it.
steady rain of debris from tumbling walls filled the street
the beast came on.

The area in front of the arena was bedlam as carriag
and palanquins disbursed. Patrons rushed to waiting bea
ers, the servants trembling with fright and frustration.
said something for the brutality of the city elite that tran
port waited. But the outskirts of the crowd were frayir
away; some chased by their screaming masters. A clump
officials rallied the Cabal arena guards and handlers in
formation. It seemed a forlorn hope against the approach
ing juggernaut.

Laquatus felt satisfaction at their impending doom. A terrible death by monster might salve away the wound to his dignity. He thought of Turg below, a slumbering fool in someone's scheme, and he hoped the entire Cabal would be slowly eaten alive.

A dementia caster below opened reality to her madness, and a stream of undead stumbled up the street. They formed a parade and advanced laughing, their clothes trailing rags showing hints of past color. Rusty bells rattled, and a chorus of tinny horns sounded as more approached the dragon. Unholy mirth dragged sodden laughter from their rotting chests.

One bellowing voice overrode the noise below, and the ambassador looked down to see Lieutenant Kirtar directing the action. The Order representative oversaw the retreat of those patrons still trapped back into the arena.

"If necessary escape through the rear exits," Laquatus heard through his enhanced hearing. The officer waved pit fighters to join the city guards as noncombatants retreated inside. Down the avenue, the corpses' merriment reached its peak as the parade met the beast.

The street opened into a square, and the zombies surrounded the dragon, throwing themselves at it. The monster's tail began to sweep in rapid strikes, each movement leaving a trailing bundle of rotting flesh. Some zombies seemed to explode as they thudded into thick building walls. Others disappeared inside weak façades, though the sound of collapsing walls suggested they were not spared destruction. Those undead that missed buildings entirely skidded along the cobblestones, shedding flesh and bones until the remains looked as tattered and strewn as the moldering graveclothes. Some avoided the tail and reached the beast.

The giant body thrashed from side to side as a wave of guardsmen followed the undead and reached the great reptile. Spears leading, they charged in support of the merry corpses. They appeared to battle their way onto the monster's hide, and Laquatus for a second increased his sight's magnitude before it blurred back to simple enhancement.

The green fur that seemed to cover the reptile was in fact a blanket of vines. Wrapping the huge beast in innumerable strands, the greenery protected it by a thick covering of long thorns. The figures Laquatus saw clinging to the animal's side were nailed there as solidly as any crucified slave. The zombies tried to crawl to the dragon's head and left a trail of their few remaining threads, then what remained of their skin. Still the summoned corpses laughed and trembled in crazed mirth.

The lieutenant and his supporters advanced, power creeping along their limbs and armoring them against thorns. Axes and swords glowed as they were enhanced, golden flames running along the metal. Spears and javelins arced high in the air, then pierced the dragon's hide. Enchanted metal cut deep, and the monster paused.

Its mouth gaping wide, it poured out a green mist, the emerald haze flowing down the street. The ambassador could still see, but the scene was blurred. Only the frog's ground-hugging nature and his high vantage point allowed him to view all the combatants. For those on the street everything was lost in the attack. The head of the dragon swung skyward, and the ambassador realized that the monster could still see. It came forward as the lieutenant hurled forces into the air.

Burly warriors threw small raypen, their spindly legs trailing as they spread their deformed arms wide. The

agic flowed, and their arms doubled in length, feathers
urting from their skin as sorcery gave them the wings
at their ancestors gave up millennia before. Four bird
arriors climbed higher and began shouting reports to the
eutenant below. The ambassador swore as the Order
rces moved forward. The destruction of his host's city
ould have pleased Laquatus greatly.

Shouts of surprise sounded from the fog below. Like the
opical jungles of the south, ivy and kudzu spread over the
uildings and streets. Wild growth exploded out of window
oxes. Plants and vines unfamiliar to Laquatus curled around
indows and doorways as thick grasses and brush tore
arough cobblestones. The street swiftly became impassable.

Weapons once ready to battle a dragon tried to cut a
ath. The fallen zombies vanished as plants tore apart what
mained of their bodies. The Krosan dragon forced its way
arough the street, its tons of armored flesh finding the
lants only slightly less navigable than the fog that pre-
eded them. Its tongue searched the air for traces of the
ow hidden troops.

The raypen called out reports, and the Lieutenant
esponded from below. The bird warriors banked and
wooped toward the dragon. Long darts fell as they pulled
p, the projectiles slicing into the animal's head. The crea-
are bled profusely, one of the attacks tearing open the
cales near the eye. Weeping red tears, the giant blew forth
geyser of green mist. It swept through the sky, its concen-
ated green a verdant club that swatted at the flyers, hiding
nem from sight.

The raypen climbed out of obscurity, wildly pumping for
lear air. Then they screamed, their limbs flexing spasti-
ally. Their cries choked off, and Laquatus could see them

coughing up gouts of green as they went into seizures. The magic failed, and they plummeted, diving into the tall gra covering the street and vanishing from view.

The ambassador felt the lieutenant drawing more pow as the Order warriors reacted to the deaths of the flyers. Th figures blazed gold as they tried to protect against infesta tion, but soldiers collapsed as the green fought again them, the invisible seeds of destruction sown in the fir moments of battle.

The barbarian Kamahl advanced from the arena, his swor a long whip of flame that burned a path through th brush. Bursts of searing red light emanated from his bod wilting the plants nearby. Laquatus hoped for his death the jack cut a channel through the fog. The sweeps of h weapon burned others free as he reached Kirtar's positio and continued past, ignoring the bird warrior's shoute orders. He trailed supporters in his race up the street.

The dragon's head dipped to devour the impudent ba barian, but the sword's long flame charred a line of fles over its nose. Fresh gouts of the mystical growth hor mone washed over the street, but a spreading cloud flame burned out a circle of safety. The beast tried t maneuver, but fiery knives arced up and exploded on th dragon's side as it turned away. The fires swept awa stretches of the thorny vines protecting the animal hide. Cabal armsmen who had run to the roofs of su rounding buildings found their courage, and a few arrow and bolts sought the gaps in green armor. The huge ta brought down more structures, whipping in painf frenzy as rubble cascaded into the verdant growth Clouds of dust set the combatants choking as they disap peared from view.

There was a fresh bout of screams, and Laquatus watched the ıgon's claws hooking a hapless fighter into the cloud. Unable see into the green haze, he summoned a wind. It took pre- ›us seconds, but the mass of dust blew over the rooftops, com- :tely blinding those archers and spearmen with the courage be exposed. The merman ignored them as the cloud began clear the street. He saw the dragon whip its head, catapult- ; a screaming soldier through the air to intercept the barbar- ı as he came into view. Laquatus clapped with delight.

"Good show," he called, ignoring the looks of the ıporter. The barbarian and his humanoid projectile sailed to a faceless building, which shot out more dust as inter- .l walls collapsed. The roof pitched sharply, and refugees the street battle screamed as they slid off and fell to the nbers and stone blocks below.

The lieutenant ordered a retreat, driving the fighters and the v remaining observers at street level down other avenues.

"We'll hamstring it as it tears into the arena," he shouted. ıquatus started as he saw the beast coming closer. The ybox began to drop, cutting off the view of the action.

"Take us back up!" he ordered the importer, furious at ıe interruption. It was the merchant's servant who ıswered him.

"The energy to the transports is being redirected to the :fensive shields," the pilot explàined, directing the craft a cradle against the opposite wall. "They must be plan- ng to drive the animal into the decay field to kill it." ne ambassador could feel the deadly spells below grow- g more powerful.

"Why would they think the beast headed here?" he ked. "Surely it will chase the cowards running away rather .an attack an empty building."

This time it was the importer who answered him.

"It comes to answer the cry of distant kin," Touste explained. The merchant was nervous, and the merman cou~~ tell the human tried to control his own fear by showing h~~ superior knowledge. "It will break its way in and kill whoev~~ it finds when it sees and smells the corpse of the dragonette~~

The ambassador looked to the sands below. Turg lay ~~ if dead, stuffed to bursting on wild ass and the monste~~ caller. There was no way to raise him from his slumbe~~ though Laquatus sent command after command to th~~ amphibian's mind. His enhanced hearing could hear th~~ slamming of bolts as every gate closed in an attempt ~~ keep the beast inside after it broke through.

"I am sure they will kill it before it can devour you~~ champion or reach us," the importer said nervously. Th~~ ambassador grasped him by the throat and with a sing~~ motion threw him to the sands below. Maggot-ridde~~ meat struck the floor, and the merman's guard did n~~ even wait for the order, hurling the skybox attendant ov~~ the side of the conveyance. The mercenary retired bac~~ trying not to catch his master's attention.

"I will trust these incompetent animals to protect me~~ Laquatus said to himself. "These dry, ungainly fools, unwort~~ of all responsibility!" he screamed as the guard tried to ma~~ himself smaller. "I spit on these air-breathing tube worms!"

The ambassador sent his call forth again, compellin~~ absolute, immediate compliance. But his demand did n~~ split open the skull of the comatose pit frog. Instead th~~ orders passed through the rock beneath the arena, resona~~ ing in the caverns below. Laquatus felt the surge of pow~~ as his waiting armies prepared to attack.

CHAPTER 6

"Bloody hell," rasped Kamahl as he opened his eyes. The fighter ached over every portion of his being. His mind fuzzed, and he tried to remember where he was. It came back to him as he coughed up dust and smoke. The fight with the attacking monster, the concealing clouds of dust, and the impact of the thrown soldier. All of it surged into focus as he pushed his way to his feet. Plaster and lumber sloughed from his back as he looked to the gaping hole that his flight had left. The small fires started during his impact were growing and at his stern glance died down, the smoke whistling through every crack in the houses structure as his will compelled the flames.

Kamahl looked for the soldier who had rammed him. A congealing pool of blood leaking from another pile of debris told the barbarian his likely fate. He shoveled away wreckage with his hand and exposed a dead face. A support beam nailed the corpse to the floor as firmly as a mountain. The mage could hear cries of the beast and stumbled outside, his steps becoming firmer with every second. His sword hung from the outside wall, the blade sunk deep in oak. Kamahl threw power into the steel and ripped it free in a hail of splinters. Armed and aware, he cut his way to the street.

The grasses and bushes that blocked his way had grown only a little after his unexpected withdrawal. Rubble from newly demolished buildings covered a lush growth that continued to push its way toward the sun. The barbarian climbed carefully up a slope of debris, accepting the risk of a fall for a better view. The tail of the dragon lashed across the street, each beat bringing fresh destruction. Kamahl saw no sign of the other fighters and wondered if the beast had killed them all.

The monster reared up against the wall of the arena, its front two legs digging at the stones. Thin panels of fine rock fell, revealing the brick that formed the walls. Kamahl knew the beast would claw its way through in minutes. Whether any yet remained inside was unknown, but they would surely die when the dragon pushed its way through the ramshackle structure. The barbarian sheathed his sword on his back and walked up the street toward the stadium, the grass and brush grasping at his legs.

The mountain warrior stopped and concentrated, ignoring the caresses from the growing plants. Kamahl hurled a continuing barrage of knives drawn from his mind. The blades burst into red and orange flame, casting shadow a

ey spun before sinking into the waving tail of the mon-
er. The dragon's reflexive movement from the pain batted
ide some of the projectiles, imbedding them in buildings.
he weapons started fires as they discharged into walls and
ew trees, the smoke promoting fresh cries of panic as those
uardsmen hiding in rubble and out of sight found their
nctuaries set alight. Despite the secondary damage, the
agon's tail dropped limply to the ground as Kamahl's
tack burned through bundles of nerves.

The beast, maddened with pain, spun in the square
fore the arena. The monster's hips brushed against the
xposed brick core of the pit walls. The masonry frag-
ented and stained the creature's upper legs a dark ochre,
atching its dusty claws. The beast slowed as its dead, trail-
g tail robbed it of speed, dragging through the rubble and
atching on exposed beams before the monster's power tore
free. Kamahl continued his assault, more magically forged
ives spinning on their trajectories toward the dragon.
ity guard corpses were still impaled on the creature's
orny armor, and the barbarian's attack thudded into the
ooling bodies. The monster's thorny armor and the dead
egan to burn as the mystic metal vanished in gouts of
ame. Kamahl knew the impromptu funeral pyres were the
ly ceremony the guardsmen were likely to receive in
abal City.

The dragon recovered, finishing its turn and roaring at
e barbarian, its teeth red with the blood of those already
ain. Kamahl drew his sword, waiting for the beast's charge.

A new flare of magic lit up the street, surprising beast
d barbarian. The combatants froze in the glare, the
onster blinded and the city guards diving for cover.
amahl stretched out his mind, trying to trace the origin

of the power rippling through the ground. He felt for th
stability and strength that he knew from his home moun
tains, but from the depths an alien magic seemed to poiso
the very street he stood on.

Pools of light expanded out of the ground, their blu
radiance growing stronger and attacking Kamahl's eye
Frothy ponds formed, stilled, and dimmed, and creature
erupted into the upper world.

Giant crabs surged from the holes, spreading out in a re
tide. Their massive frames broke through the welter c
brush. Claws tore out the dragon growth by the root
revealing the cobblestones that had vanished under th
beast's attack. The snapping of small tree trunks sounde
across the battlefield as the crustaceans cleared a beach
head, their pincers shredding those obstacles they could nc
simply uproot by sheer strength.

The dragon blinked at the sudden activity, frozen in su
prise. Then a building front, damaged by the battle, ca
caded into the street and broke its trance. The monste
breathed out a cloud of green mist, beginning a new bout c
berserk growth. The potent breath swept up the street, se
tling over the scuttling crabs then reaching the barbariar
Kamahl closed his eyes and concentrated. Small flame
leaped up from his clothes and gear, then grew until h
entire body was encased in the pale flame. The sound of th
fire was echoed in the hiss and crackle of new growt
sprouting everywhere in the street. Cobblestones cracked a
trees and bushes forced their way to the surface. The flame
leaped from Kamahl's clothes to the ground and new ter
drils of growth withered. The warrior started forward, th
fire of his will burning a path through the resurgent vege
tation. The flames lit the mist, and he moved as if in a fo

The barbarian used his sword now, his fiery armor thin-
ng, leaving him more exposed to the mist. The energy
ing to his sword and each swing of his weapon cast a
thing whip of power ahead to clear his path. The blade
ened the way to the crabs' clearing.

The pools were still lighting the fading mist with their
liance. Kamahl felt immediate antipathy to the light. Its
lor pierced the eye, and his weapon's flame curled back
hind him, expending his irrational hate into the vegeta-
n at his back. The dragon was coming into view, and he
uld not afford distractions now.

The sea walkers showed no reactions to the barbarian's
iergence from the new jungle, continuing to cut back
iwth. The dragon breathed again, its concentrated wrath
lowing over the clearing. Many of the crustaceans were
vered with growing plants, but they continued working,
eir claws now trimming grass and bushes from their fellow
irkers as well as the clearing's edge. A new surge of mer
ces began to crowd the clearing. The crabs moved on,
eir claws now raised and threatening.

Kamahl cut his way along the perimeter of the encamp-
:nt. The warrior surmounted a mound of rubble enabling
n to look over the crab's clearing. New creatures dragged
emselves from the pools, and the crustaceans charged the
igon. The giant reptile reared up, four legs waved in the
as it spun, its tail skimming through the crabs. The sea
hters were thrown up against a building front, their shells
cturing with a series of crackling sounds. The dragon's
ad tail still had mass, and the reptile used it like a club,
mming it into the structure's façade. Rubble cascaded
wn over the broken shells.

The giant monster moved into the arena's square, the

street's buildings blocking the barbarian's view. Kamahl n[...]
had to skirt the new forces creeping out of the pools. Sm[...]
humanoids with huge heads crawled out onto the surfa[...]
gingerly, their whiskers trailing on the ground. The barb[...]
ian recognized the amphibians. The tresias were sometim[...]
found in highland caves. The street was filling with the
new arrivals, and Kamahl swore as they blocked the w[...]
The blind creatures' great claws scraped over the rubble a[...]
slashed mounds of mown grass into mulch. The barbari[...]
was nearing the square, and his lashing flame blade scyth[...]
away the undergrowth. The dragon screamed and ca[...]
back into view. It stomped a crab into jelly, and pounds [...]
meat squirted out between the animal's clawed toes. [...]
began to move up the street.

The amphibians' oversized heads rose up, orienting [...]
the giant monster. A surreal and hypnotic radiance puls[...]
out toward the common enemy—faint in the sunlight a[...]
dust of battle but commanding all the same. Kamahl caug[...]
only a brief glimpse, and it mesmerized him. The bat[...]
faded away as his mind lost itself in a play of color. [...]
training strained to break the silken mental bonds, [...]
reassert his mastery. The barbarian's struggles cleared [...]
mind, and as his sight came back, he found himself turn[...]
around, facing down the street, away from the dragon a[...]
toward the tresias. He shifted his eyes away, avoiding t[...]
hypnotic trap that tried to ensnare him once more. Fr[...]
the corner of his eye he could see more crabs coming fort[...]
these falling upon the rubble and vegetation to expand t[...]
beachhead.

As the hypnotic power of the tresias seemed to dim,
new wave of reinforcements crawled from the depths belo[...]
Kamahl shuffled to the side in atavistic reaction as the n[...]

arine fighters rolled and oozed over the landscape. The
phalid soldiers hauled themselves by their tentacles out of
e pool. Bags of flesh, they left a trail of slime as they slith-
ed over the cobblestones.

Though they lay like dead jellyfish cast up on the beach
y a storm, each grasped a weapon. Spear guns and tridents
ıg at the dirt as the invaders rested for a few precious sec-
ıds then resumed their drive on the still-bemused mon-
er. The hypnotic tresias light vanished as each amphib-
n collapsed, hanging their heads and starting to crawl
ıck on their fragile limbs toward the pools to the under-
orld. The cephalids and crabs parted as their blind com-
ıtriots returned, their manner showing the same disquiet
ith their allies that the barbarian felt.

Kamahl scaled the side of a building, his bruised hands
aving a tacky film of blood as he swarmed up the side. The
a forces had cleared a path, but he would not trust their
ompany. By the time he reached the third story, the dragon
ıunded again, fury in its voice as it overcame the amphib-
ıs' spell. The barbarian chinned himself to the rooftop and
ırned to run toward the giant monster, finally free of the
ıdergrowth and mer warriors below.

The cephalids attacked the dragon, propping their
:ojectors on rubble and bodies from the battle. The
ıafts flew wildly, and Kamahl congratulated himself on
·eking higher ground. Incompetence and inexperience
ıuld kill as quickly as malice. A few bolts from spear
ıns snapped into reptilian flesh though most landed on
ıbble and cobblestones. The projectiles discharged
ıowers of sparks, and the barbarian detected the same
ıergies that fed lightning storms. The mountain war-
or conjured an axe of flame and threw it with all the

force at his command. The conjured weapon sp[u]
through the air and slammed into the shoulder of t[he]
convulsing dragon. A charred circle expanded as t[he]
magic destroyed the thorny armor to show the hi[de]
beneath.

"There's an aiming point!" Kamahl shouted to t[he]
forces below. The cephalids were silent, their tentac[les]
locked around their projectors as they compacted sprin[g]
and loaded new shafts for another volley. The barbari[an]
forgot the clumsy fighters in the street below as he hea[rd]
the battle cry of the Order.

Lieutenant Kirtar maneuvered on the rooftops as we[ll,]
ceding the ground to the invaders from the forests and se[a.]
Kamahl could see city guardsmen coming up other stree[ts]
from his four-story vantage point. The dragon was clawi[ng]
down brick and timber over the cephalids and the remai[n]-
ing crabs. The sea fighters scrabbled to get clear as the mo[n]-
ster tried to bury them. Another barrage of bolts sputter[ed]
and arced, but the huge beast seemed to not notice t[he]
pain. It hopped from foot to foot, crushing the cabs.

Kirtar was a fountain of energy as he crossed the roofs. T[he]
Order champion's attack slammed into the giant creatur[e's]
hip, tunneling its way to the bone. With a crack audib[le]
throughout the street, a joint gave way, and the creatur[e's]
rearmost leg spasmed and dragged. The giant tried [to]
breathe more fog, but only a few wisps came out. It tried [to]
back out into the square as everyone closed for the kill.

Kamahl was accelerating as he jumped to the final ro[of]
and conjured another weapon in his free hand. He hurl[ed]
the axe at the creature's side, aiming for the thicke[st]
remaining patch of the beast's thorny armor. He was in t[he]
air in a long leap when it exploded, devouring a bro[ad]

wath of the deadly vegetation in a wave of flame. The barbarian's sword smashed into a mound of muscle as his jump landed him on the beast's side. His plunging sword burned a deep wound, and the dragon screamed again. The giant tried to scrape the mountain warrior off against a building, inflicting even more damage to itself in an instinctive response to the attack.

Kamahl levered himself up and over the rise of the animal's spine, his sword and an axe acting as pitons. The rumble of cascading rubble drowned out the barbarian's angry cry as a barbed tendril of the creature's remaining armor sank its thorns into the fighter's thigh. One hand held his buried sword as the other tore the vine free. Below him, the beast heaved and pitched as the warrior cupped his hand and drew flame into the world. He clasped the summoned fire against the wound, hissing at the pain. A wave of cold swept his body as his flesh tried to shrug off the burn. As he lay panting, the mer forces attacked again.

Soft-bodied sea warriors raised their spear guns, discharging magical projectiles to little effect. The dragon's head dipped, and its claws scrabbled, tearing apart some of its tormenters. The mer eeled their way into mounds of rubble, and others suctioned their way up the outsides of buildings. The forest creature took advantage of the ascending invaders and snapped them down from the buildings. Even as it devoured its foes, the crabs made a run for its flanks. Though most died under the dragon's heavy stomps, some scuttled under the massive frame, and now giant claws nipped at the injured leg and tail.

The barbarian saw the crustacean warriors moving wildly below, their claws shearing at the huge tendons. The middle leg on the left collapsed, and Kamahl jumped for safety as the animal went down, rolling to crush the sea fighters. The mountain mage's sword lashed into a building wall, and the pull of gravity dragged the steel down. The power of the blade left a trail of smoking brick as Kamahl arrested his slide. As he slowed, he pulled the weapon free and fell the remaining distance to the street. His leg protested, but he ignored the shallow wounds. The back of the beast lay toward him, and he could see the street coming apart under its pounding mass. He closed with the downed beast.

Lieutenant Kirtar called for all forces to finish the monster. A mer fighter finally showed some marksmanship and shot a charged spear beneath an armored eyelid. A shower of ocular fluid soaked the fallen grasses, pouring from the empty socket as it writhed. The few remaining crabs began to climb the body.

The barbarian watched the cephalids retreat back to their pools, then he could see only the monster. It filled his vision as it tried to rise to its feet. Kamahl raised his sword and plunged it near the spine. The beast somehow got its legs under its bulk, and the barbarian was nearly catapulted free. Only his grip on his sword allowed him to stay with the monster. The dragon was stumbling away from the arena and up the street, headed for the sea fighters and their pools. The crabs tried to climb the slack tail, but they failed as the giant swayed from side to side. The beast was killing the warriors almost by accident as it crushed both hard-shelled and soft-bodied fighters from the sea against the broken bricks of Cabal City.

Kirtar stood opposite Kamahl on a building roof, sure footed despite the slope of the crumbling structure. The barbarian saw a predatory grin as the aven unleashed another flight of his conjured birds. The mountain warrior swore and breathed out a cage of flame, concentrating even as his uncontrolled mount tottered beneath him. The golden sparrows swooped down and swept over the great reptile, their wings of light shaving away the remains of the dragon's thorny armor before rising to the sky. The spell wrought creatures threw themselves as living knives at the beast's head, vanishing in concussive bursts that carved away hide.

Determined to get the kill, Kamahl forced power into the long blade of his sword. Inside the monster a scalpel of flame cut its way to the backbone. Massive vertebrae parted as the barbarian's will sought out the thick cable of armored nerves. New magic impacted on the dragon's flanks, but Kamahl was locked in directing his final attack. Bone and nerve sundered under Kamahl's lethal surgery, parting the spinal cord and killing the beast.

The mountain warrior turned to jump clear, but he was crushed against the beast's back as a huge crab came from the rear in a wild rush. A crustacean had finally managed to climb the dragging tail, and now its vain attack only put the barbarian at risk. Kamahl was bowled over and barely avoided the huge claws, which clutched for something to hold on to.

The dragon fell and the barbarian could hear Kirtar shrieking victory. New attacks impacted against the already dead flesh as additional surges of magic burrowed into the slowly collapsing corpse. Fighters left off their attacks, running for their lives as tons of flesh gave up life.

The barbarian snarled, trapped under the crustacean. He forced his way through legs, the spindly limbs landing like clubs as the mer fighter panicked, and the pair began to fall free. The barbarian and crab were directly under the beast and both bolted for the closest bit of clear sky, trying to race under the beast as the wall of descending flesh loomed over them. But the panicked crab yanked the barbarian back, its claws gripping his armored belt as it tried to pull itself to safety. It only doomed them both. Pressure threatened to smash Kamahl like a bug, and his breath exploded out his mouth. Pain flared all over his body, and he fell into darkness, his senses fading as blackness smothered all.

CHAPTER 7

The stench of burned flesh and destruction was sweet in Kirtar's nostrils. The aroma was nectar the bird warrior savored as he stood with his eyes closed. The crackle of fires soothed his hot blood, the destruction of the Cabal structures an unexpected benefit. The beast had torn a great wound in the city's fabric and like draining blood, the citizens flowed into the streets.

The attack had caught him deep in the arena, and it had ken precious minutes to force his way through the crowds. he plaza had been a madhouse, bleeding guardsmen form-g defenses to manage the crowds. With his warriors still st in the clearing stands, the lieutenant took control, stilling order into the fleeing cowards, clearing the way

for the coming battle. True, he was forced into a tactic
retreat and the sudden arrival of the mer empire forc
turned the contest. But it was his own blow that laid th
beast low when all was finally done.

The bleating of the wounded irritated him, and h
directed those of his order with healing skills to ply the
trade among the injured. He pointed to the mer forces
receive healing first. The monsters of the deep at least wer
brave fighters and far more worthy of aid than the corrup
gamblers of the city. The lieutenant moved down to th
street level as he saw his orders being relayed. The fe
Cabal officers he saw looked thoroughly cowed, and nor
disputed his authority.

"This is the natural order of things," he whispered t
himself.

The crabs dragged away the corpses of their dead, despit
the Cabal servants' furtive attempts to secure the bodies fo
the city's use. The crustaceans sorted through the rubbl
their immense strength allowing them to move all but th
largest beams. The exposed corpses not from the mer real
were discarded on the rubble piles to be snared by guard
men. Kirtar made a note to have his own forces colle
their dead in Cabal territory.

A centaur staggered to the street, the simian face visib
over the high grass. He started toward the Order officer, car
fully trying to find a clear path. Kirtar's mystic senses detecte
a change in magic. The arena defenses, still unbreached, wer
coming down. Servitors slowly walked toward the growt
obstructing the streets holding staves. One took the lead an
his staff of black wood and iron passed among the stalks. Th
plants withered into brittle husks as the lieutenant watche
The other Cabal reinforcements joined in.

'Ware the street cleaners," the champion called out
h derision. A few of the workers bristled but none chal-
ged his appraisal. Kirtar expected nothing more from
h cravens.

'Lieutenant," called the centaur, moving into the cleared
et, barely avoiding a "mistaken" swing of a withering staff
lded by an angry guardsman. The centaur bared his fangs
l shook the huge club that he used as a walking stick.

Kirtar recognized him as the fighter allied with the barian. The injuries he had sustained appeared half-healed,
l the officer assumed that was the reason the forest
ter had not joined in the battle. He confessed to him-
f that the warrior, Kamahl, had at least shown rash
rage during the fight.

'What is it?" he asked. Then trying to explain his short-
s, he continued, "As you can see there is much to be
ne, and our hosts seem incapable of doing it." Kirtar
ored the efforts of the Cabal to clear the streets and the
am of carts arriving to haul away the rubble.

"The beast was a Krosan dragon," the centaur said. "It is
nd only in the forests of the far northwest." At the signs
the bird warrior's exasperation with the lesson, Seton
de his point. "It has absolutely no business being here.
mething is wrong, and this attack could be only the sign
greater troubles."

"I appreciate the information, sir," Kirtar said, speaking
h excessive courtesy, "but what am I to do?" He waved
the destruction caused by the single beast. "How does the
struction of a pit like this concern the Order?"

"For the dragon to appear this far east, the reverberations
whatever is disturbing the forest must cover leagues."
ton explained, his voice showing offense. "As an officer

in the Order, sworn to protect the Northern Reaches a
hoping to extend your authority south, I thought you wo
be grateful for the insight. Excuse me if I misundersto
your seriousness." With that the centaur moved away, t
haft of his granite-capped club beating a tune of anger
the cobblestones.

Shaking his head at the vagaries of forest warriors, Kir
turned back to supervision. But there was little to do, as
army of Cabal workers fell to work in concert with t
remaining crabs.

"Of course they are ready now," the lieutenant mumbl
to himself. More movement caught his eye, and he turn
to see Laquatus, the mer ambassador, and Turg, his amphi
ian champion, coming from the arena. The frog mov
slowly, and his eyes were glassy. Kirtar had not paid atte
tion to the arena match and wondered if Turg was injure
The frog squatted on his heels, slowly rocking from side
side as the ambassador came forward.

"Congratulations on your brilliant victory," the merm
hailed. Laquatus gave a short bow that good manners demand
the lieutenant return. "The beast would have surely destroy
the city if not for your quick action." The ambassador look
pained as he said it, and Kirtar felt obligated to inquire.

"Did you take injuries during the battle?" The lieutena
had seen nothing, but it must have been a madhouse insid

"No, no," replied the merman. "The spells protecting t
arena sealed me and my champion away from combat. Tu
was trapped on the arena floor, and a few others and I we
locked in a skybox during the actual attack. I fear t
excitement was too much for my companions. In a fit
desperation they tried to leap free and perished in the fie
protecting the audience from the arena floor." Laquat

oked quite distressed, reining his voice in with difficulty.
's desperately sad. One of the deceased was an importer
ith some knowledge of the attacking beast. He said it was
type of dragon that came in response to the beast my
ampion killed."

Kirtar frowned.

"A centaur told me that the beast never left the north-
estern forests," the officer said. "He was quite convinced
at such animals were never here. To come in response to
cry means either the animal was tracking the one killed
that it was in the general vicinity." Kirtar wondered if
erhaps the centaur was on to something. There could be
continuing danger.

Another bird warrior flew through the air. The four in
irtar's party had been killed, so this golden-winged fighter
ust be a messenger from the north. The lieutenant waved
s arms to signal his presence, but the sharp-eyed flyer was
ready swooping down to him. The raypen folded his wings
d shook the still settling dust off his feathers.

"Greeting to my First," intoned the raypen, its high tenor
ping as it recited the message from memory. Messengers
ere specially trained to give messages word for word to pre-
nt written orders from being intercepted. "There have
en attacks of forest creatures all along the western borders
the high plains. You are to return north directly, collect-
g information and offering aid to those whom need it. The
llages under the Order must be protected. If necessary you
ill stay and oversee the southern defense. We must find out
hat is happening. Pianna, Captain of the North."

Kirtar cursed the bad timing. Fighters from across the
ntinent were here for the contest, and representatives of
e other continental powers had arrived as well. Here was

a chance to forge new alliances, and the Captain had just ordered him back to the barely civilized plains to protect scores of nameless villages. His huge hands clenched in anger, but he relaxed them with a conscious effort. The captain was head of the Order, and he must believe that she knew what she was doing. After all, he thought to himself, he didn't want to stay in this pit of a city anyway. There would be other chances to make his presence known. News of his victory would help convince others that the Order direction was necessary for the common good.

"I am afraid I must leave directly," he said to the ambassador, waving the messenger toward the main camp. "I am sorry to miss the championship rounds, but am sure Turg will triumph now that I will withdraw from the contests." He looked toward the amphibian, but he had vanished from sight. Looking for the frog brought the officer's gaze back to the sight of the mer forces diving into the pools, dragging their dead behind them.

"I was very surprised to see your soldiers streaming from the ground," he stated, his eyes narrowing as he turned back to the ambassador.

Laquatus seemed huge, his form giving off vibrations that seemed hypnotic. Kirtar could feel his pulse slowing as the violet eyes of the merman expanded to fill the world.

"But of course you knew of the soldiers under the city," the velvet voice insinuated. "They attacked at your orders being already under your command. Don't you remember?" Kirtar fell into darkness ringed in purple as the ambassador took hold of his shoulders.

* * * * *

"I must therefore leave immediately for forest's edge."
ne words resounded in Kirtar's head, and he wondered
no was saying them. It was with some surprise that he
alized that he was the speaker. "This attack is but one of
zens that have issued from the west. The Order is the
ly force that can protect those villages without the walls
d guardsmen of Cabal City," he said to the assembled
y elders.

Kirtar stood on a rough platform against the arena, look-
g over the square. The fall of rubble punctuated his
eech as work crews tried to clear the streets. The dragon
at he had slain filled the street, and blood from the great
rpse slowly drained into the storm gutters, the smell issu-
g from the sewers under the arena. The crowd of hench-
en and ordinary citizen ignored the odor. Kirtar knew
em to be used to such odors in this pit. He gritted his
eth in anger.

Why was he giving a speech to the Cabal, he wondered
vagely. The city was contemptible. Only the grave breach
civil order had convinced him to fight the dragon attack.
abal City was a sour taste in his mouth. Only the sight of
e mer ambassador, his invaluable advisor, prevented him
tting in contempt onto the arena square. He ignored the
owing mutters at his long silence to regard Laquatus, his
osest ally. The merman was the first to see the importance
uniting the continent of Otaria, saving its fragmented
story.

The mer agreed it was long past time to impose order on
e land. The underwater kingdom would lend arms to
lp the lieutenant pursue his dreams. The guards the
abassador put under his command proved invaluable in
feating the huge beast. It was the first and richest fruit of

the inter-power alliance that the Order wished to form.

How lucky the ambassador had ferried his personal gua to the catacombs under the arena. Kirtar wondered at th expense of shifting so many water breathers. It was fort nate that the drowned caves had been available. Eve though the forces proved effective, he still chuckled at th naivete of the ambassador. It showed the merman's inexpe rience with the dry land that he would bring wat breathers as guards against land-bound dangers. After a how many flooded caves could there be? He nodded to th ambassador, grateful for his support and resolved to do h best in protecting Laquatus from his own foolishness an inexperience.

The officials began clapping after long seconds, and th crowd belatedly joined in. The Master of the Gam heaved his heavy bulk up to the podium beside the lie tenant. Kirtar dragged his attention back to the officials the Cabal, despising them but determined to act polite for his ally's sake. The mer ambassador nodded appro ingly, and the bird warrior felt a burst of pride at his ow statesmanship.

"We thank you for your leadership in combating th dragon in conjunction with Ambassador Laquatus's guard The Cabal functionary sent an ill-favored glance towa the water dweller as he mentioned the valiant sea fighte It was the base nature of the pits that made them so susp cious of such timely aid, the lieutenant said to himself. Th speaker turned from the ambassador as if snubbing him an gestured broadly toward the Order officer and his guar behind him.

"Hurry up, you bag of wind," the aven warrior mutter to himself.

In recognition of such bravery and valor in cause of the
mon good, we gladly offer the pick of the prizes to Lieu-
ant Kirtar."

A polite clapping sounded as a representative of the
der went to select a prize from the mound of treasure
led from the arena. The champion was unable to
train showing at least some contempt for the proceed-
, and he chose an elen to carry the prize. Though the
nt bird warriors stood close to ten feet tall, the gray-
ned humanoids were of the serving class. The lieu-
ant doubted his hosts were intelligent enough to read
 insult of the great robed figure going through the
zes like a ragpicker searching a garbage pile. The elen
ected an object, the round sphere almost lost in its
antic hands.

The ambassador and his frog both looked to the prize,
oring the rambling official. As Kirtar agreed to this farce
y as a favor to his ally, he wondered what could be so
portant about a bauble plucked randomly from a pile.
e elen walked slowly, appearing almost introspective as
came nearer the officer. The giant bird warriors were
own for their lack of magical talent, and it appeared, out-
e everything Kirtar knew, that the huge servant tried to
 magical senses to probe the metal surface. Intrigued by
at would drive such a mystical incompetent to such
orts, the lieutenant stepped forward to intercept the prize
rer. The walker showed no awareness, continuing
vard the baggage train where the bauble was to be stored
h the other luggage. The officer plucked it out of the
n's grasp, seeing Turg step forward as if to admonish him.
en all thoughts of the frog, the Cabal, and anything else
ished from his mind.

The sphere erupted in a shout of power. The dull m[e] surface seemed to burn away, blurring Kirtar's eyes w[ith] tears. The magic that called so softly now filled the wo[rld]. As the flare of energy subsided, the lieutenant held a gl[obe] of perfect crystal. The clear depths called to him, draw[ing] his spirit away from Cabal City. The aftermath of the ba[ttle] and the stench of the street were gone. Purity and glory s[ur]-rounded the bird warrior. The audience showed its essen[ce] stupidity in staring dumbly at him, ignoring the vistas t[hat] opened at every side.

Kirtar saw himself striding through a field of enem[ies] each frozen and impotent against him, and his spells sw[ept] them away to oblivion. The banner of the Order flew o[ver] the field in victory. The aven's heart sang as he knew [the] triumph, the glory, that waited to be seized.

The images dimmed until he saw once again the m[ag]-nificent globe filling his hand. Kirtar heard the excla[ma]-tions of the crowd but ignored them. They were not wor[thy] to taste the future he had seen. This city was trash a[nd] could be ignored now that he held real power. His h[and] hand closed over the prize, gripping it as tightly as his m[ind] gripped the visions it bestowed.

CHAPTER 8

"Everything was going so well," thought the ambassador, stunned by the surge of magic. "How, by the stormy seas, have things gotten so out of control?"

The ambassador was finally able to rouse Turg from his digestive slumber only at the end of the battle. He was required to lay actual hands on the amphibian before he could break the near coma. Seeing the pit fighter too stuffed for any use he forced the ma-noid to expel much of what he had eaten. Thank-ly, no one witnessed the thoroughly unpleasant scene, t Laquatus pledged the frog would not be allowed such havior ever again.

Even as Turg scraped his face clean, a soldier from the

underground army had found the ambassador and repor
on the battle. The cephalid shifted down the seats of
arena and collapsed as it fell from the high walls to
sands below. Laquatus thought the tedious importer wo
have looked very similar if he had not dissolved av
under the then-active defenses.

"My lord," the warrior had said in a muffled voice, nea
inaudible as it tried to speak out of water, "the beast is fal
and our forces clear away the debris. Captain Satas has s
those who cannot live long outside the water back throu
the portal. He has been forced to retire as well and w
further instruction."

Laquatus cursed the poor timing that found so few warr
able to live long above ground. More amphibians would hav
be found for further battles. The cephalid's tentacles were nea
white from exhaustion, and it needed to get back to the wat

"Tell the good captain that there is no need for furt
operations on the surface at this time," the ambassador s
carefully. "Sound the recall of all troops. It is not necess
for our fighters to act as servants to the inferiors inhabit
this land. I will meet with Satas later at the usual place."
paused, wondering just what the situation outside was.

If worst came to worst, he could always find refuge in
deep caverns. It was unlikely that any would be able
invade the dark subterranean rivers. Whatever happen
he needed to do as much damage control as possible. T
presence of a secret fighting force must be explained a
assurances offered to the Cabal. Briefly Laquatus regret
the necessity of sending the army back below, but furt
action would undoubtedly create substantial casual
without any lasting gains. If only the cave digging crews l
opened up more of the underwater cavern systems.

He returned the cephalid's gesture of obedience and
watched the soft-bodied soldier scale the wall. Captain
Itas had responded promptly, and it sounded as if the
quick action of the tresias had saved Turg and the ambassador from having to contend with the dragon. He resolved
to closet himself with the diminutive amphibian in the
near future.

The destruction of the city streets put him in a better
humor. The rubble and still-visible bodies made him cheer-
fully overlook the insults he had suffered for the moment.
Though whoever made him and his champion an object of
fun would someday pay the price. He saw the last of the
marine dead being dragged into the pools as he arrived to
talk with the lieutenant. The self-important champion had
succumbed easily to the ambassador's spells, and he dragged
the officer into a gaping building as his mind overrode the
men's. It took only a few minutes of apparent conversation
to set a cover story in place.

Kirtar now believed that days before the ambassador had
told the bird warrior of a secret guard foisted upon him by
the emperor. Unwilling to insult the ability of his Cabal
hosts, Laquatus had hidden them in the secret tunnels
under the arena. Realizing that the lieutenant was the pre-
eminent military power in the city, the ambassador offered
his troops to the Order as an emergency reserve. The attack
of the dragon revealed how incompetent the Cabal was in
military matters, and only the lieutenant prevented a complete disaster.

The decision of the emperor to send additional troops
showed the wisdom of the underwater monarch. At the
conclusion of the battle, the badly damaged marine formation retired back to the deep wells under the arena and the

embassy. Laquatus created the fantasy of a tempora[ry]
alliance that even now worked at the bird warrio[r's]
memory. When Kirtar went north, he would take with h[im]
the absolute conviction that a permanent alliance was t[he]
natural next step with the mer empire.

"Lieutenant Kirtar, we have orders to escort you to a ce[r]-
emony honoring your leadership." A gravely voi[ce]
announced almost in the merman's ear. Laquatus broke [off]
his mental manipulations suddenly, leaving the lieutena[nt]
to stumble and look about vaguely at the sudden release. [A]
section of city guardsmen stood at ease, one holding a cle[an]
standard that contrasted with his torn and dusty uniform. [It]
appeared that the city was wasting no time in honoring [its]
hero. The ambassador smiled brightly.

"A great honor indeed, Lieutenant," the merman sa[id,]
gripping the bemused warrior's arm and starting off for t[he]
square. He ignored the guardsmen who had to step out [of]
their way or be trampled. The Order's men had be[en]
unwilling to interrupt a private conversation, but the c[ity]
soldiers seemed much too arrogant.

"Perhaps an object lesson is in order," the ambassad[or]
said to himself.

Turg was resting somewhere in the surrounding buildin[gs,]
making himself scarce as Laquatus rearranged the lie[u]-
tenant's reality. The merman could only make a simp[le]
request as he shepherded the aven to the ceremony called [by]
the city. The aristocrat's usual close mental link with t[he]
amphibian was strained by the necessity of keeping Kirta[r's]
mind quiescent. Laquatus had no idea what he was saying [as]
he continued to impress Kirtar with images and ideas und[er]
the cover of the conversation. The ambassador receiv[ed]
only a split second of warning as Turg acted on his spite.

The wall from an upper story fell out, the heavy cornice
d brick an irregular boulder that flattened an impudent
ardsmen like a overripe fruit. The ornate carving was fol-
wed by a rain of other bricks that broke arms and heads
d grew a bumper crop of pain among the escort.

Laquatus shouted with loud dismay and pointed to the
en, calling for aid. Even had anyone looked up it would
ve been difficult to spot the camouflaged Turg scamper-
g away in manic glee. The ambassador knelt by the men
Kirtar called for a surgeon to treat the fresh bout of
oken bones. The merman hoped to watch the men as
eir bones were set, but additional guardsmen came to
cort them to the delayed ceremony. This time the inter-
ption was much more polite, and Laquatus curbed his
npulse for Turg to create another accident.

"We thank you for your actions," the fat man said, as the
rder leader stepped to the stage. "In the hour of our need
. " he droned and Kirtar stood in the background, still lost
the grip of the merman's spell. Laquatus dared not use his
agic in the presence of so many. The official was looking
kance at the ambassador as the subject of the mer forces
me up. The aristocrat gathered himself to respond only to
ve Kirtar step forward.

"The decision to use the forces was mine," he said, claim-
g the cover story that Laquatus had implanted. Victory
as sweet in the ambassador's mouth as his new puppet
ayed his part. The lieutenant told the assembly that the
rces were under his command during the battle. The aris-
crat looked on benignly as the farce played itself out on
e stage.

The selection of a prize was supremely unimportant to
aquatus, and it was only as the hooded elen brought back

the diminutive dull-gray ball that the merman took notic
The pit frog had access to the ambassador's abilities, and I
was first to feel the beat of power produced by the spher
The ambassador started from his machinations and look
on it as well. Then both stared.

The flare of power blinded Laquatus. The metal ball,
muted before, reflected the sun in a brilliant spray
light. The strength of emissions from the sphere blacke
out his awareness of other spells, and it was only his gr
on Turg's arm that maintained his control. The unbelie
able mystic assault died down, and the ambassador trie
to cast a spell of detection, just to convince himself th
he had not imagined the event. His spell detected not
ing but reverberations. It was only when he focuse
directly of the object in the lieutenant's hands that I
sensed something unusual. Like a night animal starir
into the noonday sun, all knowledge he might learn w
washed away. The confluence of might was too much fe
even a mage of his ability.

The Cabal officials appeared stunned, and many of th
pit fighters competing in the games stood like dumb oxe
as the lieutenant mumbled a few words and walked away.
Cabal official's incredulous look of disbelief turned to ange
and he spun on the Master of the Games. The tall, spa
man jerked the fat fool back toward the arena, whisperir
furiously in his ear. The ambassador imagined that quite
few hard words would be said to someone who allowed suc
a treasure to be given away or offered to all comers. Laqu
tus smiled even as he quickly walked after the lieutenan
The Master of the Games's head would likely pay for th
insults in the arena.

Kirtar continued on, his aides and soldiers gathere

ound him, their instinct in times of uncertainty to protect
eir commander. The ambassador tried to close with the
rd warrior, but the press of people prevented him.

"Lieutenant, we need to talk," he shouted, but the offi-
r was still lost in his contemplation of the object. Such
ower was fascinating, and Laquatus ached to peer within
e orb for himself. Mastering such power will take time, he
ought and waved to a servant.

"Find out where the Order party is going," he instructed,
oking to see whom else he could command. "Meet me at the
mbassy as soon as you have the information. Find one of your
lows to keep watch if there are any changes." Laquatus was
most at a run as he headed for the embassy. The sphere was
completely new factor in his plans, one that upset his machi-
tions in the city. The challenge was exhilarating.

By the time the servant returned with his report of
e route, the embassy was a madhouse. Workers rushed
out, closing up rooms while the permanent staff was
cked over blueprints for new architectural wonders. If
e ambassador left the city, he would take advantage of
s absence and expand the residence. It was becoming
o cramped for his ambitions. In a city of spectacle, his
ome must be the most impressive.

"A system of waterfalls with a twisted channel of pools is
e most interesting," the ambassador said to a harried
amberlain. "You will have to construct a spur to the aque-
ct and bribe the Cabal to divert enough water."

"Most impressive, your Excellency," the man said sub-
rviently, "but where shall we procure the funds for such a
eat expansion?"

Laquatus waved the concern away.

"The coastal shipping fees are being collected by our

agents for the quarterly shift to the treasury. Divert all yo
need from that source," the ambassador said, feeling expan
sive. When he gained control of the sphere he would nee
a dwelling to reflect his new status. And perhaps it was tim
to accelerate his plans for reentry into the undersea cour
He looked over the drained grotto, the artificial reefs bein
broken by slaves with sledgehammers. He had been chi
fish in a small pond for long enough. The horrified look c
the chamberlain's face reminded him that he must still wi
his new status.

"I assure you that it will be cleared with the emperor
Laquatus said and forgot everything as he noticed the se
vant sent to the Order camp. He walked with the man t
the entrance of the grotto. Making sure that no on
observed them for the moment, he pulled the man into th
secret room. A crab filled the enclosure, a sentry reportin
to the caves below. After the ambassador closed the doo
the crustacean lifted the cover and vanished into the poo
Captain Satas dragged himself clear moments later. The tre
sias paused for a moment, then moved toward the ambassa
dor and messenger, drawn by their nearly imperceptibl
movements and breathing. Laquatus shifted as quietly a
possible, but the tresias adapted, altering his course. Th
merman was unimpressed with the tresias's performanc
during the battle, but it appeared the captain and his kin
could adapt well to the land.

"How may I serve, my lord," the small amphibian said i
his quiet, dead tone. The ambassador waved the spy t
speak, noting that his hand's passage in the air was tracke
by the captain as well.

"The Order will be traveling west to the forest's edge t
catalog the reported predations of woodland creatures.

e man said, opening a pouch and taking out a map. "I
ught this off a Cabal servitor able to sneak into the
ain tent." He laid it on the floor and weighted it down
th a dagger and a few coins. Then he looked at the blind
nphibian, flustered how to use his acquisition. The
mbassador also wondered how the tresias would know
ow far the cave system ran. To Laquatus's surprise,
stead of calling for a sighted retainer, the cave dweller
uckled and drew a stone from his own pouch.

"The sound of paper and mention of routes suggests it
a map lying on the floor," Satas stated, rubbing the dull
m between his hands. "I have always found such meth-
ds of little use and came prepared with a substitute."

The short creature tossed the jewel to the ambassador
ho caught it. A spell whispered new knowledge to his
ind. A variant of the false memory spell, it left him
ith a sensory map of the explored caves and cleared
nnels. The underside of the continent was suddenly
ore familiar to him than the memories of his child-
od home. Captain Satas's skin broadcast his amuse-
ent, but entranced with the novel method of informa-
on transmission, the ambassador did not even feel
ger. He did, however, experience irritation as he
lled his new memories and the map of the lieutenant's
th together.

Kirtar's route led west. The underground rivers did
derlay the route, but they were unexplored and sure to be
early impassable. Miners connecting the underworld to
e sea would have to be moved farther inland. The lieu-
nant planned to swing north and an explored cave system
y nearby. Laquatus could catch up with the party and cap-
re the newly revealed power source.

"Captain Satas, the northern caves allow us to intercep the group of landsmen and crush them. It is absolutely nec essary that an amphibious force be available for extende action out of the water. Find me soldiers and send them t the Cave of Knives." The memory of sharp stalactites an stalagmites in the north prompted the name.

"I will send what forces I can, but we are very short o long-duration patrols," Satas said in a pun, the uninter tional humor irritating the ambassador. "It may be necessar to find air-breathing slaves to meet you and supply bodie to soften up the adversary."

Laquatus nodded reluctantly, regretting the lack of force able to operate out of water. He dismissed the officer an thought of whom he could meet in the forests. Perhaps th Cabal could be of aid. He smiled and clasped the spy's hand

"Excellent work!" he cried and hugged the man in appar ent fellowship. Laquatus raised power and cut into th other's psyche. Experiences withered, and memories gre confused. He worked at the servant's mind, creating a fals shadow of drunkenness and nameless female companions. I was hard work, and the fellow proved fairly resistant. It too real effort, and Laquatus wondered if death wasn't a bette solution. But as his talk with Satas proved, he lacked walk ing servants. He continued to mutilate memories, wishin he had the resources to just kill the fellow and swim away

* * * * *

Kamahl breathed and was struck by deja vu. Buried twic in one battle.

"I am no mole," he muttered.

The warrior coughed and tried to turn over. He could no

essure prevented him from more than breathing. Even his
ad was locked in position, his cheek pressed against stone.
he barbarian could remember the dragon falling and the
ab getting in his way.

"I despise seafood," he muttered. More sensations
truded, and he could feel multiple small points of pressure
gging into his back. He remembered the crustacean's armor
d realized that he must be trapped under it. He tried to
ove again, his muscles bunching in agony, but nothing
ifted. He remembered the great dragon falling as well and
th a shock understood that two great beasts lay atop him,
eir mass making a mockery of even his powerful muscles. It
as a miracle that he was not pulped as well. The cobble-
ones underneath him seemed jumbled, and over the smell
the dragon and the crab he detected strong odors of mold.
e could hear the dripping of water and e scuttle of a rat.
he street must have collapsed under the weight and crushed
sewer. The stench of filth was the stench of life, and
amahl laughed before coughing spasms ended his momen-
ry merriment. To owe his life to a poorly constructed drain.

The barbarian wondered if anyone would rescue him. He
membered the disregard of the lieutenant and the crabs
d hoped he could count on the Cabal forces. At the very
ast, someone would have to take care of the giant corpse.

"Perhaps they will enchant it and have it walk away." The
ab might weigh over a thousand pounds, but he was sure
at he could get out without the tons of flesh holding the
ell in place. He imagined a giant undead monster crush-
g the crab and the life under it into oblivion as it tried to
se. Kamahl thought of his killing blow. He realized that
ith no intact spine, it was unlikely that even raised, the
onster would be able to move. It seemed colder somehow.

The tremendous ringing of magical energy made him believe that he was dying, and new planes of existence called to him. Then his senses located the source of the power. A locus of exultation, a shout of birth, it lay some distance away. His mind demanded he move, run to the source, but his body stayed relaxed, impotent under the great weight. His thoughts grew hazy as the energy retreated. He had sensed this before, though it wasn't as strong. The treasure room! He recalled the sphere behind the sword. Someone else must have seen its value and called forth its essence. His mind swirling, he tried to imagine what champion might hold it now. It was harder to think, the air thicker. He could not call power, the pressure on his body seeming to squeeze the magic out. Just a few more minutes of rest and them he would cut his way free. After all, a victory without being alive to enjoy it seemed pointless. Just a few minutes more. . . .

The sound roused his attention at once. The rhythmic cuts of a sharp edge into flesh transmitted themselves through the corpse. He might have been gathering himself for a few minutes or for days, but he shouted loudly, pushing the sound out despite aching, compressed ribs. There was a pause in the beat and then it resumed, louder than before.

The leathery scrape of scales signaled the shifting of the dragon's mass. Pressure spiked and eased as the giant corpse slumped to the side. Shy beams of light peaked under the crab's shell, and the crunch of metal in chitin showed the worker was near.

"Have a care," shouted Kamahl trying to shift the beast above him. It gave a little, though it still seemed pinned down on one side. "The crab is right on top of me!"

A great hand wormed its way under the shell and another
ned it. The knuckles went white as the shell lifted a frac-
n. The barbarian forced his complaining body to lift as
ll, and the additional force flipped the crustacean to the
e. Kamahl reeled at the release of weight, and the light
t his eyes watering. Seton stood, his sides heaving, with
loody axe beside him. As the barbarian moved out of the
llow depression, he could see Cabal servants advance on
e crab, sledgehammers falling as they smashed armor and
ew fragments into a nearby wagon. Other servants with
ge cleavers attacked the dragon's corpse, a steady stream
bloody lumps of flesh falling to the street. The meat went
other carts, and some rumbled toward the arena.

"Waste not, want not." Seton laughed as he came closer
Kamahl. The barbarian allowed himself to lean on the
nt.

"What happened?" the mountain fighter asked, speaking
th difficulty from his chapped lips. He waved a water car-
r over from his round of the Cabal workers.

"What happened?" the centaur replied incredulously.
ou are standing in the largest open-air butcher shop on
e continent, and you ask what happened? As if you
ssed a few seconds of a play?" The simian face writhed
th suppressed merriment.

"I don't mean this," Kamahl said irritably, dismissing the
ttle, his triumph, and his near death with a wave. "What
ce cried out so loudly long after the dragon fell?" The
ntaur moved away from the other workers.

"The Cabal presented a prize to Lieutenant Kirtar for
ling the beast," he whispered. "When he held it in his
nds, it released such power that all the city was stunned
it. He left for his camp and soon after went north. Word

came of other attacks by forest creatures, and the Capta[in] called him away." The centaur knelt, bringing his mou[th] closer to the barbarian's ear.

"They say the Master of the Games has disappeare[d] punished for giving away such power. He has gone to fe[ed] the beasts I wager. I heard the ambassador's servants tel[l] Cabal officer that Laquatus would be leaving the ci[ty] shortly for 'consultations.' " Seton looked over the destru[c]tion and the blood running into the gutters. "What ha[p]pened here is merely the beginning."

Kamahl thought of the prize that he desired given to th[e] Lieutenant.

"They rewarded Kirtar for killing the dragon?" he sa[id] hotly. "They gave him what was rightfully mine, and he h[as] run away north." He began to pace, his injuries moment[ar]ily forgotten. He ran to the pit where he had fallen, shou[l]dering aside the workers. Kamahl went to his hands a[nd] knees, looking determinedly over the ground, ignoring th[e] complaints from offended servitors. Seton followed a[nd] quelled the comments with a frown. Kamahl stood su[d]denly, his great sword in his hand. The long blade whipp[ed] through the air, the dragon blood burning away in a trail [of] smoke.

"I will go reclaim my prize from Kirtar," the barbari[an] said, steel ringing in his voice. "I will have my rewa[rd] though the entire Order stands in my way."

CHAPTER 9

The early morning dew made the grass-
lands a jeweled vista, the sun's rays glitter-
ing off the small droplets. The rider nudged
the sides of her steed and set it through
the tall grass.

The woman looked alertly over the
landscape, the slight fold of her eyes
hiding some of the intensity of her
observation. Her black hair trailed down
her back, bound in a long rope by sil-
vered ornaments. One arm rested on
her saddle pommel, encased in leather
and steel. The bracer's ancient power
was temporarily quiescent. A tall asym-
metric bow tilted forward in its case, the
he wood of the box repelling the morning moisture.

The unicorn ran easily, its gait almost gentle but cover-
g ground faster than a horse could run. Its horn glinted,
e delicate spiral supported by steel laminated and magi-
lly bonded to its skull. The mount's saddle was a tangle of
aps, and the rider's legs were half-enclosed by the stirrups.

101

The need for such careful securing was obvious as the ur
corn turned at an incredibly sharp angle, altering its run
response to a nudge from its rider's knee. Dirt showered
the steed accelerated, its enchanted hooves casting pebb
and dirt clods up into the air like slings.

The loudest sound was the jingle of the woman's sca
mail and the slap of the long cavalry sword against h
back. A field of tall wild flowers lay in a depression, ar
she directed the steed toward them. The tension was obv
ous in her first strokes as she tried to loosen her muscle
The first cuts took great swathes of flowers as she struggle
for precision. She turned the unicorn in a tight circ
almost peeling her out of the saddle. Again she wer
through the flowers. Now the sword strokes took sing
blossoms, and she nodded in satisfaction at her skill.

"If only the forest beasts were as easily understood ar
directed," Pianna, Captain of the Order, whispered to he
self. For weeks, animals from the west appeared and acte
unpredictably. Solitary beasts that naturally subsisted alor
now roamed in large groups. Skittish herd animals becan
insanely aggressive. Beasts plowed through the fields ar
villages of man doing destruction but only sporadicall
leaving some settlements completely alone while only a fe
miles away numberless herds destroyed everything. She ser
messengers to druids and other holders of wisdom, but n
answer issued from the forest, only more animals that pu
sued some unknown path or goal. The purposeless attacl
were becoming the Order's crucible.

For years she had extended the Order's message of ne
unity, and now it was being put to the test. Unfortunatel
it was a test the organization was failing. The raids contir
ued despite her best efforts. There seemed to be no plan c

rection to the strikes. Animals and monstrous plants
peared at villages and struck out in frenzy. Sometime the
racks stopped before much was destroyed, even if a hamlet
d no real defenses. Other times the assaults continued
til all was destroyed and the inhabitants were dead.

The Order-sponsored militias were swept away by the
relenting aggression. For a second, Pianna regretted the
ck of war machines imposed by the Strictures. In the past,
echanisms might have turned such assaults without casu-
ties. Her losses were precious members of the Order.

"But such machines breed more destruction and con-
mpt for life because they are so easily replaced," she
minded herself. The legend of Urza provided a chilling
sson of the madness artifacts led to. Armies of unques-
ning automatons fought wars for centuries, stripping the
orld down to a husk from which it was still recovering.
en after a century, there were still vast fields of machines
ing found, the rusted and crushed instruments of a world's
struction. Each one an opportunity for evil, to be rebuilt
til an unquestioning army might march again. The Order
ight be beleaguered, but it was still a living expression of
oble ideals.

She fingered the sword at her side, her hands running
er the pommel worn smooth by generations of com-
anders. It had belonged to one of the original members of
e Order, a symbol of authority transferred from leader to
ader, its steel in service for hundreds of years. But it acted
the choices of its wielder. It was an extension of her soul,
t a free-ranging engine of destruction. Her skill was what
ntrolled it, and before every fight she dedicated her life
d ideals to the Order. If it could act on its own, such a
rvant would dilute her involvement in her soul's journey.

In such a case, she would throw it in the crusher that ve
second.

The crushers were devours of the past, great engines th
size of a manor, their interiors filled with swinging hamme
and blades. Their power derived solely from the gre
wheels turned by knights and squires. The engines were a
extension of the individuals like a sword, or so the capta
told herself. Pianna hoped that the machines were not co
rupting the Order even as they tried to save the worl
Those artifacts and instruments of the past, which had l
the world so astray, were committed to the bowels of th
device, ground between wheel until only small scra
remained. What was left was sold to blacksmiths and ti
kers. What corrupted the world was devoured by the for
and rendered into simple blades and pots. Those items
unusual lethality were melted down and cast into ingo
the metal bars hidden in Order fortifications or droppe
into the deep waters of the ocean. Better to rely on on
own humanity than sacrifice it for soulless fighters.

The unicorn's hooves carried her far as she ruminate
and her shadow on the ground lengthened. On the horizo
a line of trees was visible, stretching several miles acro
The mount accelerated as the captain used her heels, h
hands checking her equipment as they leaped forward. Th
wood lay in a section of the plain, exposed like an ou
runner of the forest. The copse was only a few miles acro
but the trees soared hundreds of feet into the air.

Villages grew nearby, and races of all description tried
make a living through the forest's bounty. Those brav
enough harvested the wood, depending on the isolat
nature of the grove to prevent attacks from dangerous ar
mals found in the forest proper. But Pianna had recent

eceived disturbing reports of animal attacks and missing
illagers. A small detachment of the Order followed behind
er but farther west. The captain continued alone to ques-
ion the heads of the villages about these recent occur-
ences.

The forest was a wall, and she still saw no sign of the vil-
agers. Where was the smoke from cooking fires or signs of
imber wagons working the forest's edge? It had been years
ince she came this way, and perhaps her trail sense had
nisled her. The road might have shifted or the loggers
noved to new ground. She doubted such rationalizations
nd drew her bow from her case. The laminated layers of
vood, horn, and metal were smooth in her hands. She
hecked the tension of the string, and her pluck sounded
lmost lyrical as the various components vibrated and pro-
ided a rich tone. Her spirit settled, the single note calm-
ng her worries. Her quiver was full and her bow strung, her
nastery practiced and ready. She moved laterally along the
orest edge, the sure hooves of her steed laughing at fallen
rees and gullies. Still no sign of life, and she nudged the
nicorn to a faster pace.

Howls seemed to rise from the ground as she rode around
green peninsula. The stumps in the clearing revealed a
leep cut into the forest. Dozens of dire wolves ran from the
orest, joining the giant pack that surrounded an isolated
ree. In the branches of a giant pine, a group of loggers
vaved their distress. A grove of whisper trees sighed softly
n the breeze, their branches swallowing the yells of the
nen and the screams of the horses.

Whisper trees grew in small numbers, and somehow the
novement of their branches muffled sounds. Such groves
vere notorious for traps, but a lively market in paneling

that absorbed noise was in high demand in the larger citie Men of wealth lined homes to cut off the bustle of the town introducing pastoral quiet in the most densely packed mar kets. Plotters and conspirators paid a premium to line room where their councils might be kept from prying ears. Pris ons were said to have rooms where the screams of starvin and tortured souls were never heard.

But now the loggers might pay the price of their craf She knew that there would be guards to protect the logger somewhere nearby. Harvesting trees from the forest wa dangerous and often disturbed creatures that only well armed fighters could discourage. Her own troops were acros the forest, and Pianna doubted they would arrive in time Only the vagaries of the afternoon air had allowed her to hear anything at all.

There were still loggers scaling the lone tree, trying to ge out of reach of canine teeth. Ropes swarmed with men as circle of wolves around the trunk contracted. The rotter gaping wound on the tree's trunk explained why it had no been harvested. A lurch of the bare branches suggested tha it could not bear its current crop of panicked men for long

Most of the wolves seemed little interested in the men rooting through the wagon scattered and overturned in th clearing. Red jaws howled silently as the beasts rose from feasting on the draft animals still in their traces.

Members of the pack leaped from the tumbled wagons dragging away equipment as they worked furiously. What ever the animals were looking for, Pianna could tell tha they were not finding it. Now the mass of animals seeme to find new energy and converged on the few men stil fighting on the ground. A few loggers swung their axes an heavy chains, giving their fellows time to ascend the rope

he number of men on the ground shrank, but each suc-
essful retreat made the rearguard's job more difficult.

Her arrow was laid and launched in a heartbeat, the shaft
riving through the ribs of a wolf to drop it in its tracks.
)thers followed, her shoulder muscles rolling as she sent
iissiles flying. The wolves did not turn as she killed the
ear animals. The whisper trees masked her attack, allowing
er to slaughter at will. However, the wolves did not cease
heir attack, and she watched a logger get dragged down.
he dire wolf was the size of a small pony, and the man
ame apart like a sickly rabbit as the canine head tossed his
ody. Pianna could hear no screams thanks to the sur-
ounding trees.

Power flowed through her veins and into the threads of
netal in her bow. Her bracer glowed brightly as she let loose
nother arrow. This one flew to the head of the pack, and
ts discharge was blinding, the flash leaving wolves writhing
s their eyes tried to adapt. The loggers were blind as well,
nd one went down, tripping over a rolling wolf. The
nimal did not attack, but the man's own axe laid his leg
•pen. His enemy's lolling tongue lapped at the blood as
veryone's vision cleared.

Pianna drove the unicorn closer, more magic singing
hrough her bow. Now the projectiles swelled until they
eemed javelins, nailing the wolves to the ground. The ani-
nals still did not react, bizarrely intent on the men on and
round the tree despite the ample carrion everywhere. The
aptain drove her steed into the rear of the pack. The uni-
orn's horn dipped and punctured sides as the pair tried to
urn the attack from the loggers. Finally, her slaughter made
he wolves react in self-preservation. The beasts spun and
ore at her, but the Order leader's magic rose as a shield.

Golden light encased Pianna's legs and the unicorn's side as she tried to draw the pack away.

Her steed was a kicking and screaming demon, it hooves shattering skulls and ribs as the wolves tried t overwhelm them. The captain swore as she saw there wer still loggers on the ground. She rose in the saddle and fire back toward the tree, killing a beast tearing off a logger leg. Two wolves leaped as she provided covering fire to th final men. Power still flooding her bow, she swung it like stave. It struck, destroying the animal's ribs. The othe beast's jaw stopped inches away as the unicorn twisted it neck with a sinuous grace, stabbing its horn deep into th wolf's side and piercing the heart. The weight of the fores hunter nearly toppled her steed, and the equine weapo flared with power as it shook the corpse free.

The pack was converging on her, and Pianna spun th unicorn on its rear legs to ride free. She killed an attacke as it tried to duck under her steed. Another wolf tried t hamstring her mount, but the invoked armor defeated it teeth. More converged, but the unicorn's acceleration stopped them from being buried by the pack. One beas nearly defeated the captain as it clambered on top of its fel lows and leaped to snatch Pianna from the saddle. The unicorn reacted to the captain's sudden signal and turne again, flattening into an all-out run. The wolf's out stretched paws hooked her quiver and tore it open. It wa only the strength of the unicorn and the semi-locking stir rups that prevented the leader of the Order from bein dragged to the ground.

The unicorn's pace took it out of danger, but Pianna hauled her steed about, looking to see if the pack still fol lowed. The wolves were turning back to the men at th

se of the tree. The branches looked overloaded, and
esperate loggers cut the ropes to the ground, spilling a
w straggling climbers. One person in the crown had a
ght crossbow and loosed a bolt. The projectile did noth-
g more than return the wolves' attention back to the
ncircled woodsmen. Pianna cursed the man's vain
tempts even as she circled her steed and raised more
ower. She was not as strong as her lieutenant in the
ystic arts, but bursts of power left her bow despite her
ck of arrows.

More of the canines dropped, the shafts of energy burn-
g away limbs and exploding inside the animals. Many of
he crippled animals were torn apart by their fellows as the
easts raged out of control. In a second, the circle around
he tree was breached, and the men on the ground died,
espite the captain's flurry of arrows and rain of impromptu
eapons from the loggers above.

The animals were insane killing machines, snapping at
verything. Pianna turned her steed to ride out of danger
ow that the men on the ground were dead. A branch
roke, and two men fell to their deaths. Each extracted a
easure of vengeance as they crushed the wolves they
nded on, but they died by the jaws of the others. The cap-
in's arrows swept the successful killers away, but the pack
id not turn. The animals threw themselves against the
ee, which shuddered, revealing the rottenness at its core.
ianna saw the despair on the loggers' faces and sent the
nicorn forward once more.

The captain's bow shot shards of pure energy, but she
aid a steep price for each shot. Pianna's skill as a archer
reated arrows that enhanced her power in concert with her
pirit, bow, and bracer. Now the magic flowed like a river

and drained away the mystic armor from her legs and steed

She was surrounded now, using her magnificent bow as
club until it was dragged away by foamy jaws. Her swor
arced out and cut down the wolf that thought her helpless
Now bare steel carved into the pack as Pianna directed a
her power into armor. The mesh of power over her and he
steed grew as tattered as lace as her last reserves of strengt
drained away. The silence of the battle made it seem
dream as she readied herself for death.

A shower of javelins and spears fell from the sky, prom
ising life like spring's first rain. Pianna drove toward th
tree, her sword cutting through the snarling wall as mor
weapons plummeted from above. At last she was throug
and turned her steed, backing into the rotting cavity of th
trunk. The armor on the unicorn flanks evaporated. No
only a thin web of armor on the unicorn's neck and fore
quarters offered resistance to the dire wolves' teeth. B
that thin protection was enough as an Order aerial un
came to the rescue.

Griffins dived from the sky, their shrieks of rage lost i
the whisper trees. Another flight of javelins stabbed int
the wolves as the soldiers used the last of their throwin
weapons and closed with the pack. Talons flashed. Th
fliers snatched up the maddened animals. Beaks and swor
were red with blood, and the flying steeds and their ride
pulled clear. Other griffins landed out in the clearing an
advanced on the tattered edges of the pack.

The elite soldiers swung long flails and maces. Th
wolves turned to overwhelm the reinforcements. Bon
exploded as the enhanced weapons swatted the anima
away. Some of the animals tried to run, but most close
with the fighters. The fresh mages were encased in magic

wer and nearly immune to the dire wolves. The detach-
nt reaped the clearing free of their opponents, the furry
dies pinwheeling away. A few mounted archers overhead
leashed waves of mystic arrows, peppering the wolves in
nt of the tree that still tried to reach Pianna. The loggers
erhead might have screamed with joy, but the captain
ıld only guess, for the whisper trees smothered every
ınd. Pianna's magic faded away, but the battle was over,
d the pack broke apart.

A few remaining wolves fled deeper into the wood, the
es preventing aerial pursuit. Many of her command dis-
ıunted, but Pianna sent her tiring beast in front of her
cuers. Using battle sign, she directed them to help the
ıunded woodsmen. They obeyed, the power that armored
ɛm fading as they prepared to heal those still hanging
to life.

She waved for the leader of the griffin riders to follow
d took the unicorn away from the whisper trees, the
ınds of the plains once more in her ears as she left their
ıere of influence.

"Sergeant Paige," Pianna said, her arms feeling the
ɪn of her archery, "what of the villages nearby?" The
ffin riders, due to their speed, were the premier scouts
the Order.

"Captain," he replied, coughing up dust, "the villages
ve all been set upon by creatures of the wood. Bears and
ıer monsters are common, and there are rumors of great
ɑsts annihilating everything in their way. We escorted
ɔse willing to come to the fort before returning to check
you." The soldier showed the irritation that all ser-
ınts had with too-brave officers. "You were fortunate
ɑt we arrived to . . ." He paused, his lined face working

as he considered her bland expression. " . . . support yo
charge, Captain. I am sure you were moments from victor

"In protecting those under my care, there is no choic
Paige," Pianna answered. "We need to get these peop
back to the fort if their village is evacuated." She consi
ered the wagons rolling away now from the whisper tree
"But how many we can move away from danger, I just dor
know."

* * * * *

Despite its crude construction, the fort looked lil
heaven to Pianna. The walls were nothing more tha
upended logs, standing only fifteen feet high. Clumps
longer trunks provided cover for archers, but it was nothin
compared to the mighty ramparts of other Order fortresse
The fort was on a broad rise, surrounded by a dry moat ar
the wooden wall. An artificial hill rose some seventy fee
and it was capped by a large tower providing the final refu
from assault. The tower was constructed of treated timber
and the Order's sigil flew from the top of pole.

Any cover would be welcome, for madness seemed
grip almost every animal of the forest. Large predato
attacked, even though instinct should have sent them mil
from such a large gathering. Groups of normally solita
hunters erupted from the grass and were fought off on
when almost all were dead. The villagers' accompanyir
herds of livestock were ignored, their owners the targets
tooth and claw.

The gates were open, and Pianna and her party roc
into the fort. It became nearly impossible to move, th
numbers of refugees filling the enclosure. Soldiers stoc

scaffolding along the walls, runners moving on the ele-
ed paths rather than daring the tangle of people. Many
hose seeking shelter inside the walls were woodsmen
loggers. Their glassy faces showing the shock of being
en from their homes. Children ran and played among
tumult with the easy care that youth could bring,
le their parents and guardians were too numb to rein
m in. Traders and merchants of all descriptions sat with
ir goods piled high. Pianna resolved to cache such car-
s outside the walls. A group of hunters stood by, their
hing and manner marking them as Cabal minions.
ey laughed at the crowd, and each shocked face going
provoked a new burst of merriment.

he keys and chains in their stack of gear told the cap-
a they were pit hunters. The Cabal paid well for a fresh
v of creatures from around the continent. Pianna had, in
uting the forest edge, come across the leavings of such
st caravans. Starved and sick animals were abandoned
hout even the benefit of death. The predators trailing
h columns lost their fear of people and associated them
h food.

he group noticed her regard and grew silent, then
ned and looked in other directions until her attention
diverted. The Order was pledged to protect all peace-
e people on the plains, and the Cabal was careful to obey
letter of the law.

Orderlies made their way through the crowd, moving
ard the wagons of wounded to conduct them to the
lers. Pianna wondered bleakly how many had died on
way to the fort. Her warriors tried vainly to magically
l wounds when the bulk of their training was inflict-
them. She was unable to have a healer flown out

because of the current crush in the other Order holds.

The captain dismounted, her hand pressing against [ ]steed's side as the unicorn was finally led away. The stab[ ]were full of refugees, so the animals were being picke[ ]outside. The griffins screamed, so all could hear their [ ]pleasure at being refused their own stalls.

Pianna headed for the gatehouse. The officer in cha[ ]of the fort rose to his feet, giving her a salute that s[ ]returned absently. A sack of beer lay on the table, a[ ]she filled an empty flagon and washed down the dust [ ]the road.

"Sergeant Sumer," she said, her voice raspy from herd[ ]a column of refugees, "what news?" She wiped her ey[ ]clearing away dirt and wondering if the bathhouse [ ]plugged with asylum seekers as well.

"Not much of a change since this morning," the serge[ ]answered, a long scar down his face created the illusion[ ]a leer. "The refugees are still coming in, and all reports c[ ]firm widespread attacks." He turned to the map behind [ ]table, a cluster of pins showing attacks and sightings of a[ ]mals. It appeared random, and the sergeant tapped [ ]blank spaces representing the forest's interior.

"These attacks might presage an attack by the weste[ ]tribes," he opinioned. Pianna's snort of disbelief punctu[ ]the soldier's theory.

"I see no benefit to the forest folk in arousing our defen[ ]and clearing the villages of hostages against our behavic[ ]she said, reining in the temper which the journey l[ ]roused. "The random nature of the attacks mean we [ ]looking everywhere. Whatever is directing these attack[ ]doing so for no benefit other than destruction." She walk[ ]around the desk and considered the map more closely.

The only pattern these attacks have is that they radiate
n the Krosan forest." Pianna thought of the patrols that
ured the edge of the woodlands. "Perhaps the focus of
se troubles lies elsewhere." She looked to the southern
:hes of the map.

Is there any word of Lieutenant Kirtar?" she asked,
nking how valuable he and the other aven would be.

There was a dragon attack which he defeated, and he
he will be back after sweeping the southern sectors."
e sergeant's faint tone of distaste reminded Pianna that
ny considered Kirtar and his bird warriors to be arro-
t and abrasive.

He is your superior officer, and he and his people have
ver we need." She regretted that most of the lieutenant's
ple were far to the northeast and insular except for those
ing service in the Order. "He should be able to rally the
th. I know that he hoped to impress the Cabal and Mer
pire in the pits, but we need him here. Once again she
sidered the map. The concentration of her forces along
forest was drying up her information sources.

Maybe Kirtar will discover something in the south," she
I finally. "We need to know what is going on, but for now
must protect our own."

CHAPTER 10

"I hate the fores
Laquatus snarled as
exited the transp
pool. Days swimm
through caves a
river systems und
the continent h
left his eyes u
prepared for
light and he
of the up
world. Turg ca
out of t
pool behi
him, his ar
hurling sodden luggage. Crabs scutt
and set up a tent for shade as Captain Satas sat in the su
The amphibian's blind eyes sought the orb's warmth ev
as his skin burned, exposed to light nature never meant
his people.

"I trust you will be available should I need aid,"

bassador said as he walked to a chair parked under an
ning and settled into it. The blind officer tracked his
vements.

"I serve your will, but I must travel slowly as we map out
tes through the underwater caves," Satas announced,
king his claws together as he gasped in the heat. "Until
re warriors and miners arrive from the sea, you must
end on hirelings," Satas said, his skin beginning to peel
ay. His eyes were growing dim and sunken as he stayed
the hot, dry air.

"Turg can handle any small difficulties, my good
ptain."

Laquatus sipped from the goblet left by the chair. How
fortunate that decent attendants must be left underwater.
wever, it was a willingness to make sacrifices that defined
at leaders, he thought to himself. Besides, a trail of dying
vants would have attracted far too much attention.

"Stand ready to reopen the portal should the mercenar-
prove unable to meet my needs. You are sure you can
en the portal directly beneath me?" Laquatus asked as
rg slunk into the tent and settled in a sullen mass. The
ge amphibian's skin was already looking dry, and the frog
uld be difficult to control if the situation went badly.

"The stone calls out to those who know it, Your Excel-
ncy," Satas replied, having given the merman a tresias
ne. "Finding you will never be difficult while you bear it.
is reaching you that will be hard. Once you begin travel-
, I cannot guarantee immediate support."

The ambassador only nodded before remembering that
tas was blind and dismissed him and his men.

Though he appeared at ease, in reality Laquatus seethed
th anger and frustration. The lieutenant's path kept him

from the explored system of caves and the undergrou
rivers. Those that did exist were clogged with falls and ti
diverging passages. To truly develop the underwater roa
would take decades of effort. So instead of leading
attack by mer forces, he was condemned to once m
work with drylanders.

The lands were hilly and dusty, a buffer between t
plains and the forests to the west. No buildings or civili
tion as those above water considered it. Turg moved in t
tent, and Laquatus heard breaking glass. The gurgle of po
ing liquid told the ambassador the jack had found his cac
of seawater. He considered disciplining the frog, but t
heat of the day drained away all initiative. His hatred f
tered as he wondered how long it would take the mere
naries to arrive.

The first scout into the camp surprised the ambassad
interrupting the merman's sulk in the heat. The man v
small and covered in more warts than the aristocrat's jac
He dismounted and bowed.

"Your Excellency—" he began.

"Surely there is a spokesman less repellent than yo
Laquatus interrupted, looking back the way the scout h
come. "I paid for the best, not the worst." The merm
watched teeth grind as the man reached for a sword. Act
ally, the discolored skin reminded the ambassador of certa
breeds of fish, but he was bored and needed entertainme

"I will return with my captain," the red-faced merc
nary ground out. Laquatus waved and watched the fell
jerk himself into the saddle and start up the trail. T
ambassador went into the hot tent to rouse his protect
Turg lay somnolent, broken glass all around him. Laqu
tus found an unopened bottle of salt water and smash

against the tent pole bracket, ignoring the shards that
[..] on his champion. The merman took a long draught
[..]d poured the rest over his body. Already the frigid
[..]terways down below seemed a dream in this heat. He
[..]ked Turg viciously in the ribs, driving him up and out-
[..]e. Laquatus saw the broken glass slash the frog's feet.
[..] followed, resigning himself to only petty cruelties
[..]til he could once more call upon mer warriors.

*   *   *   *   *

The village was only a wide spot in the road, com-
[..]tely overwhelmed by the caravan camped around it.
[..]quatus hammered his heels into his steed and sent the long-
[..]ffering mare forward. The brisker pace cooled the ambas-
[..]dor down, his sodden garments losing heat as they dried.
[..]e mercenaries leading him watched sourly as he passed,
[..]ter dripping down to the ground. The aristocrat had
[..]propriated and emptied most of the column's canteens.
[..]e fighters' drinking water dribbled down the ambas-
[..]dor's back to the dirt as he passed. The mercenary leader
[..]s lost in a cloak, trying to seal off the heat. Laquatus
[..]uld feel Turg closing from behind as he sprinted from a
[..]d hollow to get to the camp. The hot breath of the
[..]phibian seemed to fill the merman's lungs as he crowded
[..]ainst the column commander.

"All the hunting parties bring their captures here," the
[..]an said pointing to the swathe of activity. The encamp-
[..]ent was swollen with the cries of animals and people.
[..]ars, cougars, and wolves were caged, as well as fauns and
[..]osan dragonettes. A huge elk, nearly the size of an ele-
[..]ant, was secured to a stake by a nose ring. Though the

noise enveloped them, it was without the frenzy expec[
from wild animals. Many seemed docile, even lost as th
lay within the enclosures of steel. The hum of controlli[
spells called to the ambassador. The merman felt his cha[
pion slowly entering the camp behind him and drifti[
toward the pens. Laquatus broke the spell, and Turg star[
at the surge of will. The amphibian ran to his mast[
goaded by the aristocrat's bad humor.

"Sorry ambassador," called Laquatus's escort as t[
mercenaries peeled off for other duties, leaving him a[
the amphibian with only the company of their bagga[
"It takes some effort to avoid the magic controlling t[
animals."

Laquatus nodded in recognition. The Mer Empire spec[
ized in spells of control and illusion, and a profitable busin[
was made in training and equipping the hunters who enter[
the forest.

"Without the spells provided by the empire it would[
impossible to manage these animals," the ambassador m[
tered, taking control of the giant elk. His mental blu[
eoning sent it rampaging across the camp, its painful cr[
of no interest to the ambassador. Despite its matted hi[
and sores, it still had enough power to rip the stake out[
the ground. He nodded at the ease with which he co[
hijack the spells.

The leader of the caravan approached. At le[
Laquatus thought him a leader in his finery. The m[
was tall and slender, his clothes of sturdy leather dyed[
subtle hues with fancy stitching. A sword with a jew[
encrusted handle hung at his side, and in his hand[
carried a quirt made of bone or ivory wrapped with ma[
shades of leather. The merman could feel the quiesce[

gic humming in the tool as the man came closer.

"How may we serve your Excellency," he said, bowing
l sweeping his hat low as if at court instead of a dusty
np. The mercenary knew Laquatus as the backer of the
avan, having been hired in Cabal City.

'A valuable bauble has mistakenly come into the pos-
sion of the Order," the ambassador said carefully.
.eutenant Kirtar received a prize that belongs to the
·r Empire. The officer was called west before I could
·ieve it."

'Indeed, the Order can be most troublesome about
bles," the man said and nodded to a group of wagons.
quatus could see the loot of many a rediscovered battle-
d. Such expeditions must be hidden lest the Order take
ense. The Order routinely fed almost all recovered arti-
ts into great crushers. The ambassador feared that the
ze might be destroyed in the name of such stupidity.

"If you are as determined to reach Lieutenant Kirtar as
ur earlier communications indicated, you might find this
interest." The mercenary led the aristocrat to a wagon.
ained by the foot to a wheel and lying in the mud was a
ight of the Order. Burns and knife cuts recorded the
np's hospitality. An arm was torn off, the stump wrapped
blood-soaked bandages. He was feverish and mumbling
delirium.

"He's perfect," breathed Laquatus, considering the miser-
le prisoner. Kirtar would welcome him anyway, but a pres-
t always made a guest more popular. This rescue would
o diffuse some of the nastier rumors that the lieutenant's
n might have heard during their time in the city. With
ot of coaching and an array of false memories, the fallen
ight would make a splendid passport. The only question

121

was whether the miserable tool could survive reach Kirtar's forces.

"How far is the good lieutenant?" asked the ambassac irritated that he must be dependent on these mercenar "I would bring this pitiful wretch to his commander as sc as possible." The mercenary captain looked at Laqua kneeling down and laying soothing hands on the capti The merman saw a flash of pity on the mercenary's face the ambassador opened the shirt and inspected the wour His wounds were nasty, but he might survive a hard ride the saddle with proper incentive.

"Kirtar is at least five days' ride west," the caravan lea said, turning to stare down the road. "In these condition could not guess how long it would take you to reach aven."

"What do you mean?" said Laquatus, already imp tient to continue.

"The creatures of the forest lie in your path," the m cenary explained, gesturing to the ranks of animals c tured in the camp.

"Creatures are no threat," Laquatus said with a snc "You capture the dumb animals wholesale."

"But something disturbs them," the mercenary said w riedly. "We followed in the Order's wake, hoping to capt what remained, but the beasts circle ahead of us. Mov continually, they block the way and sweep across our pa My men and I have hunted for years, and never have I se the beasts so disturbed save during a fire or sudden stor The animal world is in upheaval, and I have no explai tion. Something west drives the beasts to a frenzy."

"Yet you control your camp," the ambassador said acic standing up. If this was an attempt to extract hazard pay

uld go hard for the mercenary. Turg raised his head from
upply wagon he was stealing from at the merman's pique
d began to move closer, anticipating violence.

'The spells of the empire close their minds," the captain
d, fondling the carved ivory wand. "They move in a par-
se that we control and mold. But out there, a continent
on the move, and no one knows who shapes events."

'I need a small band of attendants to bring my knight with
," Laquatus said, nudging the wounded man with his foot.
The ambassador let his silence at the mercenary's wild
cpourings show his contempt. If the animals of the wood
sed a danger, he would handle it. If only Satas had
olored more of the western caves instead of forcing him
deal with these fearful idiots. The mercenary called to
 aide and gave orders for a small group of riders to
company Laquatus and the prisoner.

'Does the Order know you are in this village?" the mer
stocrat asked, looking beyond the camp to the few houses.
There were no signs of the inhabitants save for the smoke
m the chimneys. The caravans had a bad reputation. The
bassador knew that on occasion his employees took
ves for use and sale to the pits.

"Kirtar's scouts are oriented west. I doubt they know we
 here," the mercenary captain said, looking toward the
n selected rousted from eating and sleep.

"This brave member of the Order will be useful in earn-
 the organization's trust," Laquatus said, licking his thin
s. "But the risk of witnesses telling how he chanced into
 hospitality . . . No, I think it best if this village and its
habitants die now. Unknown and nameless."

Turg leaped toward the houses. The amphibian pushed
np workers out of the way as he raced to the closest cottage.

The stone-and-timber structure was covered in moss. hunkered down in the plain, the heavy walls stubborn resisting the elements and those who would attack. T windows were small, and heavy shutters shielded the insi from view.

The door was seasoned wood, thick and hung wi care—the builder's attempt to keep the dangers of t world outside. Turg summoned his power, drawing on t ambassador's magic. A thin stream of lightning flare blinding those foolish enough to run after the amphibia The jack closed his inner eyelids, cutting the glare as looked through the thin shield of flesh. The lock a screws holding the door shut glowed as power arced ov the door. An agonized scream sounded as someone in t house tried to brace the panel. Rock-hard boards sunder in quick succession, coming free in a series of concussion

Turg, impatient to get inside, smashed into the door, I hide smoking briefly as it touched the charred wood. Laqu tus stood, lost in the rush of violence, savoring each dea as the amphibian rampaged through the structure. The me cenary's distaste was plain, but he called to his men.

"Clear them out!" he shouted, pointing to the remai ing houses. He drew a short sword to lead squads in t unpleasant task. Animals started at the noise, and t ambassador felt the animal herdsmen increasing t strength of the spells calming and misleading the beas Death and deception played out in the caravan and t village, and Laquatus stood in appreciation as the jack a the mercenaries began to kill off anyone who might der his scheme to lull the Order once again.

An explosion shattered his contentment. What fe was employing such spells in a simple bout of murde

ne merman looked to the perimeter. Bodies popped as
me burned its way free of fighters in his employ. As the
ercenaries fell, Laquatus could see two riders charging.
o, not riders, but instead a centaur and his mounted
mpanion advanced on the camp. A glimpse of brass-
lored skin placed the pair. Seton and the barbarian fell
on the caravan, killing without hesitation as the vil-
ze was massacred.

"Destroy them," the ambassador bellowed, dragging Turg
vay from the easy slaughter with a mental command. The
ards left off their half-hearted killing to face the attack-
s entering the camp.

"A rich reward to whoever brings me their heads!" the
erman called. Greed and self-preservation sent warrior
nverging on the pair. The merman laughed, sure that
urder would solve most of his problems.

CHAPTER 11

Kamahl closed his eyes as the axe exploded in a ball of flame, the pulse of magic leaving an afterimage even through his eyelids. His horse shied, nearly toppling him despite his precautions in turning the mare's head away from the spell. Seton roared and sprang, his apelike features furious as he raised his mace and swung at a caravan guard. The man shattered under the force of the blow, blood spraying and spotting the centaur red as he moved toward a new target.

The pair had tracked Kirtar and his forces west for days

e Order rode hard, and the barbarian and the forest war-
r had closed slowly, if at all. Then the tracks were
cured by a caravan. Seton had sworn loudly as wagons
l herds of animals obscured the trail. Casting along the
d to see if Kirtar had left the western highway consumed
n more time. It appeared that the caravan followed the
itenant, and Kamahl stopped tracking and rode hard,
nbling that Kirtar would not change his path until they
sed the obscuring travelers. They had hit the outer
imeter, and Seton watched the frog, Turg, break into a
lding and other guards from the caravan advance on the
agers. Such evil would not go unpunished.

Kamahl hurled flame. The magic congealed into dull red
bes that sank into the bodies of the cowardly murderers.
e caravan guards laughed at their apparent immunity to
attack. They came a few steps closer, then stopped and
ped as the barbarian's spell began to burn its way out.
mahl felt a wave of weakness as the mercenaries charred
ash. His anger was drawing too much power into the
ll, and he paused to control his rage. His horse shifted
der him, and he jabbed his heels, sending the mount into
fight.

Seton rampaged through the camp, his club spraying his
ponent's brains each time it landed. The caravan guards
d in vain to corner him, but the centaur's prodigious
ps carried him free. Seton then turned to take merce-
ies from behind. He pushed his way through the herd of
tive animals to reach their tenders. The barbarian could
his club raising high, then falling again.

Kamahl's horse froze, then began bucking under him.
e beast that had stayed controlled through so much
ult went wild and spun. The barbarian could feel the

horse dropping and beginning to roll. He threw hims
from the saddle, drawing his sword in midair. He landed
a run, turning to see what creature attacked his mour
There was nothing tearing at the beast, though it scream
in rage and fear as it twisted in the dirt.

A leather-clad mercenary charged toward him, an ivo
baton raised in the air as he regarded Kamahl and his hor
The leader waved as if in introduction and turned towa
the animals closest to the barbarian. A herd of simple cat
stopped chewing their cud as one.

Kamahl knew that magic controlled the animals, f
these cows were huge with heavy horns that stretched mc
than three feet from side to side. These were not dairy co
or animals being driven leisurely to the butcher but anim;
with fighting spirit. Whatever spell had kept them doc
ceased, and he found their attention focused upon him. Tl
cattle bellowed and charged, three bulls forcing their w
to the front of the herd in their rush to close with him.

Kamahl spun a pillar of flame around himself, but tl
maddened animals disregarded it. He threw himself to tl
side as a long horn hooked through his shield and scored l
armored belt. He gasped, his air knocked out by the impac

The barbarian did not want to play the butcher to liv
stock, and he ran under a wagon as the rest of the herd close
The cows collided with the freight wagon, and he hobbled f;
ther into the camp, gaining new strength as he shook off tl
bull's blow. A mercenary considered him an easy target as l
struck from the rear. Kamahl's sword sheared through tl
falling club and cut the man's arm free. The stricken gua
could not even scream as Kamahl's return stroke set his he
free as well. Guards closing with the barbarian slowed, waitil
for others to converge on the mountain warrior.

Seton broke into the ring of guardsman, trailing his own
ump of pursuers. The centaur's club was covered in gore,
nd every swing sprayed blood wide. He moistened the
ub's head anew using Kamahl's opponents, smashing men
own in three quick strokes before leaping. The barbarian
uld see the forest fighter's fangs clearly.

"Too slow!" the centaur shouted, raising his club like a
andard. Blood ran down it and drenched his arm. "Where
e your nets and snares now, hunters?"

He swung and knocked the wheel off a wagon, the oak
nd iron flying away in pieces. The centaur's arms fell again
nd wretched the other wheel free. Seton jumped to the
de as the heavy freight bed tipped over and spilled a load
f furs and hides over the ground. A heavy skin reminded
e barbarian of the centaur's own hide.

"Murderers!" The cry was bestial in its fury. The giant
ropped his club and leaped upon a guard, grabbing him up
n two hands. Seton tore the man apart, hurling limbs.

Kamahl threw fiery knives into the stunned guards, reap-
ng a deadly harvest before they turned to respond to this
ew attack. The outmatched mercenaries were caught
etween the barbarian and the crazed centaur, and Kamahl
hought they stood no chance. Then they seemed to disap-
ear, sidling into nonexistence. The mountain warrior
ook his head violently and loosed a barrage of darts. Wails
f pain sounded, and a guard faded back into existence,
creaming as the projectile burned its way to his heart.
hen silence fell again.

Kamahl threw more darts as he dove for cover, scrabbling
ehind an overturned wagon as he considered what was
appening. Malign magic pulsed in the encampment. A
age was clouding his senses, hiding his enemies from him.

An opponent might be running to stab him from behind a
this very moment. Kamahl hurled more darts behind him
but there were no screams. That meant nothing. Wild
sprays of weaponry could not long protect the barbarian
and Kamahl focused, trying to see past the spell. He shoved
his sword into the ground, taking strength from its solidity
He must see his enemy before he was struck down.

His vision wavered, images fading in and out of focus like
a mirage. For a moment, everything was clear, and he could
see the mercenary in the fancy clothes stepping carefully
over the corpses of his men. The ivory wand was raised, and
Kamahl focused on that as he willed the magical tool to
combust, to explode into flame. The barbarian reached into
the center of his own innate magic and brought it forth
The mountain warrior had to prop himself up with his
sword as the ivory began to char. The panicked captain
threw it away, and it blossomed into flame as it left his
hand. The force of the magic took the man's arm, the fancy
leather shrinking under the fierce heat and closing off the
amputated limb. A fire elemental rose from the wand'
remains.

The summoning grew greater; the inferno seemed to float
a few feet off the ground, its colors pulsing. Shafts of ruby
red flame danced in the heart of the creature. The center o
the elemental was in constant motion, and a tendril of fire
dipped down to the earth. The dirt fountained up as it
burned, throwing off ash and clinkers. The soil had sand
and glass began to form. Obsidian began to solidify and
merge with the debris orbiting the flame. The barbarian
could feel his creature and its appetite. The elemental
existed to burn, to devour substance. His hate, rage, and
even fear had called with uncommon strength, and the fire

eature crouched, ready to sweep away the enemy. Kamahl
atched it drift, and a lick of flame reached out to a guard.
efore he could make a sound, the elemental was on him.
esh shrank away, and bones flared as the mountain war-
or's summoning grew a little larger. Within seconds only
h remained to merge with the volcanic glass that hissed
d popped as it fell away from the creature.

The cattle that chased Kamahl still followed the cara-
n's leader commands, and they charged from the wagon
ey had reduced to splinters. The elemental jumped to the
rd, and the smell of cooking beef filled the air. There was
ly the sound of searing fat as tendrils of the creation
erced the thick hides and destroyed internal organs in an
stant. The elemental grew larger still as it rendered the
imals down and sucked up their bones and horns. These
anced inside the flame as hunger temporarily gave way to
riosity. The remains of the bulls dwindled away, shards of
of and bone becoming encased in glass as the fire weak-
ed, then strengthened in new hunger.

"Such a marvel," Kamahl said and groaned in frustration.
was too strong! A creation to fight armies, and he had
lled this chaos. The barbarian looked around. Seton still
ellowed, now some distance away, his club turning merce-
aries into clumps of broken bones. The caravan animals
ere waking from their spells, and they voiced their confu-
on. A few houses in the village still appeared intact, but
ho knew how much longer that would be the case. His
eature was hungry, and there were too few meals for its
ppetite. He caged it in its current place, ready to send it
way. Regret at banishing so fine a creature filled his heart.

Turg jumped from a crowd of animals, his fist drawn back
he swung at Kamahl's head. This time the barbarian was

not mired in spell, and he dodged. The mountain warrior
sword swung as he dropped, and only the amphibian's wil
contortions in the air kept the monster from spilling bloo
onto the ground. The jack seemed to vanish as it landed i
a pack of wolves. The beasts circled uncertainly, giving con
fused cries. Throughout the camp animals vented their con
fusion, and Kamahl vaulted to the top of the freight wago
to see if perhaps Seton was responsible.

There were few living guards anywhere nearby. Kamah
and the centaur had cut a bloody swathe, and no on
seemed brave enough to close with the pair. Seton wa
standing amongst stacks of cages. The barbarian could se
him ripping locks off to release the confused animal
inside. He looked for signs of Turg, wondering where th
treacherous frog lay hiding. As his eyes swung back to th
village, he saw the ambassador and a group of mounte
mercenaries.

Laquatus smiled. The merman waved, and Kamah
looked around, trying to see whom he was signalin
Mounted next the ambassador was a knight of the Orde
The figure swayed, and the barbarian could see the man wa
missing a limb. He wondered why Laquatus would includ
such a wounded man in his party.

"I see you and your companion decided to join our littl
expedition," the aristocrat called mockingly, his hors
shying as more and more of the captured animals vente
their distress. "It appears the centaur has found one of hi
relatives," he called. Kamahl turned to see Seton back a
the wagon reverently lifting the pelt of one of his peopl
from the dirt.

"You will die," yelled Seton, laying aside the hide an
grabbing up his bloody club. The few mercenaries not wit

he ambassador were running from the camp, leaving every-
hing behind to avoid the coming battle.

"There are more important matters than you to attend
o," the ambassador called back. "Besides, you will be far too
usy taking care of all these animals to worry about me."

The ambassador was casting a spell, and it echoed over
he encampment, redoubling in strength as old commands
ombined into new purpose. Kamahl felt it coming and
rouched into fighting position.

The animals that had milled so uncertainly minutes
efore turned toward the barbarian and the centaur. Bears
hat Seton had freed from their cages snapped at the druid.
Kamahl could see the surprise on the giant's face as beasts
urned and saw him as an enemy.

Animals screamed in the remaining cages as Seton
moved away. The malign spell picked up intensity, and a
giant elk charged the centaur from the side. Its sore-
matted hide still covered impressive muscles, and it threw
self at the druid with horns lowered. The line trailing
rom a ring in its nose caught a wagon wheel, and the
eavy oak circle skidded through the dirt as it came at
Seton. The centaur threw himself sideways, his flanks
eavy with effort after the fight and his grief.

Kamahl threw spears of fire that formed a barrier against
he approaching animals, covering the druid's escape. The
arbarian looked to his penned elemental, the boundless
unger of the primal being perhaps the only answer to the
arnivores that struggled from the cages and pens.

Bears, cougars, and wolves moved together toward the
air. Two Krosan dragonettes struggle from their enclo-
ure, the six-legged reptiles ignoring the surrounding car-
ion as they closed.

The mountain warrior eyed the ambassador. Perhap killing the merman would end the unnatural animosity. Bu the aristocrat and his escort had already disappeared, los behind some piece of landscape or illusion. He readied hi sword and the elemental—the coming slaughter of spell bound beasts a foulness to his soul.

"On my back," Seton commanded as he threade through the flaming barriers Kamahl had formed to stop th animals. "If we stay, we only do the ambassador's will."

The barbarian looked for his horse, but it was lost in th madness.

"We can return once the spell has run its course, or have turned it, but for now we must be away."

Kamahl paused only to free the elemental from his cal "Another time you will feed," he promised the flame. Th ruby shafts in the creature seemed to pulse in agreemen and then the glass and ash collapsed to the ground in superheated pile of debris. The barbarian sheathed hi sword and swung himself up on Seton's back. The centaur muscular body was as wide as a draft horse, and Kamah resolved to reclaim his mount as soon as possible.

"We will meet again, Ambassador," he promised.

The animals came around the flaming barriers.

Seton left at a run.

CHAPTER 12

There was a stillness to the air around the camp. Lieutenant Kirtar sat in his tent wondering if he dare look into the orb he had won in Cabal City. The globe brought visions, dreams of glory and control. He had imagined such possibilities throughout his life. He ached to smash the power of the Cabal, to finally order the restless mages of the Pardic Mountains to the southwest. Everything seemed possible if he just had time to investigate the orb, experiment with it. His huge hands clenched as he restrained himself from digging through his baggage for it. The visions became so compelling that he lost himself, and he could not afford the time—these meaningless patrols along the forest.

Kirtar stood suddenly and went outside, breathing deeply to calm himself. A fragrant breeze brought him a whiff of the forest, and his face pinched at the smell. Give him the cold, clean air of the plains, he vowed. He moved to the camp perimeter, absently accepting hails from his soldiers. The forest had always been chaotic, unstructured. He regarded the line of trees with a deep ambivalence. The tribes and races of the forest interior cut themselves off from the rest of the world. Kirtar felt contempt for such behavior. The world cried out for a firm hand, he thought, and his knuckles cracked as his fists tightened once more.

"Lieutenant," said a soldier bringing wood in from the trees. The fires for the night were being laid. Another day spent here.

"I saw bison moving deeper in the trees," the soldier volunteered uncertainly, obviously new to the unit. Kirtar wondered that the sergeants had not beaten such hesitation from the new recruits. Let the lower ranks police themselves, he thought to himself.

"Bison are no danger except when surprised or in breeding season," Kirtar reassured the soldier.

The sentry still looked nervous, but the bird warrior ignored him and walked on. The anxiety in the lower ranks was quite disgusting, the aven thought. He must admit that the sheer number of attacks, sometimes from animals well known for their timidity, was unsettling, and the frequency seemed to be increasing. Nevertheless, it was no excuse to be a coward. Nature was chaotic, and it was only natural that it must, occasionally, be curbed.

The rumble of thunder made him look to the darkening sky. No sign of rain clouds. The rumble became stronger and more continuous, never breaking. He turned to the forest. The soldier he left dropped the gathered wood and ran for his gear. The bison came out of the trees, a dumb relentless tide.

"To arms!" Kirtar yelled, echoed by others throughout the camp. The Order tents and animals were atop a small rise, and the lieutenant could look down to the forest's edge. As far as he could see in the dimming light animals were coming out, not driven by the weather or any sign of fire.

"Stand your ground," Kirtar bellowed, as he move to the line of men and bird warriors forming in the path of the bison. The beasts were coming up the rise, slowing but still advancing. Why, he wondered. A raypen launched himself into the sky, his wings spreading in the setting sun as he flew over the camp.

The sergeants in the line began chanting, a song of the Order's glory. Magic flared as warriors united their will and cloaked themselves in power. The bison slowed but still came closer, the leaders not pushed by those behind but advancing on their own.

"They are only dumb animals!" Kirtar cried as he strode to the head of the line. The mass of animals seemed a personal attack after his words to the sentry, and he responded as he would to any attack. The magic flowed to his hands and left them as golden birds. The power flew to the leading bison and struck like a catapult burst, killing the animals instantly. There was a moment of silence as others looked at him.

"Attack!" Kirtar yelled, and other projectiles followed. Arrows and javelins arced into the air, but the dead were lost in the mass of new animals, and Kirtar howled in anger, determined to stop the assault. Perhaps if the ground were better, he might have succeeded, but the animals lapped around the growing bulwark of corpses.

Kirtar's cries to his men were lost in the noise and confusion of battle. Bison circled through the camp, their humps more than eight feet off the ground. Calves bawled and tripped, finding their feet with difficulty as the torrent of animals ebbed and flowed like a river.

Kirtar wondered how thousands of animals might remain unseen in the forest. They continued to leave the trees, all apparently aimed for him and his men. The beasts were disorganized and showed little of the frenzy of previous attacks, but the sheer number of bison made them dangerous.

Ten-foot-tall elen stood with long pikes set, a steadily growing wall of corpses protecting the hooded bird warriors. The massive soldiers were proving useful, despite their lack of magic. Simple muscle might carry the day.

The line of soldiers contracted as sergeants tried to form a perimeter. Now relentless pressure spilled bison into the lines. Trapped bulls gored the men who turned to oppose them. Kirtar watched a soldier fall to the ground, the sudden thrusts of the heavy horns splintering the man's chest. The lieutenant leaped forward, his fist encased by power, and broke the bull's spine. He called out in triumph as he stood over the beast he killed with a single blow. However, the victory was lost in the unrelenting tide of animals.

In the skies above, the raypen swooped and dove. Kirtar could see them exulting in their flight. The flyers swept down and plied their long maces and lances before rising again, untouched by the sprawling chaos below. The rumble of hooves made speech impossible as the animals milled, fresh reinforcements constantly coming to test the camp's defense. Aven were lost in the midst of the herd, occasionally appearing atop animals they killed, but soon disappearing back into the crush of bodies. Kirtar felt a thrill of pride at how the bird warriors succeeded while the other races vanished under the milling hooves.

A group of bulls threw themselves up a pile of bodies and forced their way among the elen. Now long axes rose and fell, two feet of heavy-edged steel hewing its way through bone. The raypen congregated over their land-bound brethren, and darts showered down more heavily. The giant bird warriors rolled the bulls back down the pile of corpses surrounding their position.

The lieutenant saw it all from his perch at the center of the camp. Poised on top of a light wagon, a steady stream of power flowed from his hands in the shape of golden sparrows. He directed the magic to support his fellow aven, a flock falling suddenly to create barriers of cooling flesh. The buffalo still flowed over the rest of the plain, their numbers seeming endless, as he was forced to direct more attention to protecting himself.

Kirtar had been fighting and patrolling ever since leaving the Cabal. Most of the attacks were over in seconds, and the monsters that destroyed towns were rarely sighted. A series of pickets and militias pushed the incursions back, but these waves of buffalo were unprecedented. Now he received reports of vast herds washing over positions, their numbers absorbing all the power that the Order could bring to bear.

Lines of small trees along the forest's border cracked and were trampled as more of the bison came out of the woods. The raypen swooped and trailed flails behind them. The iron bars rang against the bony skulls, but the stampeding animals came on regardless.

"Use your magic," he cried, and a single bird of power flew to take down a small cow. The raypen wheeled in the air, their feathers dim as they exhausted most of their energy in enhancing their attacks.

"We will bring back aid!" they cried and flew away east. Kirtar cursed them tiredly, though he knew they had spent themselves into impotence. At least the elephantine elen still fought, but he could tell by the turning of their hoods that they watched their brethren flying away.

A fresh surge of beasts threw itself against the wagon, and it tumbled to kindling as the lieutenant fell. His magic now armored his flesh and his fists. He fought his way through the maelstrom to the piles of dead animals killed before they could reach the wagon. A bull took him to the ground, the heavy skull battering at his shield, threatening to crush him. Two strikes of his dagger marked the animal, and it was swept away.

He threw himself between two huge corpses, wondering for a moment if he should just hunker down, wait out the attack and protect only himself. The snapping of tent poles changed his mind in seconds. He should have been unable to hear the sound of breaking ash staves, but some portion of his being had waited for the sound throughout the battle.

The lieutenant's tent had been erected amongst a clump of boulders and by happenstance the silken walls withstood the tide of animals even as warrior mages fell. Now its respite ended, and the structure collapsed, shrouding the bull that had torn its way into the tent.

Fresh strength thundered through the bird warrior's limbs as he thought of the sphere, the wondrous ball whose power inspired such visions. The Order's future—and his as Knight Champion—was in danger. He came out of hiding like a striking snake. A lance of golden power burgeoned from his fists, and the point parted bone as it stabbed relentlessly. Without the power of a steed behind it, the golden spindle still exploded through ribs, the showers of blood churning into the soil as still more buffalo swirled into the combat.

He held the lance high, calling for his warriors to rally, but his brothers were trapped behind the walls of corpses. He was alone, and the herd still tore through the camp. As stubbornly as any bull, he forced his way closer to his former pavilion. The long lance slapped against the ribs of animals in the way, the enhanced spear breaking ribs as Kirtar beat his way closer to his objective.

Then he saw it. His prize, his destiny was being kicked by the wrapped bull. Like some monstrous pillow, the bull inside the tent's fabric rebounded off the ring of boulders, its splayed hooves tearing at what remained of a knight's pavilion. More animals spilled into the ring of boulders, and Kirtar flew to a low stone. The metal sphere, which had glowed with such promise, was duller, its glory muted.

"You've soiled it!" cried the lieutenant and threw his lance through the trapped bull and pinned it to another animal. He dived into the scramble, the sphere tucked behind his feet against a rock. The attack seemed to be dying down, and there was less noise, but he stood furious and with bare hands beat the animals trying to escape. His blows, which once shattered boulders, rebounded from simple bone and hide, but still his arms rose and fell. The ring of corpses trapped the animals. Kirtar's opponents soon dripped blood from their noses and ears. A cow tried to crush the bird warrior against the boulder, but he grappled still, his power healing broken bones even as he killed the animal with an especially frantic blow that shocked the heart into stillness.

A figure blocked his vision, and he almost swung before recognizing the massive form of an elen. The robe enveloping it was torn, and the gray skin was bruised and swollen. The long axe cut the spines of wounded animals, the pain of their broken bones washed away by death. Cries for help sounded throughout the remains of the camp, a surprising number of soldiers still living despite the length of the assault. Kirtar stooped and tucked the sphere into his purse, taking a moment to regard it. It was less brilliant, but the echoes of his former visions lurked in the corner of his soul as he tried to will it to its previous glory.

An aven bird warrior strode over the hills of dead flesh, coming to deliver the report on the survivors. "Sir, the mounts have returned. The outrider managed to save the string and brought them back."

The company's steeds had been hobbled some distance from the camp, and a quick-thinking guard managed to herd them to safety as waves of buffalo swamped the camp.

"The wagons and most of the equipment were destroyed though efforts to salvage what we can have begun. The wounded are stabilized and await the efforts of the more powerful mages."

Kirtar laced up his purse and strode away toward the steeds.

"We have no time to waste healing bruises," he stated to the officer, who gaped as the lieutenant raised his voice. "Men, we have triumphed over the forest in spite of its attempts to destroy us. We have lacked only the will to seize our victory."

Most of the soldiers were stunned, but Kirtar could see he lingering battle madness in the faces of his bird warriors.

"It is long past time that we took action against the easts that disturb our dominions," he announced. "We ust recognize our duty and destroy the forces that would verwhelm us!" He pointed toward the disappearing buf- lo.

"The herd could not sweep us aside and withdraws to enew itself in the hidden glens. Would you fight it again?" Ie swept his hand over the destroyed encampment. Would you fight twice as many beasts when someday there re half as many of us?" The bird warrior drew himself up roudly.

"Tired and exhausted as we are, I know that only by con- nuing the attack can we win this war." A feeble cheer ent up, but it was magnified a thousandfold in Kirtar's isions.

"Mount up and ride into the forest," he commanded. We will kill until nothing remains to oppose us!"

Ignoring frantic signs from the healers, he took those arriors who could move to the steeds and mounted. He led ne charge against the retreating heard. A bestial sea flowed efore him, and he vowed to empty it, one sword stroke at time.

CHAPTER 13

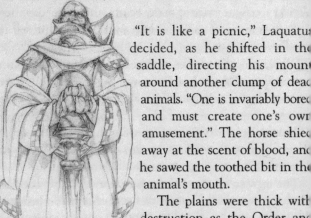

"It is like a picnic," Laquatus decided, as he shifted in the saddle, directing his mount around another clump of dead animals. "One is invariably bored and must create one's own amusement." The horse shied away at the scent of blood, and he sawed the toothed bit in the animal's mouth.

The plains were thick with destruction as the Order and the forest's forays clashed. After a week of piled corpses and devastated towns, Laquatus ached for a change. The death of drylanders was always enjoyable, but even a favorite dish might loose its appeal if sampled too often.

Turg felt the ambassador's lack of interest, and the amphibian did its best to enliven the journey. Forbidden from attacking the villagers along the way and banned from

144

ssaulting the mercenaries, it took a few days for the frog to
ct. Laquatus could feel his champion drawing on the
merman's cunning though he lacked enough interest to
interrogate his servant.

A horse's scream made the ambassador look up, wondering if they had fallen into an ambush. One of the pack-
horses fell and thrashed, a caltrop sunk deep into its hoof.
Laquatus could see iridescent glitter on the metal and knew
it to be a deadly poison. A mercenary ran to care for the
beast, stooping to draw the iron from the leg. But Turg
seemed to appear, blocking the way.

"It appears to be poison," the ambassador called as the
tired servant hesitated to force his way past the frog. "If you
touch it, you will be too weak to walk within the hour. If
you cut yourself, you might as well dig a grave." The frog
nodded emphatically and turned to the downed horse. Bor-
rowing a knife, he slit the beast's throat, moving slowly as
if expressing grief. The ambassador would be ill at the
mawkish sentiment if he were not sure that Turg had
dropped the caltrop into a pouch.

The mercenaries patted the frog awkwardly on the back.
They expressed that night their gratitude for his quick
thinking. They saved him the first cuts of the dinner. The
merman sneered at their stupidity. They neglected to ask
how an aristocrat from the depths of the sea might recognize a poison on sight, especially one volatile enough to be
deposited for contact use. Did they think him a sage to
know every toxin? He knew the deadliness of the concoc-
tion because he carried a good supply of it secured in the
depths of his luggage. The frog was cheered at dinner, and
the ambassador wondered what else might happen.

A mental command reinforced his previous orders. He

could not afford to lose any of the men, though the steeds were expendable as long as there was a surplus. Perhaps this game might keep his attention until they reached the lieutenant.

The frog did not use poison again, and the ambassador was glad. It could be an indiscriminate tool, rather like the amphibian. Instead the jack amused himself and the merman by daring the mercenaries into dangerous lapses in judgment, primarily by example. The frog took to taunting the forest animals who were gripped by the strange compulsion. He seemed to turn his back on them with unconcern. Laquatus knew the champion's peripheral vision was extraordinary, especially in seeing movement. But to the ignorant, and there were few air breathers who were not, he appeared oblivious.

The frog also took to helping with the horses, always quick to step in when a strap came undone or a stone was in a shoe. The animals shied away from the champion, showing better judgment than the fools riding them. However, even Laquatus was hard-pressed to see the camouflaged frog sabotaging the packs and saddles. The merman wondered at the ingenuity of the amphibian. The race was known for its savagery, not playing petty tricks and doing small injuries. It could only be the mental link, the ambassador decided. With other things to control and plots to tend to at the Cabal pits, Laquatus was the overwhelming dominant partner. But now his aggression and deceit flowed in ever-increasing amounts to the jack.

It doesn't matter, he said to himself. Joining spirits was a difficult task, but surely his control would prevent things from getting out of hand. If only they could reach the lieutenant. He forced himself to look at their prisoner. The knight smiled absently, the stench from his wound strong enough that none cared to ride close. In camp the confused man was left alone.

The knight was already broken, and it was the work of a few minutes to invade his mind, inserting new memories. Now he could only babble that the ambassador was his savior, his rescuer from forbidding odds. Occasionally he would lapse into spasms and blurt out the names of his supposed tormenters. Laquatus amused himself by inserting the names of fighters who had irritated him. Kamahl and his noxious partner Seton had prominent roles. But like a pie, the situation's humor grew more stale every day. Furthermore, he must force his temporary minions to care for the madman.

The next morning the knight was still alive, though Laquatus doubted he would last the day. A perfectly good plan ruined by the lieutenant's stubborn insistence on staying hidden. There were villagers, but the ambassador wanted a performance for the Order. A preview was performed for the cheap crowds, but he moved on before the man could say more than "He rescued me," and name a few names.

He stopped only one time at a village. The headman, seeing the poor condition of the knight, offered hospitality. The ambassador was forced to influence his mind and leave a cover story with the others.

"The messenger," he explained, "suffers from an infection of the blood. Only healing magic might offer a chance."

So they continued. The merman opened his kit of poisons and drugs. Some elixirs were deadly but in miniscule amounts could give temporary strength. The knight rallied, his eyes growing brighter. No longer did he lie strapped like a sack to the back of his mount, his arm tied to the bridle. He tried to sit up, to move with his steed. But it was a feverish energy that gripped him, and Laquatus knew they were running out of time.

Turg was free of scrutiny as the ambassador worked on his project. The malice that the merman planted in the jack took full flower and blossomed as Laquatus mixed another stimulant for the knight.

The mercenaries set up the midday camp, making a bed at Laquatus's orders for the knight. The dying man was cut from his saddle. The ropes parted to let him fall to the piled blankets.

"We must continue," the wounded warrior insisted, trying to rise, only to fall back. He attempted to push himself up with his hands, forgetting somehow that he only had one. The stump bled once more, even through the heavy cushion of bandages.

"Perhaps a sedative or a smaller dose of the stimulant," Laquatus muttered, boiling water to prepare an infusion. All that he carried was deadly, and he tired of trying to make poison give life rather than take it. Rarely had he worried his potions might be too effective. Laquatus tried to calm the knight's spirit even as he worked to rebuild the body. False memories and commands were increasingly useless as the captive's mind lost itself and could not remember the impulses he implanted. He mixed more powerful drugs, knowing that he was buying hours without sustained rest or magical healing.

The merman needed time to mix the potions properly, and he went to the perimeter of the temporary camp. He concentrated, tying a spell to the line he traced around the tent and mounts. With each step Laquatus took, a subtle cry sounded from the ground. "Look elsewhere," it seemed to say. "There is nothing here," the magic whispered. The wards were based on misdirection and would keep beasts away from the camp. The ambassador had grown piqued at being unable to command the bizarre attacks of wildlife. He could no longer command the animals by his magic, but he could mislead them.

Turg and two of the hunters made for the perimeter, watching for signs of danger. Laquatus mixed the poisons inside the tent. He wielded the mortar and pestle, selecting the herbs and sealing everything into a porous bag. Then he went to the fire; to the eyes of the ignorant he was brewing a healthy tea. He wondered how long they would survive if he invited them to share with the patient.

His champion watched a swarm of insects pass, their buzzing creating background noise. Like a rolling cloud, the tiny warriors dipped and flew over the plain. Sometimes they moved with the wind and at other times against it. Barely aware of them, Laquatus measured out a cup of the tea.

Screams sounded from the perimeter, drawing everyone's attention. One of the soldiers was outside the wards, twisting on the ground. A mercenary ran outside to help him, then swatted at the air. Stinging insects boiled from the ground, settling on the would-be rescuer and pumping venom into his body. The first man down convulsed. The rest of the soldiers took a few steps to help but stopped, unwilling to risk death for one already doomed. The warrior still standing turned and came back to the camp in a drunken stagger. The mercenary's face swelled until he was blind. He called for help, his bulging throat choking off the cry in mid-word. Turg grabbed a spear and put out the butt end. As the dying man came closer he pushed him, the jack's muscles sending his victim reeling head over heels backward. Unable to stand, the man crawled. He set off away from the camp, having lost his bearing in the fall. After only a few yards he collapsed and was still.

"Stop!" commanded Laquatus as other mercenaries grabbed weapons, closing on the frog. He poured the tea down the knight's throat ignoring the sputters, sure his minions would hold until he finished the unpleasant chore. Swords whispered from scabbards, and he stood up, livid, seeing a few fools edging closer to the champion. Turg stood hunched over with arms spread wide. The ambassador could see the gloating on his face. The merman threw the filled teapot at the bravest fools, the hot metal burning a man, putting him down.

"I said, stop!" Laquatus bellowed. He stalked to the edge of the wards, slapping armed men out of the way. "Leaving the camp is death!" he shouted. "The moment those two men stepped outside they were dead!"

He stalked to the leader of the mercenaries and hissed into his face.

"If your incompetent minion had crossed back into the wards, they would have fallen. We would all be kicking our last!" he said, inches from the warrior's face. "Now tell these fools to sit down and wait until the insects pass."

Fear and loathing was in the other man's eyes, but he nodded curtly and stamped back to the fire, his hands holding an animal prod. Those still standing against the frog saw the hatred rising off the man and slunk away, not wishing to call attention to themselves.

Laquatus moved back to his tent and put away his poisons. Once his equipment was packed he called Turg to him with a mental command. The moment the amphibian let the tent flap close the ambassador bludgeoned him immobile with a mental assault.

"You have had quite enough fun for one trip," the merman whispered, looking into the frog's spirit. The flow between them had changed the jack. The amphibian's intelligence had soared, and mentally he bore little resemblance to the near animal he once was. Laquatus pondered the champion, wondering at the signs of familiarity the new creation showed.

"Why, it's me," the ambassador said. His murderous impulses and controlling nature had bonded with the frog's savagery. Like a baby taking its first steps, the amphibian was manipulating the people around it. Like a proud parent, the ambassador admired how far his offspring had come in luring the mercenaries to their death. But sadly, like a child, the frog had no grasp of the larger plot. With a faint sigh of regret, Laquatus channeled power along their connection. Turg screamed, his body thrashing as a flood of energy scoured his mind.

"Just stay out," the merman said to panicked questions from the mercenaries at the tent flap. "I am working with Turg on a question of discipline."

The mental constructions giving the amphibian its independence and reasoning power melted under the assault, dissolving like sandcastles before an incoming tide. Laquatus scarred the frog's mind, crippling its ability to grow mentally. Even as he attacked the mind he could feel the frog vainly trying to repair its shattered spirit.

"Strong, aren't you," the ambassador chuckled, bearing down a little harder. "We'll just have to make this a daily ritual then." He tore at the soul, pleased by the jack's agony.

* * * * *

It was a somber expedition that moved through the plains. The casualties kept the mercenaries close to the ambassador, scared to leave the safety of his wards. Turg was as he used to be, a sullen mountain of muscle. The frog could barely restrain himself from attacking anything that moved. The ambassador devoted more attention to managing the jack, amazed at how much more work it required, but the extra effort engaged his attention. The boredom that plagued him vanished under the workload. The soldier was in a coma, drugged to near-death in the hopes that they might find a healer. Laquatus regretted the delay Turg had created , but he must have absolute control.

The cries of battle sounded, and the ambassador stood in his stirrups. The forest was closer, but most of the land was open ground. The ground was dry, and the merman could see only the dust of the melee. He cursed the mercenaries' newfound timidity. If they were to be useful, his guards should be scouting ahead. The noise was dying down, and he feared the fight might end before he could join. The chance to finally receive accolades for rescuing the dying knight riding behind him was too great to resist.

"Attack," he ordered with a great cry, unleashing his champion as he spoke. There was movement from ahead. Mounted figures becoming visible as a breeze began to clear the scene of dust. The mercenaries broke into a charge and echoed a battle cry. Turg was obvious as he ran toward the fighting, and the guards knew that if the amphibian left the ambassador's side then the wards protecting them from observation were gone. Laquatus waved he laggards forward, his frown driving them to overtake heir fellow. Fear could create as bold a fighter as courage, he ambassador said to himself.

It was an Order detachment, the ambassador realized vith glee. The mounted knights maneuvered against reptilian beasts that gathered in a circle as the soldiers dressed heir ranks. Laquatus's mercenaries drew near the formed anks, but except for a few glances, the soldiers ignored the ough irregulars racing to join them. The merman kept back, wanting disposable minions between him and any langers. Besides, he must tend his captive, who showed igns of life as he approached a detachment of his fellows. Laquatus's passport gave a feeble cheer before lapsing unconscious. Only the straps and webbing kept the man on his horse. The merman drove his horse and that of the sick man faster. All his hard work could not expire within sight of the finish line.

The Order finished dressing its lines, and boots thudded nto mounts' sides. The knights moved forward, lances lropping to ram home. Their opponents were great lizards, heir sides heaving in the sun. Dust settled over their scaly bodies, making it difficult to count them despite their size. The knights shifted their angle of attack, their lances tearing at weaving heads and opening up necks.

Laquatus's mercenaries arrived in a disordered mob, but heir attack did more damage. Doubtless this was due to heir experience in gathering animals for caravans, the ambassador said to himself as he slowed and tried to appear nore solicitous of the wounded man.

Familiar with the species, the mercenaries dodged strikes and unleashed blows to the joints and fragile bones at he back of the head. Despite their size, thousand-pound creatures fell as easily as cattle in the slaughterhouse. The Order forces swept back to attack again, but this time they cheered the irregulars as the last reptile fell. The ambassador led his passport forward, interrupting the victory cries as he struggled to get the Order's attention before the knight could inconveniently die.

"I have a man in desperate need of healing!" he cried out, his face flushed in apparent fear for his prisoner's life. "He might die any minute!"

A sergeant of the Order threw himself from his horse, rushing to the wounded man's side. He drew a dagger and cut away the restraining cords.

"Bring blankets and erect a tent!" he ordered his men, easing the patient to the ground.

"I prayed to find someone who could help," the merman said, trying to sound relieved. "I am Ambassador Laquatus of the Mer Empire. Can you do anything?"

The sergeant ignored him, already falling into a trance. The energy rolling from his hands was almost invisible in the sunlight. Used to the rich golden color of healing, the ambassador wondered if he misunderstood the sergeant's intentions. But the one-armed man's breathing seemed to improve by a miniscule amount as more power soaked into the body.

"The sergeant is exhausted," a soldier explained, coming from a packhorse with a bundle of wood to start a fire. "We've been marching for days, slaughtering anything we can find."

He dropped the fuel and began cutting a circle of turf away for a fire pit. All the Order soldiers looked exhausted. Some stood with still bloody weapons, too tired to clean them.

"I am Corporal Vale," the soldier continued as he stacked the wood, laying down the kindling, then the heavier pieces. The warrior was twisted as if a healing had gone wrong, but intelligence glinted from the slack face.

"Why are you here so close to the forest?" Corporal or not, there was suspicion in his look.

"Attacked," came a gurgling cry from behind them.

The corporal spun, his dirt-covered knife ready to stab.

"I was attacked," the wounded knight repeated, his eyes glassy as he looked toward the sky.

The corporal crowded closer, his knife still ready but his attention on the wounded man.

"Who attacked you?" Vale asked gently. The knight's face was flushed, and the corporal motioned for one of other soldiers to continue the fire building. "How were you injured?"

The sergeant was deep in his trance, his face growing hollow as he poured more healing power into the wounded man. Laquatus watched with interest, for the stimulants and poisons he had poured down the knight's throat were nearly as deadly as the seeping wounds.

"A metal-hued barbarian and a centaur," came the implanted answer. "They fell on us behind a wave of animals, killing everyone before I was rescued. A frog carried me away," he gasped and passed out.

The ambassador restrained a wide grin, all the work had been worth it. He tried to look concerned.

"He means my jack, Turg," he said, pointing to the battlefield where the amphibian tore away raw flesh and gulped it down. "I was coming after Lieutenant Kirtar when we happened upon the ambush. We were only able to save the one man before being forced to flee. We were lucky to make it to you alive."

The corporal grunted, then knelt to catch the sergeant as he toppled. The healer looked as wasted as his patient, and

Laquatus wondered if they would both die. Vale looked lost as he held his superior's head, already tucking blankets around the drained figure.

"Kirtar is five miles farther in the forest," he said distractedly. "Follow the main path, and you will come upon his camp." He turned to the ambassador. "If you could leave a few men to help protect the wounded, it would be greatly appreciated."

"Of course I can," Laquatus said expansively. He waved three mercenaries over. "I will leave these guards here with supplies and food if you could give me one man to lead me to Kirtar."

Vale nodded, exhaustion catching up with him. Even three unknowns would be an infusion of strength to the weakened command.

"Toltas," he called. A soldier stood up from the fire building. "Escort the ambassador and his men to the lieutenant. Tell him of the aid they provided."

The soldier made no protest, looking like a sleepwalker. Laquatus accepted the guide, for the rest of the command looked like the walking dead.

The detachment appeared asleep as the ambassador's men and their guide left for the lieutenant. As they proceeded, the ambassador looked for further signs of the forest's aggression. He kept a ward up to deter attack from whatever they might meet. Scattered groups of animals lay piled, killed by the Order. The guide took them around the corpses, too tired to speak. Turg jumped to inspect each mound, but Laquatus kept firm control over the frog's appetite.

They came to the main Order camp, nearly abandoned except for five guards. They did not even challenge the mbassador and his party, their faces dull as they ate. The distant sounds of battle could be heard, and Laquatus and his mercenaries drew weapons.

"Where is the lieutenant?" the ambassador barked. A soldier eating beans gave only a vague wave toward the noise.

Laquatus looked at his guide, who was glassy-eyed and swaying in his saddle. "Stay here. We can find Kirtar on our own."

Too tired to argue, the soldier dismounted and slowly walked to the cook pot.

"Come on men," Laquatus said loudly. "The lieutenant might need our help." He put his heels to his steed's side and moved out at a bone-jarring gait. Once they were out of sight of the camp, he slowed down. "Pull up, you fools," he said to the mercenaries. Caught up in the moment, half of his riders forgot he was no friend of the Order.

"We will slowly scout out the situation, and if Kirtar truly is in trouble, we'll finish him off," Laquatus said coldly. "If he appears to be winning or there are flying messengers, we will act in support. But do nothing until I give the order."

At a mental command, Turg faded from view. His camouflaging skin mimicked the small undergrowth on the border between the forest and the plains. Laquatus fed more energy to his wards. The mercenaries and the ambassador moved slowly ahead while the frog sent mental pictures back to the merman. Laquatus threw his reins to a mercenary and slumped in his saddle as his champion's visions filled his mind.

There was a clearing in the brush, and inside it the Order laid siege to the herd of giant animals. They appeared reptilian, as large as dragons, though without wings or signs of magical ability. They sounded cries of distress like mighty elephants, as the lieutenant sent mounted squads against single animals.

The knights lowered their lances, the wood and stee[l] flickering as magic flowed through the weapons. The horse[s] approached at a slow gallop, closing obliquely with th[e] group. The hills of flesh shifted, trying to retreat farther int[o] the herd, but there was no more room. The points cut int[o] the belly of a huge reptile, tearing through the hide. Bloo[d] poured down, gallons soaking into soil. The final lance tor[e] through the ligaments of a leg, sending the animal down[.] Turg was overwhelmed by the smell of hot blood, and Kirta[r] sent another squad after a different animal.

The ambassador came out of his light trance, disap[-] pointed at Kirtar's strength. He must come in as an ally, h[e] realized. He drew his personal weapon, a trident, and calle[d] softly, "We will support the lieutenant, men."

They came out of the concealing brush nearly opposit[e] the Order. Laquatus sent his steed around the perimeter o[f] the clearing to link up with the lieutenant, seeing littl[e] point of charging into a battle before making sure the effor[t] was appreciated.

Over the bellow of the giants, the screams of griffins car[-] ried on the wind. A flight of Order soldiers came down, thei[r] weapons ready to be unleashed. However, instead of charg[-] ing the herd, a woman dismounted. Kirtar saluted her, an[d] Laquatus realized this must be Captain Pianna, head of th[e] Order. He enhanced his senses and drifted back to the brush[.]

"Captain, you are just in time to join us," Kirtar said, th[e] bird warrior standing proud. In contrast to his men h[e] seemed alert and eager.

The captain drew off her helmet and handed it to [a] mounted subordinate. "I need to speak to you alone," sh[e] said, her voice flat.

Kirtar looked to the animals, as if to mention the lack of tim[e]

"I am sure your butchery can wait." She walked away, her sword of command sheathed over her shoulder providing an easy way for Laquatus to track her movements through the detachment. Finally they were far enough away that she stopped and turned to Kirtar.

"What, by all the stars in the sky, are you doing here Kirtar? What insanity drove you to attack into the forest? I directed you to scout and protect the western villages, not initiate a war." She looked over the slaughter and the dead animals.

"The forest and its creatures are part of the natural order. Why would you order needless killing that goes against our basic ideals?" she asked passionately. Laquatus focused his attention on Kirtar hopeful that he could use the answer to good effect.

"To protect the plains, the enemy must be destroyed," the aven replied, his tone growing hot. "These attacks are only a symptom of the chaos deep in the forest itself. It is long past time something was done to tame the west and its beasts! For now, only destruction can protect our land from the contagion here."

Laquatus chuckled to himself as the captain stood stock still. "Rank hatred and insanity," the ambassador whispered lovingly. "I can make use of that."

Pianna rallied and pointed to the lieutenant's men.

"Setting aside your unique views of handling the current problems," the captain said carefully, "there is still no excuse for the condition of your men. I just came from your camp. After a flight of griffins landed, I was forced to wake your guards to find out where you were. Your men are completely spent, their magic dissipated in these pointless attacks." She pointed to the few remaining herd animals in the clearing. "You have dragged your pickets so far forward you are beyond support. You have nowhere to fall back to in an emergency. We should be back where the militias can act in concert, not driving for the depths of the forest!"

The few remaining animals broke their instinctual response to band together for protection and started for the woods. The lieutenant's men moved to attack, sending their mounts in pursuit of the giants. Their lances dropped parallel to the ground. Pianna called out for the men to stand, but only a tired blood-thirst remained in their minds, and they did not obey.

Laquatus thought quickly, the captain might obey the Order Strictures and destroy the prize. He sent Turg to find the sphere in Kirtar's camp, burning the need to stay concealed into the frog's mind.

He raised his trident and shouted, "Kill the animals!" The mercenaries followed.

The ambassador sent his troop to head the beasts off. Only after the charge began did he realize the true size of his opposition. Just the whales and great sea beasts were larger, and he wondered if the mercenaries could do anything with their swords and spears. But these men hunted the forests, and they were ready for such foes. A few nets flew up, trailing long ropes, to land against the reptilian sides. They stuck, the throb of magic bonding them to their targets. The entangled beasts trailed long lines behind them as they bolted. The nets tore trees from the ground, but the lizards fell as they became tangled with massive rocks. The Order followed, and their lances pierced the unprotected bellies, letting out rivers of lifeblood.

The ambassador swung his trident, power snapping among its tines. A lash of lightning danced along the lead beast's side, the current destroying nerves and locking muscles. Tons of flesh piled up as the Order and the mercenaries worked together in the slaughter. Laquatus turned toward the leadership, the lieutenant and the captain already mounted and closing. The griffins spread out in a half circle behind their leaders.

"Always glad to be of service," the ambassador called out, enjoying the rage threatening to boil out from the captain's demeanor. "We met a detachment of your men after rescuing one of your knights. Arrived here just in time to help you deal with these animals."

The captain visibly forced herself to be polite.

"Thank you for your aid, Ambassador. We are thankful that you could come, but it would be best if we adjourned back to the base camp," Pianna said with a tight smile.

The merman still had no response from Turg as to whether the prize was located. He needed to keep the leaders out in the field.

"Surely the best thing is to continue killing your way into the forest," Laquatus said, swinging his trident to point west. "The business of the Order is to end the threat of attacks."

"The business of the Order is what I say it is, Ambassador," Pianna said, interrupting any comments that Kirtar might have had. "We have lived with the forest for generations. It is foolish to risk everything when we do not even know why these attacks have begun or how we can stop them. We are not the Cabal to believe that death is the final answer and first response."

She turned the horses and started back to camp, forcing the rest of her troops to follow. The merman could see the rebellion in Kirtar's face. He could race after her, but that lacked dignity. A spurt of animals showered from a cluster of brush.

"Beware," Laquatus cried, and a bolt of energy arced from his trident to the bushes at the side of the trail. Soldiers drew weapons as small animals flowed out and up the legs of their mounts. They were stoats and shrews, and Laquatus cursed the fates that supplied him with such diminutive foes. He needed some great menace to impress the Order and help cement an alliance, but only vermin presented themselves.

The Order steeds pawed the ground, starting in fright as the small animals tried to scramble up their legs. The lieutenant swung a long flail with gusto, the heavy ball tearing its way through the creatures as his soldiers and Laquatus's mercenaries maneuvered to give him room. Swords and lances swung, and creatures died, though their numbers seemed undiminished.

The captain and her officers dashed the ambassador's hopes for any victory by summoning their own creatures. Several of the griffin riders concentrated, letting their steeds snap up mouthfuls of the furry foes. Huge single- and double-horned beasts set the ground shuddering as they stampeded their way into the flow of sharp-toothed vermin. Gray rhinos dipped their heads and swept the small animals away. Tiny teeth worked at their gray hides in vain as the Order directed creatures shattered the flow of small beasts.

Laquatus, however, was not willing to give up. He raised power, but the blasts that ripped from his trident barely stunned the stoats. That was not where his power had gone. The merman's sly summoning drew greater beasts from the brush, attracting creatures that had fled Kirtar's murderous attacks.

Great cats leaped at them from cover, throwing themselves on the rhinos. The horned beasts rolled and tried to scrape their feline attackers off as larger teeth worried at their hides. A few giant bulls thundered out, shoving panicked rhinos and goring the gray beasts' sides. Laquatus ceased his call, concerned that he might destroy himself in calling up more dangerous animals. Predators, large and small, attacked the Order, and the ambassador watched as his mercenaries aided the beleaguered knights.

"Hold them for a few seconds," Pianna cried, a bow in her hands. The captain's arrows flew low to the ground. The missiles were for cutting harnesses and standards, but the curving blades instead dismembered the stoats and badgers. Then the razored half-moons lodged deep in the legs of the bulls coming from the forest.

The small animals were so easily killed, the ambassador lamented, and not even poisonous. Laquatus threw arcs of energy that leaped from small animal to small animal, stunning them. He drove his horse among the unconscious creatures, cursing his horse as it failed to trample enough.

The lieutenant and his men had dismounted, swords killing the last of the small creatures before they closed with those slyly summoned by the ambassador. The rhinos returned, finally free of the great cats. Huge horns sundered ribs, and the bulls died quickly. The Order knights killed off the last of their attackers and turned to help the mercenaries.

A lion leaped at Laquatus, pulling down his horse and spilling him to the blood-soaked ground. His guards tried to spear it but missed, allowing the lion another chance to kill Laquatus. He laid his image over his horse, sacrificing the beast as he rolled away. The gaping jaws locked on the equine throat as the merman's steed did him a final service. The ambassador called for his champion, regretting that Captain Satas and his dependable minions were far to the east, still mapping their way to the Order's Citadel.

CHAPTER 14

Kamahl and Seton drove themselves hard up the road, pursuing both Kirtar and Laquatus. It took days to finally flush themselves of the ambassador's animals. They had been relentlessly pursued, the beasts continuing long after the merman and his party departed. Only the combination of the barbarian's flaming barriers to impede pursuit and the druid's constant effort to break the spell finally won them through. Each time the druid erased the implanted commands, he turned the creatures back to the forest. The repetitious contact with the animals led Seton to suspect that something beyond the ambassador and his lackeys was affecting the creatures of the west. Riding in the wake of

Kirtar's forces confirmed that something was wrong.

They returned to the village where they had battled Laquatus and his minions, but the site was deserted. Kamahl found his horse grazing in a deserted field and moved to a narrower mount, much to the relief of his legs. They continued west, looking in vain for the ambassador and his minions. Whether by magic or good trailcraft on the part of Laquatus's mercenaries, they could not track the aristocrat and his murderous cronies.

Soon enough they did find the trail of Lieutenant Kirtar. Dead animals and markers for fallen Order soldiers began to appear. Within a day of leaving the village they came upon a gravestone. The marker was nothing extraordinary, a simple boulder with the sigil of the Order and the troop name.

"The warriors of Eiglin," Seton said, identifying the unofficial symbol of the lieutenant's command. The soldier was interred in frozen ground. The dirt was enchanted to be as resistant as iron, denying scavengers an easy meal. The resting place would be recorded for eventual reburial in the mausoleums of the Order or the graveyards of the soldier's people.

Filled with hope that they would soon meet Kirtar and their search would be over, the two continued on. Instead they found more of the Order's passing slaughter.

They followed long runs of animals hunted down by soldiers until there was nothing left alive. The barbarian and the centaur were forced to backtrack as the trails ended in piles of dead flesh. Soon they neared the edge on the plains and entered the realm usually ceded to the forest.

The killing of animals continued even as the villages

were left behind, angering the druid to greater and greater heights.

"There is no sign that these animals threatened anyone. The Order destroys anything in its path. Perhaps," he said darkly, "the waves of animals are right to kill, with such enemies waiting to come within the trees."

The barbarian rode with his axes loosely tied to his saddle, instantly ready at hand. Such destruction seemed pointless to the mountain mage. The Order had the right to protect itself from attack, but such indiscriminate slaughter must provoke a reaction. Seton assured him that the peoples of the forest were not behind the current attacks. The killing would not curb further animal incursions, for the beasts lacked the intelligence to react to such dangers. To kill every dangerous creature would be the work of decades. Even though the barbarian had spent his life in the mountains, he knew that one roused the forest at his own peril. The random attacks could change into a real campaign of destruction.

* * * * *

The dust and the cries dragged the pair onward, both desperate to see at last the events whose aftermath had filled the land for days. Seton went forward, his face sick and angry at the slaughter. Kamahl followed hoping to finally catch up with Kirtar or the ambassador. A camp with exhausted Order soldier appeared as they rounded a corner of the road. The centaur charged through, drawn to the combat beyond. Kamahl followed, knowing that both of those he sought were more likely to be near the tumult of battle.

The barbarian looked to the camp as he passed, seeing the line of wounded stretched out. His heart raced as he saw the face of the injured knight, the fighter he had seen with Laquatus. But the man was down in the dirt, a surgeon and orderly working on his wounds. The knight's shirt was cut away. Festering sores and weeping gashes lay open to the dusty air. Kamahl directed his steed forward more strongly, trying to regain the time lost due to his pause.

Seton slowed unexpectedly ahead, allowing Kamahl to come closer. The big centaur crowded a man on a horse, fear and strain plain on the guard's features. The druid's club was in a carrier strapped to his body, and rather than waste time fumbling at the straps he used his hands, as he had back at the caravan.

"Murderer." Kamahl heard him growl as he swept the mercenary off his horse and turn his head until the fellow could see behind him. The dead man's steed stood placidly, apparently accustomed to death in close proximity. "Take a centaur's hide and die!" Seton spat. Kamahl assumed that the centaur had found another member of the ambassador's party. The druid dropped the corpse in the road and reached back to draw his club. Kamahl looked, but no one else saw the killing, and the dead man faded into the background with the other corpses.

"Such a criminal deserves death," the barbarian said as Seton breathed deeply. "But perhaps vengeance might wait when we find the others. Especially if they be in the company of the Order."

The giant grimaced but nodded reluctantly. The pair advanced more slowly, the detail of the fighting beyond becoming clearer as they rounded a clump of trees.

Animals of all sorts, both large and small, moved chaotically between riders and infantry. Seton turned his head, waving off a bobcat as it ran at him and tried to climb to higher ground on his back.

"Sheer madness!" he exclaimed, and Kamahl agreed with him, turning his horse from a badger headed for the trees behind him.

The druid moved tentatively into the confusion. The mountain warrior could feel energy hum as the druid neared a pack of wolves. The beasts snarled, and Seton snarled back, reinforcing the sound with a wave of the club. Kamahl stayed close to his friend as the druid tried to drive the animals away from the killing field.

"Difficult," huffed the druid as a bull elk threatened him with its antlers.

The centaur tried to nudge the animal on with his club, but the beast fenced the stone-tipped weapons with its velvety antlers. Kamahl whipped a fire lash into the ground at the animal's side, and it broke away. The centaur grunted and tried to control other animals as the barbarian raised a line of flickering flame that began to prod the animals to the side. Kamahl ached with the effort of controlling himself, but the druid wanted to stop the battle, not join it, and the barbarian felt constrained to honor his friend's wishes.

The pair worked their way through the animal refugees, turning those outside the fighting back to the forest. Now they crowded the Order soldiers. Kamahl stayed the peacemaker, though more and more he ached to smash a profane soldier to the ground. This fighting was wrong, and they must stop it. The barbarian's frustration mounted higher, and it was with relief that he found another member of the ambassador's party.

Turg announced himself by springing from ambush, as he had so often before. The faint flames Kamahl used to herd animals roared higher, drying the amphibian's skin as the creature came at him. The barbarian ducked as the frog's hind leg thudded into his mounts shoulder, his sword out of position. The jack threw himself onto the centaur. The frog was red with blood and gore from the battle. Kamahl wondered if the champion's fury was directed at him for following the ambassador or attempting to quell the slaughter. Regardless, the amphibian jumped to the druid's back and tried to rip his throat out.

The centaur showed the flexibility of his kind, turning around at his humanoid waist to fight the frog face to face. Kamahl saw them gripping arms, and he waited for parts of the amphibian to fly over the battlefield. As massive as the frog's muscles appeared, they were dwarfed by the forest warrior's mighty shoulders. He turned to his own defense as he left the centaur to his.

Without Seton's will, the animals swung back to fight. Two bears and dragonettes converged on Kamahl, and now the barbarian's fire lash burned away fur and scales. Other animals came closer, some fleeing battle, the others seeking it. The Knights of the Order came together, and a new summoning burned through the magical ether.

New creatures shimmered into being. They seemed huge mounds of crystals, some over twenty feet high. For a moment, Kamahl wondered if the Order forces were trying to construct a fortress. Then the apparent masses of rock began to move. Ponderous legs swung into new positions as the creatures started across the field. Light began to glimmer inside the crystal, rotating wildly before leaping out to engulf animals. The magic congealed, slowly trapping its victims in glowing layers. Bison and great bears struggled as if in tar until the bands of golden light hardened and left the victims immobile. The monstrous creatures knew their allies and rhinos ran freely among the trapped creatures, trampling and goring the helpless animals.

The megoliths moved their crystalline masses over their captives, both the living and the dead, and settled down for a moment. Then the legs raised the crystal bodies, and new bands of magic jumped forth to trap fresh prey. A cow kicked and thrashed as the energy tightened and locked it rigid, waiting for a rhino's killing thrust or a crushing death from the advancing giants. The megoliths had moved far enough that Kamahl could see the lane they left behind. Every drop of blood, morsel of flesh, or sprig of a plant was gone. A floor of corpses lay in front of them, and the crystal grew rosy as the mineral creatures helped the Order sweep the field clean.

"The drive is broken," Seton croaked from behind Kamahl. The barbarian turned to the centaur. The druid's face was black with an oily liquid, and water wept copiously from his eyes. Of Turg, there was no sign.

"The ambassador's jack vomited his bile into my eyes as we struggled," Seton said, peering myopically into Kamahl's face. "I wrenched his shoulder and would have pulled his arm off but for the burning of its juices."

The centaur tried to wipe his eyes clear, and Kamahl pulled a canteen from his gear. The forest warrior tilted his head back and poured the water directly into his eyes.

"I think the battle is done," he gasped and handed the nearly empty container back to the barbarian. Animals fleeing the conflict proved the centaur's word good. A bear lumbered by, giving only a glance in their direction before continuing on its way. However, there were other creatures on the field. A rhino stabbed its way through the flow of animal refugees and headed for Kamahl. His axe spun into its skull, dropping it into the bloody mud. Others converged on him, and he drove his horse forward, trying to get away from the approaching beasts. The megoliths reversed course, and energy folded over the barbarian despite his horse's efforts to outrun the spell. The mare's gallop suddenly stopped, and the horse tumbled to the ground. Kamahl threw himself free before he could be trapped beneath the body.

He rolled, the sword flying free from his grip. He came to his feet with knives of fire in his hands. Seton swung his club, snapping a rhino's horn free as he struggled against the megoliths' magic. Kamahl ran to his aid, his power severing crystal as he turned to destroy the mineral giants. But the battlefield held only the victors and the dead. The creatures of the forest merged back into the trees as the rhinos and megoliths began to fade away.

The barbarian hobbled to his horse, a deep gaping wound on her side telling him that a rhino had attacked while he scrambled to his feet. He knelt and laid his hand on her side.

"Thank you," He whispered, then stripped the saddle and gear from the corpse.

"My friend," Seton said tremulously, "I can't see you—" The centaur collapsed, rolling up against the other corpses in the field. Kamahl paused for a second and threw away everything, racing to find a healer.

* * * * *

Kamahl did not know how long he searched before he found someone willing to help his friend. He was sure that the exhausted sergeant came more because of the barbarian's sword than belief in his story. Once he checked to see if Seton was alive, the Order soldier fell into a healing trance.

The mountain warrior struggled to clear the centaur's eyes, scouting for water among the fallen to wash away the poison and quench the druid's raging thirst. Kamahl waited, wondering if he should fetch others to help, but the cries of the wounded could be heard in the distance. The barbarian counted himself lucky to have found the sour sergeant.

"I have done what I can," the Order soldier announced suddenly, standing up and moving away from the patient he had lavished so much care over.

"I do not know how to repay you," Kamahl started to say.

"Don't bother," came the gruff reply. The man stretched, his back crackling at the movement. "I saved the eyes. I don't know if he will be able to use them. Bring him to the main camp when he feels able to walk."

"I will thank you as soon as I can guide him up the road," Kamahl said. "I will do it right before I speak with Lieutenant Kirtar."

The sergeant laughed harshly. "I won't be seeing you then. Kirtar has been recalled. The captain was going to haul him back to the citadel to explain his conduct. If I know Captain Pianna, he was on griffin back within a minute of the battle's end."

All that riding and he must have missed Kirtar by only minutes. The barbarian stood rigid, wondering how he would catch up with the lieutenant now.

* * * * *

Kamahl sat in his camp, eating a piece of travel bread. Despite the tons of meat lying in the field, he had gathered none of it. Besides being no scavenger, he could not afford the trouble a fire might bring.

Seton recovered some, and the barbarian was able to lead the centaur to the Order camp perimeter, though he did not follow the druid to the healers. He left the giant and returned to his solitary tent.

He waited for a day, eating dry travel food and ignoring the stench. The barbarian meditated, but the core of his anger made his attempts to find peace meaningless. On the second day, Seton returned.

The druid's face was discolored, the apelike features splotched with what looked like blue-and-black dye. His eyes seeped a steady stream, and he advance slowly into the camp, watching where he stepped.

"It looks worse than it really is," the forest warrior said. "The healers believe that with time my sight may improve." The giant tried to sound cheerful, but it was obviously difficult. The barbarian came closer, gripping his friend firmly by the lower arm.

"I have not wasted my time in the Order's camp," Seton explained, lowering himself gingerly. "The lieutenant was called to the Citadel to explain his policy of slaughter.

"The captain sent word that all forays into the forest would cease pending further information. There is talk that the bird warrior might be demoted or transferred far to the East." Seton paused, speaking more seriously. "The Mer

Ambassador and his jack have also left for the Citadel, 'hoping to resolve the current difficulties,'" the druid repeated, the bitterness plain in his voice.

"The quest must not end here," Seton urged. "Reclaiming the orb or foiling the ambassador's plans, your journey must continue." The druid stood and picked up Kamahl's gear.

"This was not my first stop after the Order's healers released me," the woodland fighter said. "I was able to secure you another steed. Come and I will introduce you to him." The centaur picked up Kamahl's gear with a single hand and headed into the forest, not bothering to wait for a response.

The druid walked through the trees, his huge strides tentative but still forcing the barbarian to step rapidly to keep up with him. They arrived at the foot of a tall cliff after a long walk, one that obviously taxed the giant's strength. The vertical rock face climbed hundreds of feet, the limbs of trees seeming to peek out over the top of the ridge.

"Unless this steed can fly or is invisible, I do not see it." Kamahl quipped as he reached the centaur's side. The druid chuckled painfully as he dropped the barbarian's gear and looked blearily to the sky.

"Emerald!" he called. "Your rider is here!" A head popped out over the top of the cliff, eyes swiveling separately to peer down on the two below. A lizard stepped onto the side of the sheer wall, standing vertically a moment before it started down.

"Emerald volunteered last night to provide you with transportation. He fed this morning and should be ready for days of hard riding."

The barbarian moved back, nervous to be under a creature of such size descending with no visible means of support.

"Do not worry," said Seton. "Emerald's kind can walk

on a ceiling as long as the surface can hold the weight."

The lizard was at the bottom of the cliff and stepped to the ground. Its body stood as high as a horse, though it was much longer. Emerald's long tail beat against the rock.

"Exactly how am I going to ride it?" Kamahl said as he approached the beast. The centaur said nothing, swinging the saddle onto the animal's back. A long tongue darted out of the gecko's mouth and worked along the underside of the saddle. When the druid settled it all the way down, it squelched and then locked solid.

"That will hold you and your gear even if you are upside down," Seton said with satisfaction. "Though you might want to grip with something besides your knees. Now climb aboard, and tell me how it feels."

Kamahl approached cautiously and, using the saddle horn, pulled himself up. The lizard was huge, but the barrel of its body was close to the same width as a horse's.

"How do I care for it?" Kamahl said uncertainly.

Seton laughed. "Emerald is as smart as you are, even if he can't talk," the centaur explained. "When you want to get the saddle off, just tell him and lift. That tongue will smear something on its back that will break the saddle's grip. When you want to start out again, just do as I did." The druid lifted the rest of Kamahl's gear to him and helped secure it. "Emerald knows the way to the Order and how to avoid trouble. Just trust him to know where he is going."

The forest warrior stepped back and settled down to rest. Before Kamahl could say anything the gecko started with a jerk.

"Good luck in your quest, Kamahl," Seton called.

The barbarian could only wave, hoping the druid saw him as he concentrated on adapting to the lizard's gait.

CHAPTER 15

"The air is no place for a merman," Laquatus muttered as he held tightly to the soldier's waist. The ground was distant, and he was reminded of long swims in tropical seas. The clear water reveaaled the ocean floor far below. However, the air would not support the ambassador as he drifted down. He felt his jack's fears and knew only his unbending will and orders kept the frog from panic. He wondered how bruised the amphibian's companion would be when they landed again.

He had convinced the captain his contacts with the Cabal and other continental powers would help her in discovering the source of the disturbances. Laquatus hoped to get her alone and work his mind-altering magic, but she gave him no chance. The strain of controlling Turg and his own fear sapped his energy throughout the griffin ride. Now the final destination was in sight, and he could hardly wait for the feel of dry land beneath his feet.

Laquatus regretted his diminished power. He had been forced to abandon the mercenaries. Pianna was barely willing to allow the ambassador and his champion to accompany her. The merman hoped the underwater explorers had finally reached the Citadel. The promise of sea warriors and competent minions made the loss of the mercenaries bearable.

The Citadel was a massive conglomeration of stone. The castle itself was on top of a rocky hill, the only visible road to the gates exposed to attack from above for its entire length. Double walls of stone reinforced with dozens of towers enclosed the top of the mesa. The central keep was less martial, the fineness of the stone work contrasting with the crudely worked blocks of the outer walls. But however brilliant the white rock appeared, Laquatus still noticed bars on the windows.

There was a town at the base of the hill, tucked between the living rock and a stream flowing down from the north. The slate roofs of the tall houses nearly hid the cobblestone streets. The avenues looked crowded, and the ambassador could see wagons and tents in the town squares. The griffins had often soared over long caravans of refugees headed for the Citadel. The merman wondered where the additional people could be placed. The courtyard that the griffins aimed for seemed clear of any but Order officials, and Laquatus tried to guess how much longer that would be the case.

The landing was a blur as the ambassador closed his eyes. The skybox had felt rock solid in comparison to a living steed, and he wondered if his sudden fear of heights would be temporary. The griffin landed with a lurch as it stumbled to a halt. Laquatus turned and watched Turg's ride land. The moment the flier's claws touched the ground the frog was off, running his hands over the solidity of the cobbles. It took the merman several moments to dismount, his legs locked with cramps. Finally, he commanded his champion to aid him to the ground. The Order soldiers showed disgusting ease as they hurried to unload their steeds of cargo, saddles, and harnesses.

The stablemen moved slowly, as if listening for news. They looked at the pit frog and the ambassador with wide eyes, and Laquatus wondered what wild rumors would be circulating by the day's end. The officers and their guests stepped to the main keep, the several-story building looming over the merman like a cliff.

They moved into the darker room, Laquatus's eyes adapting easily to the dim light coming through the narrow windows. Food was laid out on trestles. It was an example of the journey's hardship that Turg did not immediately fall upon the buffet but squatted down at the ambassador's side. The hugeness of the hall seemed to siphon the noise of its few inhabitants away. The ambassador carefully enhanced his senses and ached at the sudden cacophony. He carefully reined in his energy, hoping that the casting of his spell was undetected. The journey had taken quite a toll on him as well.

The officers were off at an isolated table, small portions of food set before them, though neither ate. The merman's enhanced vision could see the irritation on both of their faces. The rest of the griffin scouts gave them a wide berth, and the server left a flagon of wine at the table rather than standing ready to pour. The ambassador was assaulted by thunder, and Turg stood with a threatening gesture. A serving man stumbled back with a tray of bread and wine.

"Give it here, and then leave me alone!" Laquatus grated out. The impertinence of the man to disturb him while he was concentrating. Only the importance of eavesdropping prevented him from calling for the servant's supervisor. He made a note of the man's face for punishment at a later date. His attention shifted back to the officers in mid-argument.

"I did not return to stay behind these walls," Kirtar said with obvious exasperation. "The fight is to the west, against the creatures of the forest." The bird warrior looked at the captain as if the stupidity of the original question could not be believed.

"I ordered you back to oversee the deployment of militias. Your fighting has changed nothing except to strew corpses amongst the trees." Pianna drank quickly, trying to gain breathing room, to the ambassador's eyes. "Ever since your entry in the Cabal tournament you have lost interest in the Order. Have you succumbed to the lure of wealth and prizes?"

"Wealth is a tool we can use to build the Order," Kirtar said, hammering down a goblet with a peal that split Laquatus's ears. "As for the prizes, I procured one that was worth any number of villages that fell while I competed."

The lieutenant ignored the captain's indignant gasp and opened his pouch. Pianna looked down into the pouch, her eyes locked on the sphere. The lieutenant's fingers cupped it and raised it before her. The room fell silent as Order mages detected the throb of contained power and looked to the officers. Laquatus felt a surge of envy as the lieutenant pushed the sphere back into his pouch. The ambassador was surprised by the sour expression of the officer's face and could barely hear him mutter, "It's dimmer still."

"Impressive enough," the captain said agreeably. "And I can understand your fascination with it. But what have you done since you received it?" The silence seemed to echo in the merman's ears.

"I see," continued Pianna as several seconds passed without response. "Your prize was not used nor provoked any response other than influencing you to ignore your recall and engage in indiscriminate slaughter." She shook her head sadly.

"You are less than you were when you left," she stated emphatically. "You had plans, but once you held that power in your hands you could only use violence. It corrupted you without doing anything but offering you magic you had not earned." Bitterness and resolution filled her tone. "I have never seen a better example of an artifact curbing and shrinking a soul. You must give it up."

"I will not!" replied the lieutenant hotly. "It is only that I don't know how to use it," he confessed, his pale skin flushing in the dim light. "It was bright with glory once, but every time I look at it, the visions grow fainter. I don't know what to do. I know only that this is valuable, and it represents the salvation of the Order."

"It is a chain that is dragging you down. You speak of what you can do, what you know," she said gently. "You must give it up, even if it must be destroyed."

The bird warrior started but with visible effort stifled his initial response and nodded.

"The Order and the Strictures must come first," he said reluctantly. "Only give me time to examine it a little more. You are right that I have done nothing with it other than let dreams of glory lead me astray. Give me a chance to investigate it a little more before we give it up to those who use the crushers."

The captain nodded doubtfully as Laquatus tasted his heart in his mouth. Give the orb to the fanatics who thought the past should be erased? Those who spurned objects of enchantment and condemned wonders to the grinding wheels of their one sanctioned machine? He would see the Citadel ground to dust before he allowed the orb to be damaged.

Kirtar excused himself and left. It took a moment for the ambassador to break his trance and send his jack after him. Perhaps it would take an obvious intervention to take the sphere from these fools. He hoped the underground explorers would find a route soon.

* * * * *

Turg lurked behind a pile of heavy canvas, waiting for the lieutenant to speak. The frog had followed the officer and stayed at a distance. Laquatus soon begged off any further talks with the captain or her representatives, citing his exhaustion from the journey. Now the ambassador rode the frog's spirit, nudging him closer to hear the conspirators.

At least that was merman's belief. The bird warrior left, but instead of retiring directly to his room he spoke to several knights before visiting the armory. Laquatus had a bad moment when he saw the shape of a great crusher filling a building's interior. Several squires pushed a capstan, driving the interior mechanisms. A robotic bird was thrown into the machine's gaping mouth, and a series of smashing collisions sounded, then died down as tiny pieces of the forbidden technology came out the other end. A pile of mechanical limbs and less definable work filled a basket that the presiding officer continued to empty.

Laquatus very nearly sent his champion charging for the orb at that moment. Kirtar had shook himself and left the crusher with a look of fresh determination on his face. Once more he stopped to give a message, and this time Turg was able to hear.

"The dungeon just after midnight."

The frog spent hours waiting in sight of Kirtar's quarters, but the bird warrior did not come out again. Dinner came and went, and the frog's belly grumbled.

In camouflage, he raided the remnants of the evening meal, then headed for the dungeon. Rather than the vast cavern that Laquatus expected, just several empty cells in a tower's base served as the Order's prison. Only the distinctive smell allowed the frog to find it without asking for directions. Laquatus was heartened that even the Order's ideals could not negate the need for small rooms reeking of despair and filth. The frog breathed the odor in deeply before hiding behind stores in the main room.

Kirtar arrived first, inspecting the chamber carefully. Laquatus fed a minute portion of power to Turg, and the spell, combined with the champion's natural camouflage, prevented his discovery. Other knights arrived until five moved to a table. Laquatus noticed with little surprise that all were aven bird warriors. Kirtar spoke, and the others listened silently. The door was not whisperwood, so the lieutenant talked softly.

"I and my fathers have served the Order loyally. You have all been warriors in the Order without any blemish on your service. None may say otherwise."

Turg could hear the rustling of nods and crept out a bit beyond the bags to see the conspiracy.

"But to be loyal to the Order means that sometimes the Strictures must be disobeyed, ill-conceived commands must be ignored."

There were fewer signs of agreement, but there was an affirmative air about the group.

"I won a great prize while competing in the tourney," Kirtar continued. "While defending the helpless, even in that evil city, I defeated a dragon."

Another nod of assent and a bit of pride showed among the warriors at one of their own overcoming such a beast.

"These are difficult times for the Order," the lieutenant said quietly. "The forest has risen and assaulted our lands as never before."

"Aye," said a grizzled voice as one of the others interrupted. "So many refugees have arrived that they are filling up the town. The captain says that soon we will have to start bringing families within the Citadel walls."

"Exactly," said the lieutenant, showing irritation at being interrupted. "The captain has a good heart and believes in the Strictures, but that is not enough in these difficult days. It will take boldness, and while Pianna is no coward, she is not bold. The best way to protect the refugees is to stop them from being displaced." A murmur of agreement filled the room. "We must take the fight to the forest."

The dead silence through Turg's ears told Laquatus that his extreme step was not popular. The lieutenant seemed to know that and quickly continued.

"The prize that the rumors speak of I have with me," he said, opening his pouch. The thrill of power shook everyone in the room. Turg's camouflage flickered, but such was the group's fascination that no one saw. "The captain saw its strength but in blind obedience to the Strictures wants destroyed. She would not consider using it and never held. Touch it now," Kirtar said and laid it on the center of the table.

Each bird warrior stroked it, and one and all were lost i
some interior vision. Turg tensed as Laquatus wondere
about attacking the gathering while they were stunned. Bu
they shook off their bemusement, all except the lieutenan
with reluctance. Kirtar looked dissatisfied.

"Once it filled the heart with peals of glory, but now i
is only a ghost of what it was." Disbelief showed on th
other faces. "I know what the problem is. I have let my ow
reluctance to use this power destroy the potential that orig
inally resided in this prize. I can afford to wait no longe.
The magic must be used, and we must take the Order in
new direction." The officer looked each warrior in the eye
in turn.

"Tomorrow I will take the captain's place, and you mus
all act to support me when I do."

Turg retreated as the members of the coup left.

"Treachery, always a popular choice with subordinates,
Laquatus mused as he directed his jack away from the plot
ters. This betrayal might be just what he needed.

* * * * *

"There is no reason for these attacks, your Excellency,
the captain said to Laquatus. The ambassador had begge
an audience with Pianna, hoping to find some other angl
to grasp advantage. Besides the excellent news of a powe
struggle within the Order, Laquatus had felt a whisper fror
the tresias stone during the night. An explorer had finall
proved a path to the Citadel through the undergroun
rivers. Further reinforcements followed to give Laquatu
enough power to take action against the Order.

The ambassador sent Turg below with the stone, tellin

Satas all that occurred and that he must bring soldiers as quickly as possible. It might be possible to pluck the prize right from the Order's fingers without any of the knights being the wiser. While he waited for the frog's return, he sat in the captain's office offering his services to the Order.

"The lieutenant's incursion into the forest seemed to provoke even more of a response," she said as she showed the merman her intelligence maps.

"I always believed that he might be exceeding his authority," Laquatus said in a sweet tone. He waited for a response to his overtures, but Pianna was looking at the map. Then she grabbed a set of reports and began rifling through them, checking something.

"Yes, yes, yes," she cried out, relief plain on her face. "I couldn't see it before because we never put down the dates of the attacks." She grabbed up a pen and put a series of broad arrows on the map. She ignored the rattle of pins falling to the floor. "We never saw a focus to the attacks because the center pulling the attacks shifted over time. Kirtar was what the forest reacted to."

"The lieutenant?" Laquatus said nonplussed. "He can be irritating but surely not to an entire forest. Do not give him credit for being more than he is."

"Not the lieutenant," Pianna said. "It's that damn prize of his. He was awarded it where we saw the strongest attack, and the rest of them seem to be moving in his direction when he rode to the southern plains. We need to destroy that orb immediately."

"I knew that would be your thinking," Kirtar said as he moved into the room. Laquatus could see the bird warriors lining up in the room beyond. "Anything that violates the Strictures must be destroyed."

"It has nothing to do with the Strictures, Lieutenant," Pianna replied, drawing herself upright as she heard his insolent tone. "I believe your prize is what provokes the forest. There will be additional attacks in this direction even as we speak. We must destroy it or dispose of it immediately."

"Get rid of it?" laughed Kirtar. "Even if I believed you, why would I want to throw it away?" He put his hand in his pouch and drew the orb forth. Its power once more struck the ambassador.

"Anything that can rouse the entire forest can be used to tame it," Kirtar stated. "That is what the Order is dedicated to, is it not? Curing the world of its wildness and chaos?"

The captain moved around the table, her face calm. "But what about the villages destroyed and the refugees made homeless as you search for a way to use the orb?" Pianna walked slowly toward the door and Kirtar. "As a knight, you took an oath to protect them." She raised her hand as if to pluck the orb from his oversized fist. Energy flared and coated her, locking her in place. Laquatus could see her expression slowly starting to change from determination to astonishment only to stop halfway through the shift.

"Unlike you, I know it is sometimes necessary to make a sacrifice," Kirtar said as he retrieved Pianna's sword, her symbol of Order authority.

Power poured from the orb. A growing mass of purest crystal shimmered into being as Laquatus stood, feeling for his soldiers below. The throb of ocean magic reassured him as the lieutenant turned his attention toward him. The orb's magic seemed to light up the bird warrior's features, and the ambassador bowed slightly as if to acknowledge the aven's superiority.

"I trust there will be no problems, Laquatus."

The merman nodded, thinking how he could take advantage. The power continued to grow, and the ambassador wondered if the lieutenant was preparing to destroy him. But Kirtar's look of victory changed to one of confusion and then fear. The crystal around the captain pulsed and began to grow, inching across the floor as the bird warrior gripped the orb tightly, concentration freezing his face.

He seemed to collapse inward, panting. Cries sounded beyond the room. "Mutiny" and "Save the captain" could be heard as the lieutenant once more tried to force his spell to stop. He fell, and his supporters rushed into the room.

"I can't control it!" he gushed, stricken with fear. The bird warriors looked at Laquatus, threats in their eyes, and one started toward him, murder plain in his face.

"There is no time," another soldier exclaimed. The crystal grew faster, and the ambassador unconsciously retreated.

"Let the spell take him!" With that they plucked the lieutenant up and retreated through the door.

Laquatus tried to follow, but the crystal was already too close to the wall. The stone began to sparkle, and then it too was engulfed in crystal. The merman was trapped with no way out, the spell expanding in irregular spurts. He tripped over a chair, holding the seat out as if to halt the effect. The wooden legs froze in place well above the floor.

"Turg," he called to below, "Captain Satas! Open a portal! Immediately!" He backed up against the wall. Could he cut his way through the stone? He was trying to raise power when he felt the tickle of the portal forming at his back. He fell through the wall screaming, "Close it! Close it now!"

CHAPTER 16

Once more Kamahl ran to a city, his leg
pumping. But unlike the roads to city, Caba
people were everywhere, packing the trai
to capacity. He threaded the crowds as h
once threaded razor shards in the moun
tains during his training. The traveler
were refugees from the western border'
violence. Ever since he left the gian
gecko, Emerald, he had run throug
despairing crowds. As he approached th
Citadel, there were expressions of hop
in the faces about him. However, th
crush in front of the gates seemed t
press out the travelers' optimism.

The low wall surrounding the tow
was unguarded except for a frustrated soldier trying to direc
the incoming traffic. He never saw the metal-hued barbar
ian with the great sword, his eyes nearly blind from starin
at the constant flow of refugees.

Running was impossible now, but Kamahl persevered
He shoved his way through the masses, aiming for th

reat castle on the hill. If there were guards in the city,
hey were lost in the crying crowds. It seemed the entire
world tried to reach a place to eat or sleep. Large men with
clubs stood before every inn.

"There is no room, move on. Move on," they called to
those trying to enter. The staves were not used except to
prod the persistent away. Kamahl wondered how much
onger that would be true.

The road up the side of the hill was thick with people. A
teady stream of Order uniforms came down to the town to
help with the crowds. A few refugees struggled up the path,
pressing on to the greater safety of the castle walls. Despite
all their martial posturing, the Order compromised their
defenses, so those on the road would not fail to find shelter.

Kamahl continued through the multitudes, confident
that he finally had his bearings in the narrow streets. He
arrived at the bottom of the road and there tasted the
ambassador's duplicity.

"Hold!" a sentry cried. More guards converged on the
mountain mage.

"It is the barbarian!" yelled the corporal commanding
he lower detachment. "Take no chances with him!"

The people around Kamahl tried to retreat as the soldiers
ormed up, their spears still in the air as they jockeyed for
oom to maneuver. On the walls of the fortress above, the
barbarian could see other soldiers drawing weapons. Should
he try to lose himself in the crowd?

He was sick of retreat, and if the prize were truly his,
hen he would fight for it. He threw his cloak back and
revealed the armor and bracers on his wrists. Before he
ould give formal challenge, a guard raised a crossbow from
behind the spear wall and discharged it.

His hand threw out a line of fire, and he turned durin
the split second of the missile's flight. The flame at
through the bolt, withering the shaft and melting away th
head. What was left of the cowardly attack shattered on hi
armored side. He looked at the detachment, his rage radi
ating in all directions. The refugees continued to retreat a
far as they were able, the Order tensing for his response. H
took gobs of wax from a pouch at his side and stuffed ther
in his ears. The cries of the crowd and whatever command
issued from the corporal were cut off.

Knowing that false accusations might be made agains
him, Kamahl was prepared to batter his opponents into sub
mission. Tiny black globes flew from his hands and began t
detonate. The explosions occurred well in front of th
spearmen, but the concussions spilled them back with eacl
throw. The barbarian quickly glanced up the road. No rein
forcements coming yet.

Another bolt came at him, but his magic was fully ener
gized, and it seemed to dissipate in midair. Kamahl threv
more globes, and these exploded inside the enemy ranks
Soldiers tumbled to the sides, deafened by the noise. Th
crossbowman lay on the ground, his entire body bruise
from the close detonation.

Kamahl watched his back, but the tight press of refugee
prevented guards from getting through. Signs of pani
were everywhere as civilians tried to flee, and the mass c
onlookers crippled the Order's response as surely as i
manacled Kamahl's own actions. The barbarian started u
the road.

He jogged, his footfalls thudding in his ears as he passe
people cowering on the road's surface. A man bellowed, an
Kamahl thought he heard, "The forest, the forest," but h

swept by before he could be sure. If the town believed there was an attack from the west, the mountain mage was in no hurry to correct them.

Even through the wax he could hear cries, but none seemed to mention him. He slowed and twitched his trailing cloak back over his gear. The hilt of his sword peeking over his shoulder proclaimed to all that he was no helpless refugee, but perhaps the guards at the gate were as confused as those in the town. He spared a look behind him. A wave of people was coming up from the city. The jostling masses had no idea what was going on, and he realized they sought the safety of the castle.

Even at his reduced pace he reached the gates well before the refugees from below. The passageway through the defenses was unbarred, and he carefully walked through. He dug the wax from one ear, the cries of the crowd behind him echoing off the stone walls. He moved farther into the Citadel, ready to wrap himself in flame, but there was no one. He turned a blind corner into the courtyard.

There he found the Order. They fought among themselves. Bands of knights and men-at-arms squared off. A few bird warriors stood before the combatants, wrapped in magical armor. Glowing like the sun, they called for peace, but appeals for discipline were useless. The bands of soldiers met in hand-to-hand combat. Flesh and fists reinforced by mystic will assailed foes wearing a shared livery. Bones shattered, and the fallen were dragged free without regard for allegiance by the Order's healers.

The combatants bludgeoned each other but abstained from plying their blades. Only their open hands were enhanced. The Citadel made war upon itself, but a brotherhood of centuries could not be overturned in a single day.

Individual soldiers began to come at Kamahl. He drew his sword and slapped the fighters away. He advanced along the courtyard's edge, careful to use the flat of his blade. The roar of explosives would unite the fighters and would surely bring them against him. He circled, aiming for the central keep. He knew in his bones that Kirtar would be at the center of this struggle.

Magic assaulted his senses. The spell should have been lost among the contesting mages, but Kamahl felt it, like cold stone lodged in his gut. The power was muted, but it grew. What he felt was surely only the first stirrings. He knew not what magic pealed forth, but he knew that the orb must be involved. The purity and purpose of the spell lifted it far above the crude castings in the yard. He needed to reach Kirtar and the prize.

Disdaining the low profile he had kept so far, he ran for the keep door, black pellets flying before him. The explosions wiped the guards away, leaving only the gate to oppose him. The great door had a smaller entry in one panel.

His sword arced high and then cleaved its way into the iron-reinforced wood, cutting through latches. Through his one clear ear he heard the cries of the crowds coming through the gates only to be confronted by a civil war within the walls. Another blow sliced the final latch, and he jumped through.

The orb's spell grew louder and more strident in his mind. He looked for Kirtar, but the main hall was empty. His peripheral vision caught a shadow of movement, and he raised his arm. Claws shrieked on the iron bracer, and he half-spun at the impact. Another strike fell on his back, ripping through his cloak and scoring the studded leather over his shoulder. He swept his sword in a circle, slicing through the air. The scrabble of feet led his eyes to his foe.

Turg crouched just out of reach. Kamahl lunged forward, his sword a ribbon of flame, but the frog jumped to the side, seeming to vanish as the blade curved to skewer him. The amphibian was gone, hidden, and Kamahl dug the other gob of wax from his ear. He listened but could hear nothing besides the noise of the crowd outside.

A movement close by registered on his senses, and he darted toward the foe. But the signs faded away, and his boots suddenly lost traction. Feet flying from under him, he fetched up against a wall. Turg flickered into view right over him, the amphibian's hands reaching for his calf. Kamahl's dagger punched into the frog's thigh even as the claws started to shred his muscles. He tried to extend the thrust, aiming for arteries, but the amphibian vanished, a trail of blood leading to tables of food. A loaf vanished from sight, and the spatters stopped. The barbarian's own leg bled freely. He sent fingers of flame crawling over the gashes, sealing the injury as he screamed in pain.

The hall was huge, and the frog might be anywhere inside it. Kamahl threw showers of flame into the upper reaches, burning brighter until the barbarian's eyes stung.

A cluster of odd shadows appeared, and Kamahl knew where Turg was. The barbarian charged an axe and let it fly, trailing magic as it sank into the stone floor. It vanished in a globe of destruction. Turg leaped, an arc of lightning streaming toward the barbarian. The power grounded against the wall and charred an arc to the floor as Kamahl threw himself away. He rolled several times and came up with his sword ready. A crater showed where his axe had detonated. There was no sign of the frog.

The mountain warrior looked for shadows, but the flares

above the floor were dying out, his magic leaking power. A bank of clouds seemed to extinguish them, and Kamahl saw the illusion of rain sweeping across the hall. He tried to detect the frog's energy but the orb's spell still shrilled behind him. Fighting the mer champion was not his goal and he moved into a corridor toward the source of the magic and Kirtar.

A barrage of metal plates rang against the sides of the corridor. They skipped off the floor and glanced off his wounded leg. He sent fireballs arcing up the corridor in response.

"Dinnerware," he snorted, the amusement breaking his concentration, as pain had not. More projectiles flew, and he knelt, holding his sword before him. Kamahl created an intense shield of flame to devour the iron plates that might be launched against him. Instead he smelled charred fish, and a stream of bodies vaporized in his protection. He looked to the side. A sea creature with long limbs flopped on the floor. The flying fish expired as the shield's heat dried it out.

"Find Kirtar," Kamahl growled to himself. The shield broke into shards, and he sent them flowing up the corridor slowly, blocking the amphibian's advance. The barbarian hurried, remembering the orb and listening to the spell's strength. He reached a cross-corridor and at last spotted the lieutenant.

Kirtar looked nearly dead, his pale skin somehow appearing transparent. The bird warrior was being carried by other aven, and his eyes swept over the barbarian without recognition. His hands cupped the prize. Kirtar, once so arrogant and proud, was dying before the barbarian's eyes.

"It's still spreading!" called a soldier looking back the

way they had come. "We need to get out the postern gate before it cuts us off!"

The soldiers started forward again, carrying the warrior's destiny away.

"Kirtar!" Kamahl bellowed. A door opened onto a stairway, and a gaggle of servants surged into the corridor. The leaders screamed as the barbarian thundered forward, forcing him to slow lest he crush the innocents in his rage. A circle of lightning flared, stopping him in his tracks.

The servants stood frozen. In the corridor beyond, Turg flickered back into sight, the frog laughing at Kamahl through the screen of dead civilians. He vanished from sight as illusion surged over him, and the servants collapsed to the floor.

"The frog must have raced past under the cover of the fish," Kamahl swore. He drew power, grounding it to his sword. The steel danced with flame, and he prepared to send it streaking up the corridor to flush the amphibian out.

"Murderer!" came the cry from behind him. Members of the Order stood, fury evident as they looked at the barbarian and the circle of dead innocents. All were armored, and Kamahl could hear more soldiers crowding behind them. The front rank raised maces, their heads wrapped in deadly golden light.

The barbarian threw an exploding pellet of flame, the concussion echoing off the walls and sending him tumbling back. The narrow corridor acted to concentrate the blast toward him. His ears ringing, he got to his feet. The explosion had spun him around, and he could see Turg bent over in amusement, his wide mouth a gigantic smile. A shaft of flame sped toward the amphibian only to shatter in mid-air. A wave of magic seeping through the wall had already cut off the corridor. It resonated with the orb's magical signature, and Kamahl knew he had found the source of the magical call swamping his senses.

The frog blew him a kiss and vanished from sight. Shards of fire impacted uselessly against the magic as the mountain mage realized himself cut off from the amphibian and Lieutenant Kirtar. Trapped, he turned to the coming soldiers. They were not dazed by his concussions. Completely armored in light, they only shouted with derision at his explosions. He could not hear them, but he could see their faces and knew they were beyond reason.

Pillars of fire rose up to char the plaster, cutting off his sight of the Order knights. He turned to the crystal wall, wondering if he might somehow tunnel through. A shoe had come off one of the dead servants, and he kicked it toward the barrier. It struck the border and stuck there, becoming frozen even as he watched.

He could feel his spells dying, and he saw the enhanced swords and maces smashing through the curtain of fire. Contempt was in every figure stepping into the hall, and he acknowledged his defeat. He must kill and escape the Citadel before being slain by the massed opposition of the Order.

Kamahl lifted his sword and once again the brilliant fire that could devour iron shimmered off the blade. But instead of attacking the knights, he sent the pulse of flame into the walls. Rock ran like water, and wood vanished in explosions of gas as fire gutted the Citadel's structure. Supporting walls were cut, and timbers burnt away leaving nothing to support the walls and ceiling over the men coming to kill Kamahl.

Rubble cascaded over the soldiers, burying them in a sea of dust and stone. The barbarian held his cloak over his face, unable to retreat because of the crystal wall at his back. The dust started to clear, and Kamahl could see a sloping ramp of rock leading to the upper floors. He started forward only to be caught short as his cloak held him in place. The tattered train of his garment was already frozen in the crystal wall. He cut himself free with a knife, leaving the cloak to be preserved in the crystal. He scrambled up the ramp, the stones settling as he neared the upper floors.

Suddenly reality quivered, and Kamahl froze. The orb, its echo familiar to the barbarian, was active, but its ambiance had changed. The new tone set his teeth on edge. The orb was different, and Kamahl started up the ramp again, determined to find out what had happened.

CHAPTER 17

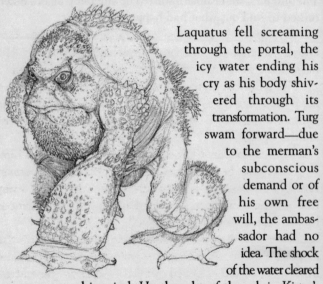

Laquatus fell screaming through the portal, the icy water ending his cry as his body shivered through its transformation. Turg swam forward—due to the merman's subconscious demand or of his own free will, the ambassador had no idea. The shock of the water cleared his mind. He thought of the orb in Kirtar's hands. The lieutenant had been weak, barely able to stand. The Order fought among themselves, and the town was bursting with refugees. This was the moment of maximum chaos. Should he attack in force?

A look at his soldiers revealed this to be an impossibility.

The transport mage was present and a few tresias, but Captain Satas and his squads of fighters were nowhere. They must still be travelling the last few miles. There was no time! He must act before the prize was destroyed or transferred to a more powerful person.

"Open the way to the surface," Laquatus ordered the transport mage. "Just inside the castle walls would be best." He began to concentrate, building on his link with Turg.

"I cannot, your Excellency," came the reply behind him. The merman spun, his composure broken as he bore down on the mage.

"Why not!" Laquatus grabbed the amphibian's whiskers, knowing them to transmit pain, and pulled them viciously. The mage hissed in agony until the ambassador loosened his grip.

"The spell that you fled touched the portal and drained my power," the mage said, pulling its whiskers through the merman's fingers. "It will be some time before I may cast another spell."

Laquatus wondered if the universe itself was against him.

"There must be another way to the surface," the merman raged, twisting in the water wildly, trying to think of a way through the rock above him. He felt trapped, dependent as he was on another to cast the spell.

"We created a permanent opening outside of the city," the mage said as its shivers of pain stopped. The blind cave dweller backed away as if to deny the ambassador further opportunity for violence. "Captain Satas ordered a permanent pool to be opened in the rough country to ease the placement of spies and travel of messengers."

"Why didn't you say so earlier?" the merman said. He gathered his champion and what guards were available and left for the permanent pool. Perhaps there was still time. In short order they exited to the upper world, the ambassador racked with momentary disorientation as he transformed into a walker once more.

Laquatus appeared at the foot of the citadel near the lower wall. Gullies and heavy brush backed the hill on which the castle sat. The thick growth made movement difficult but infiltration fairly easy. The ambassador was surprised that the Order had not placed traps or at least planted poisonous shrubs. However, he was willing to take advantage of the situation.

There were no roads or paths around the hill to the castle gates. Knowing that time was of the essence, he sank into a trance, preparing to act once more through the jack. The camouflaged amphibian worked his way to the winding road, careful to be unobserved as he dropped from above. A surge of people ascended the path below him, and soldiers came down from above. The ambassador sent pulses of illusion and misdirection, reinforcing the jack's camouflage as he climbed to the main part of the Citadel.

Explosions shook the air, and Laquatus sent the frog up at a run, tearing through the gates. He saw Kamahl force his way past the guard. Covering the intervening courtyard without becoming involved with the fighting was nearly impossible, but he did it. The jack threw himself rolling past the barbarian as the metal-hued warrior turned back to look outside. The frog made quite a bit of noise, and he ran ahead lest he be caught in close quarters. But the barbarian gave no sign that he noticed the sea warrior through the web of deceit, and Laquatus resolved to attack.

His attempt to ambush the mountain mage failed, and Kamahl forged ahead of the mer champion, blocking Turg's path to the lieutenant and the prize. Petulance at his opponent's poor timing sent the ambassador and his frog into a rage. He grabbed every thing he could from the tables to throw down the hall. Goblets, platters, and bones whistled through the air, only to be rendered harmless by the barbarian's defenses.

Laquatus reigned his temper in. Kirtar had the real prize, and time wasted on Kamahl took true power farther away every minute. Besides, who knew how far the crystal wave might travel? The castle might be uninhabitable at any moment, and he was having a food fight.

Realizing how trivial the barbarian really was, he unleashed a school of flying fish as a distraction, passing the barbarian in a cloud of deceit. The frog shied away from the white flame surrounding Kamahl, the heat drying his skin, making him dangerously lethargic.

Once past, Turg wondered which way to go, confused for a moment as to where Kirtar might be. Seeing a stairway he moved into it. A barrel of water for washing the floor delayed Turg as he drank the filthy water down, his primitive instincts overriding Laquatus's sophistication.

The ambassador reestablished control with a burst of will. He must find the prize. While he wondered where to go, clattering footsteps descended the stairs. He faded into the shadows. He glimpsed Kirtar, the object of his quest, carried past by three guards. He moved to follow, only to be blocked by a group of servants retreating from upstairs.

"I will not be denied," thundered Laquatus in Turg's skull, and lighting arced from his fingers, slaying those in his way. He ran after the lieutenant, seeing the wave of crystal already coming through the wall.

The jack moved silently, running after the warriors retreating from their master's disastrous spell. The aven stopped as the lieutenant called out.

"I must try again," he insisted in a hollow voice, the words barely audible even to Turg's excellent ears. The bird warriors kept moving until he weakly swatted at their hands, the palest glow surrounding his fists. "I command the Order, now stop!" The three did so reluctantly.

"Sir, you have tried so many times to turn the spell," one said, his eyes signaling that he wanted to run. "Why should you succeed this time."

Kirtar folded himself around the orb.

"Because I must," he said. The lieutenant's frame shivered violently, but he regained control. "The crystal devours me. Find out what is happening." The mage lost himself in a trance.

The retainers separated, one going to check on the advancing spell, the other going ahead. Laquatus watched through the amphibian's eyes as the bird warrior looked back, hesitation plain in his face. Then he turned abruptly and walked away.

Once the lieutenant has a single retainer, Turg ran down the corridor, a lance of lightning surging from his hands. The ambassador put everything into the link, the electrical arc growing until it was arm-thick. The stroke continued through the soldier's body, burning away the plaster on a wall ten feet away. The frog collapsed, his spells exhausted as the last barrier to the orb fell.

Kirtar's eyes were clear, jolted out of his trance as the amphibian crawled closer. The leader of the Order lay slack, shock visible on his face. He began to tremble once more and pushed out his palm as if to command the world to halt. Turg glanced behind him. The wall of crystal was advancing faster. Laquatus knew it was time to claim the prize.

The lieutenant cried out as Turg plucked the sphere from the aven's hand. The bird warrior faded even further as he lost touch with the sphere. The ambassador ignored everything as his champion gripped the prize. The bright mirror finish of the orb darkened, the reflected light from the spreading crystal lost as the prize changed. The ambassador forced the pit frog to retreat, lest it be entombed with the others. Rousing the will to move was as difficult a battle as any Laquatus had ever fought.

Turg blindly stumbled away, still looking at the wonder cupped in his hands. The sphere was the color of the seas, constantly shifting and changing. The blue of the tropics gave way to the gray of the northern reaches. The ambassador looked through the frog's eyes as the prize continued to change. The sphere became a globe of water—endless tides sweeping across it unhindered by the land. A world that hinted at wonders hidden under its surface.

Turg tripped and tumbled with none of his deadly grace. Only the terrified shout of Laquatus's spirit prevented the prize from spinning out of the pit frog's grasp. The globe still called to the ambassador's mind, but he resisted the urge. There would be plenty of time to plumb its depths after the amphibian was safely back in camp.

A call came from below, the calm voice of Captain Satas speaking through the ether. "I have arrived with new mages. Do you wish to return to the underworld?"

"Yes!" shouted the ambassador's spirit. Turg fell into a pool of swirling energy as the tresias, and his mages reacted to the apparent source of the call. The shock of passage pulled the ambassador's spirit back to his rightful body. He shook himself awake and looked around. He was out of the gully, his clothes torn and bleeding from abrasions. The travel mage held onto his arms and bruising covered the minion's face.

"Why am I out here?" Laquatus demanded, slapping away the blind hands as he felt his minor pains.

"You left the entrance at a run, lost in your trance. You would not stop or respond," the mage said wretchedly. "The others were afraid to restrain you physically, and my weight was too slight to stop you. I tried to ensnare you in an illusion, but you went right through them. You moved without direction, dragging me through brush and bouncing off trees. I don't know where we are." The amphibian wailed, lost in the world beyond his caves.

Laquatus had driven Turg often enough to realize that his link with the jack was bleeding back to him. As the aristocrat's spirit concerned itself solely with directing the frog, his own body responded to echoes of those commands. He would have to exercise more care in the future. But even with blood dripping from his face, the ambassador was in a good mood. Who cared where he was. He had captured the prize.

"Do not worry," the merman said. "I have succeeded in everything."

The ambassador must have come hundreds of yards in his blind rush. Now a squad of griffins fell from the sky, their shrieks of anger reminding Laqautus that the Order considered itself attacked from without and within.

"Satas," he called through his stone, "hide all signs of the portal and prepare to take me away." He waited precious seconds as the Order landed in a clearing only yards away.

"I cannot," the tresias said sorrowfully. "Like his companion before, my transport mage is spent in pulling your champion away. We cannot rescue you at this time."

The merman thought quickly, trapped with only his own resources.

"Send Turg to me through the permanent portal now," he cried through the mental plane. "Keep the orb safe until I return."

He commanded his champion to come. The frog resisted, still entranced by the sphere, but the ambassador owned his soul. With a despairing cry, the jack came through the portal, running toward the ambassador.

"What incredible luck," Laqautus cried, stepping rapidly to greet the griffin riders as they came through the brush. "Now the traitors are doomed," he said confidently. Confusion replaced the hostility on the riders' faces.

"What are you talking about?" a soldier snarled, rage burning through his bemusement. "The traitors are trapped in the Citadel. We came to question you," he added, driving his steed closer.

"Monstrous!" the ambassador howled, as the sound of Turg breaking through the brush made the riders turn. "My champion has been chasing the brigands, trying to cut off the barbarian's allies." Turg was torn and bloody, his wounded thigh once again seeping.

"We saw Kamahl meet with warriors dressed in hooded robes less than an hour ago. We then informed Lieutenant Kirtar of the notorious murderer and his confederates. He assured me that he would act to protect the Order," said the ambassador. At the news, a few soldiers sympathetic to Kirtar took it upon themselves to heal Turg.

The detachment head appeared lost, uncertain of everything.

The news of the mutiny must have been unbearable to most of the Order, the ambassador knew. The captain was very popular, and Kirtar was a fool not to kill her secretly. However, he knew any organization would accept outright lies to preserve the respect for its leaders.

"Take me to Kirtar this instant," Laquatus demanded, betting on the bird warrior's death.

He and his champion were mounted once more on griffins, and they flew toward the Citadel. The ambassador fought his fear of flying by dreaming up contingency lies. People streamed down the road from the castle, a few soldiers rushing from entrances. A hole was blown out the upper stories.

"Damned barbarian," the sea mage heard his rider mutter.

They landed, and Laquatus and Turg were rushed to the current leader of the Order, Pianna's sword in his hand.

Laquatus stepped forward to spin his tale, confident his story would be confirmed.

* * * * *

Laquatus rode through the city gates, accepting the accolades with a dignified nod. The knights and soldiers of the Order were drawn up and saluted him and his champion as they started their brave ride for the sea.

The new captain was very understanding of the ambassador's need to leave, not trusting anyone as he struggled for unity with soldiers still reeling from rumors of murder and mutiny.

Officially, the barbarian Kamahl and unnamed conspirators infiltrated the fortress, and Kirtar had discovered it too late. The lieutenant took control, rushing to protect Captain Pianna who had already fallen to internal betrayers. Kamahl fought his way through the protective guards to join the murderers. Kirtar fell in personal battle with the barbarian. The mountain warrior cut his way out of the castle to the plains. There was no sign of Kamahl, and Laquatus doubted the new captain would waste time looking for the barbarian when he had traitors to root out. The ambassador wondered if the lie would hold. But what matter the fables of the plains? He had captured the orb, and the Order could believe what it wanted.

After an hour they stopped, the merman anxious to leave his new retinue behind. Laquatus conducted a series of personal interviews, and the convoy continued on without him and his champion. The ride back to the portal was tortuous, the road seeming far longer. Turg moved in camouflage, while the merman rode in a borrowed cloak. Selective illusions took them past soldiers and regular travelers.

At last they left the path and headed for the portal open outside the city. It was dark as they made their way through the brush and into the gully. The pool gave off a feeble glow, the light caught by the overhang above. He reentered the underground, sliding through the transformation with ease. Only a small squad awaited him, and he wondered where Captain Satas might be.

"Where is the rest of my escort?" Laquatus called as Turg swam for a cache of supplies and fell to eating. A tresias approached and the ambassador noticed the heavy bruising that he himself had inflicted hours before.

"Captain Satas has gone ahead to the emperor, carrying your captured prize," the blind amphibian said, keeping away from the merman. "He decided such an important artifact must be conducted to his Imperial Highness as rapidly as possible." The small creature swam backward and crowded against the wall, fearing an angry explosion.

Laquatus did nothing. The captain led him by hours and with his smaller stature and better routes could not be intercepted before he reached the sea. The tresias formed the backbone of the officer core and messenger system that he used to communicate with his forces. There was no way to reach his personal retainers. Perhaps he could fly overland and beat Satas to the sea? But he did not know the Captain's route and access to the underground was under the bastard's control. He might be unable to even reenter the subterranean rivers.

The prize had slipped beyond his fingers once more, and worst of all, it had fallen into the hands of the emperor, his master.

CHAPTER 18

Aboshan, Emperor of the Seas, reclined in his palace listening to a courtier. The cephalid shifted his tentacles, sliding back into the throne. No mere chair, the pile of coral was covered with short growths endlessly moving over his skin. The organisms cleaned and feed small amounts of power to him drawn from the building's essence. He turned and let the multicolored polyps move over another area of his body. The brilliant azure of his skin competed against the array of color on the throne and walls. His eyes idly moved as he luxuriated in the comfortable embrace. Tentacles left vortices through the water as he turned and sent a magic call to the fish colonizing the palace walls. An animal darted around, and he caught it, appreciating its jewel-like colors before devouring it.

The huge room was formed out of coral. The unique species excreted a dense mesh, becoming as tough and resilient as anything in the sea. Two large doors opened out to the ocean, and several gaps in the dome's roof allowed fresh currents of water to flow. The ceiling and walls glowed as tiny plants funneled light through the structure and spilled it out. When the sun disappeared from the upper air, other organisms would feed light through the palace. Aboshan wondered how those on dry land could bear to live in dead structures.

The emperor dragged his attention back to the speaker. The brown fur of the courtier rippled as his body slowly rotated, the selkie using unusual restraint as he reported about the land. The seal could take on a human's appearance much as Aboshan could form legs. The emperor, of course, avoided such transformations as much as possible. He considered the land contemptible. The fact that the courtier by nature could move among the land bound with ease made him suspect in the cephalid's eyes. He breathed water down, reveling in another advantage. The selkie needed air, and only a special spell allowed the creature to remain at court without withdrawing every few minutes.

"The Order is in disarray," the selkie continued, darting his head briefly toward a fish swimming close by. "The new leader is a warrior named Bretath. He conveys his respects and his gratitude for Ambassador Laquatus's aid in the recent troubles."

"As if we took any notice of land-bound troubles," the

emperor drawled, his boredom plain to all. "Surely you have some news of interest beside the business of savages and their meaningless tribes."

The selkie somersaulted with agitation before settling down. The emperor yawned, used to the courtier's flighty nature. He firmly believed that air breathers should deal with air breathers, being already contaminated. Some sages believed seals, whales, and others needing air to be refugees from the land. Their ancestors were right to flee back to the sea, but Aboshan shuddered at the thought of such a lineage.

"Of course, your Imperial Highness," the seal answered, his tone hesitant as he searched for a new topic, one likely to interest the monarch. "There are problems regarding the treasures gathered inside the continent."

The emperor's attention focused on the selkie. The land might be filled with contemptible peoples, but it held the lion's share of past wars' spoils. The battlefields had only occasionally moved over the sea. Many of the prizes were lost in the ocean's abysmal depths where even the emperor's warrant had little weight. His beak snapped as he considered the dry kingdoms' salvage activities in retrieving ships lost at sea. It was only proper that his nation empty the land's treasure troves.

"Our explorers and diggers locate and transport the reclaimed prizes easily enough," the selkie said. "Bringing them to the coast is not the problem. But now that we move more of the discoveries to the court, we are having difficulties."

The seal spoke slower, for a thunderous expression grew on Aboshan's face. The emperor had instituted the policy of relocating the machines and objects of power from above the waves to below them. For decades, isolated stretches of coastline and caves on rocky islands had held the empire's loot recovered from ancient battlefields. The monarch had decided that such potential power must be brought under his direct physical control.

"Many of the mechanisms are delicate, and we find them difficult to repair," the selkie continued. "Fetishes are composed of materials that break down in the water. Worst of all, we have few trained to repair them. Perhaps it would be simpler to trade with the Cabal who is positioned to use them."

Aboshan swam free of the throne, his trident held in two tentacles as if to attack. The selkie froze as the guards became more alert. The trident was the symbol of the emperor's might, but now he used it as a simple weapon, laying the tines against the seal's neck.

"We find your suggestion unacceptable," the cephalid said, his voice freezing the courtier, as previous signs of displeasure had not. "What we have recovered is for our use," he said, the trident's barbed points puncturing the courtier's fur. Blood clouded the water, and small cleaning fish from the walls swam to dispose of the perceived garbage. Aboshan's weapon pulled free of the seal's neck muscles. An electric shock surged into the school, sending the selkie into a series of convulsions as the fish died and floated toward the dome's roof. Hidden guardians appeared momentarily as they struck at the ascending food. The cephalid gripped the seal and pulled him closer, his suckers marking the hide as the frozen selkie quivered in fear.

"The land dwellers have held the keys to the past for long enough. We shall gather hold of power and harness it to our own purposes." He moved his tentacles, and the fur began to tear free of the muscle beneath. "If you are unable to oversee

he care of our treasure, then arrange with the Cabal Patriarch for workers to come here. Now go, and let it be done."

The emperor swam back to his throne as the selkie
floated, then talked excitedly to an aide, which left.

"Even air breathing swimmers are incompetent,"
Aboshan said to himself.

He regretted asking for workers from the Cabal. However, the preservation of fetishes and totems were unknown
in the undersea kingdom. Most objects of power were living
organisms. The care of dead magic was a rare art.

The doors against the wall opened suddenly, a wave of
ink surging into the room. The current began to flow faster,
pumping more of the darkness among the courtiers.

"Guards, defend your emperor!" Aboshan ordered as he
called up power. Huge cuttlefish moved through the doorway, their sides flashed colors so quickly that the eye was
uncertain of their shade from one moment to the next.
More ink gushed from them, moving into the crowd.

The darkness coiled evilly through the water, its touch
paralyzing those who could not evade it. The selkie swam
for the upper openings only to contact a trailing cloud. It
went into convulsions. Bubbles rose from its frame as it
lost control of its body and the spell allowing it to breathe.
The seal drowned in seconds, its lungs full of water and
then poison.

Sea warriors swarmed through the doors, their skin covered in a translucent gel protecting them from the ink.
Their spears and tridents started to work at the crowd as the
emperor readied himself for battle.

The throne room's hidden guards responded, surging
from the crevices and crannies that lined the walls. Octopi
weighing hundreds of pounds jetted toward the cuttlefish.

Their long arms wrapped over the animals' heads as the attackers tried to escape, their hides flaring with panic. Huge moray eels swam out, their jaws closing over the waists and limbs of the attacking mer. However, illusions swam into being, misleading the beasts' strikes as the invaders continued toward the emperor.

A school of barracuda swept through the upper exits to the open ocean. Directed by exterior guards, they flew into the invaders before the cephalids could react. Limbs separated as the living knives carved apart the attackers and a few of the paralyzed victims. The fish flexed wildly, smashing into the walls in explosions of gore as the diluted ink destroyed their ability to control their direction.

Aboshan gestured with his trident, and the current reversed. The water's speed intensified, and the ink flowed to the outside. The paralyzed courtiers and the bodies of the slain swirled out through the gates. The emperor stopped as he realized his spell prevented reinforcements from reaching the throne room. Two attackers had survived every counterattack and closed on the throne, their weapons raised for regicide.

Aboshan swam toward one, his trident focusing his will. Water surged again but in a much narrower area. A thin liquid thread cut through the rebel's upraised weapon and the merman's torso. The jet dispersed blood and flesh in a huge cloud rolling toward the walls. The ruler turned, his weapon meeting his last attacker. They locked tines, the tridents contesting for supremacy.

Aboshan forced the rebel down, rolling the cephalid and disorienting him. He grabbed the helpless throat, his magic crowding through the enemy's body, rendering him helpless. Reinforcements came through the gates and the upper works, unable to find any living enemies. A few guards began gath-

ring up the paralyzed, hauling them away to the healers
or care and antidotes.

The emperor turned the rebel's head from side to side,
studying it in hope of recognition, but he could not remember him. He shook the slack body violently, the eyes suddenly opening in shock and surprise. Aboshan laughed as
the rush of surviving sent him into a manic mood.

"Who sent you?" he cried into the still face. "Who is
behind this treachery?"

The monarch eased his magical grip on the merman's
nerves, and his victim gasped and grimaced as he regained
some control.

"No one had to send us," he rasped, his voice husky from
the abuse Aboshan inflicted on his throat. "You are everyone's enemy under the sea."

The emperor dragged his trident down the rebel's flank,
letting blood into the water.

"You lie," said the monarch, sending the tines deeper
into the trailing tentacles. "You came at the instigation
of our wife, Llawan. Why did she send you to kill me?"

"The ocean is marred by your armies and forts," whispered
the rebel, lines of despair evident in his face. "None may
trust the other for fear of informers in your pay." He breathed
in polluted water and paused. "The denizens of the upper
ocean must bow to your will or flee. The cetaceans suffer
from your contempt and whale songs grow bitter. How can
any not rise up and strike you down?" The fighter began to
talk with more strength, the emperor's magical hold weakening as the offender further roused the imperial temper.

"We are only the first lapping of a wave sweeping you
aside," the captive said more boldly. "You dare not leave
your palace unless escorted by schools of guards. You

cannot hope to chain the seas with your decrees."

Aboshan was bright red with rage, the muscles holding the trident quivering with anticipation.

"You shall fall and Llawan, Empress of the Sea shall reign in—"

The monarch cut the speech short, plunging the bronze barbs deep into the cephalid only to withdraw and stab him again. The emperor's skin pulsed a howl of rage as he executed the prisoner.

"Bring me the captain of the guard," the monarch commanded, letting loose the rebel to drift with the current. The captain was a pale blue as he approached his sovereign.

"I am trying to find out how the attackers infiltrated the palace, sire," he said in a trembling voice. The emperor jetted back and forth, his skin still pulsating in rage.

"I know how the scum came into our presence," Aboshan said and came closer. "The question is merely one of your incompetence or active treachery."

"I assure you that I live to serve only you, Majesty," the captain said excitedly. The monarch regarded him narrowly, the pulses of color slowing.

"We think not. We think you serve the self-styled Queen of the Seas, Llawan." He swam closer to the officer. "We think you would see another on the throne, so take your seat!"

Aboshan forced the captain onto the organisms that groomed the ruler, the soldier jarring against the underlying rock. His taste was not the emperor's, and the polyps turned upon the perceived usurper. Venom seared into the officer's scales, killing him as broad swathes of flesh swelled and burst. A look of unspeakable agony showed and the face was washed away by the throne's caress.

"Let him be cast into the abyss," Aboshan proclaimed. There to be devoured by worms along with his brethren in treachery. Let others of the slain be displayed as proof of our justice and continued power."

The captain's former command gathered up the dead and retreated to do the monarch's will.

It was some time before the next guard commander dared report to the emperor. Finally, a sergeant stationed in the palace came to speak to the monarch in his private quarters. Aboshan had retired to regain his composure, though a clerk to conduct official business accompanied him. The imperial rooms were lit by light pumped from the upper world. Long kelp plants swayed in the currents, and small edible fish and crustaceans scurried over the floors. The emperor saw distrust in the sergeant's face as the soldier regarded the restful scene. Aboshan hoped fear of poisons and hidden guardians would give others pause when they plotted against him. The attendants who usually filled the rooms waited elsewhere until his temper subsided.

"The attackers appeared in the palace through use of a transport pool," the commander began without preamble, anxious to discharge his duty and leave. "The cuttlefish filled the outer rooms with poisonous ink, and the rebels prevented the flow of reinforcements from inside the defenses. Most of the troops were unaware of any problems until the attack was over. All the invaders perished resisting capture or during the assault on your person. At this time we have no leads as to who might be responsible." The soldier dipped his head, the emperor and his servant half-hidden from sight by the room's growth. He left at Aboshan's nod.

The monarch turned to his clerk. The privilege of serving as private secretary to the emperor rotated fairly often. The civil service assured him that it was awarded on the basis of performance. Aboshan wondered if the ministers overseeing the palace staff really thought him so dull witted. The secretary was a tall spindly crab holding a stylus and a sheet of wax, ready to take down his orders.

"We charge the army to investigate all signs relating to the recent conspiracy to unseat us," the monarch dictated, plucking a tiny urchin from the floor and splitting it open, the pain from the quills spicing the coming meal. "All communications with the southern court of Queen Llawan are to be closely scrutinized and correspondents questioned rigorously as to their connections with our estranged spouse."

The cephalid sucked the urchin's innards down and tore at the flesh with his beak as he considered further actions. His maleficent wife and her pawns had breached his palace. Yet to act against her would provoke a civil war that even in victory would leave the kingdom crippled. He needed uncontestable proof of her guilt. The emperor thought of her rumored alliances with the cetaceans and the monsters of the abyss. Perhaps he should increase efforts to infiltrate her court as she had so obviously violated his own.

Aboshan thought of Laquatus, banished to play ambassador to the land because of his unfortunate ties to the queen. Perhaps his close experience with the land might promote sympathy for imperial plans. He thought of the arrogant and cruel merman doomed to scrape before air breathers and land walkers.

"I recall our ambassador from the Cabal to serve our
leasure once more, his successor to be appointed after
lose consultation with our loyal friend, Laquatus," the
mperor said. He waved the crab away to convey his
rders to the palace ministers.

Undoubtedly, Laquatus would serve Aboshan to regain
avor. Most of the world waited for a ruler's firm hand. The
monarch would establish a new dominion over sea and
and. The emperor's mirth showed in a shower of colors
owing over his skin, and he rang for his maidens to
ttend him.

CHAPTER 19

Laquatus looked at the capital as he swam through the water, enjoying the comparative warmth of the ocean after days in the caverns under the continent. Turg swam alongside, his clumsy strokes amusing the merman as the ambassador continued down. The light grew dimmer as the bottom gained definition. From the surface, the city could not be seen, but it filled a huge stretch of the continental shelf.

The buildings below lived, straining nutrients from the water to repair themselves and repelling pests. Steady streams of mer people swam through and above the city. A pod of whales called to the ambassador as they herded a school of fish with sonic calls toward the capital. Once

sign of tribute to the emperor, the cries sounded of oner-
ous duty to the merman's ears. But what did he care for
the opinion of air breathers? He felt the flutter of his
gills to prove his superior nature.

The whales grew silent as mer warriors swam up to meet
them, their lack of song more telling than any call. The soldiers' magic now herded the fish, their command lulling the
school to an army encampment.

Laquatus noticed many soldiers and a distinct lack of
traffic other than warriors. Wondering if some great danger
threatened the kingdom, he headed for the palace. Perhaps
a great feeding spiral of sharks swept through the ocean.
Laquatus remembered that the seas could be suddenly violent as well as tranquil.

He neared the imperial residence and noticed a great
dome inscribed with glowing characters. The huge gazebo-
like structure was the exhibition site for traitors. The
merman wondered who suffered there now?

He swam below the roof, nodding to the guards who
observed him as he neared the dead. Several corpses floated
in anchored nets, their bodies in pieces as cleaner fish and
crabs slowly snipped off small bits of rotting meat. Uniden-
tifiable parts of several different species were in some nets.

"Imperial justice, as swift and careful as always," he muttered as he swam to the wax placard inscribed with symbols.
A guard, stationed to tell the illiterate what the sign said,
relaxed as the ambassador looked over the words.

"CONDEMNED BE ALL TRAITORS WHO WOULD
KILL THE EMPEROR ON HIS THRONE. THOSE WHO
WOULD SERVE OTHER MASTERS ARE ETERNALLY
DEVOURED HERE AND IN THE ABYSMAL DEPTHS."

"Guard," the aristocrat inquired in a bored tone. "What happened to bring these traitors here?"

Laquatus had left the seacoast having heard just that a message had arrived for him. Fearing that the coastal mission might have orders to arrest him, he continued to the capital, hoping he still might intercept Captain Satas.

He and his champion had swum through the caverns in pursuit, leaving all behind but a single guide for fear of the soldiers' loyalty to their captain. The ambassador wanted nothing to prevent the appropriate action, should they catch the tresias. They had swum without rest through the arteries of the continent. But Satas could travel the more direct paths, while Laquatus and especially the massive Turg made costly detours. They missed the good captain by days when they reached the coast.

The frog kidnapped a servant whom the merman interrogated before releasing with false memories of what occurred. The ambassador knew that he was recalled, not the reason for it. He and his jack left immediately for the capital. Only the knowledge that doom might await him tempered Laquatus's joy to be free of dry land. Now he hoped to hear what news might influence his return.

"These and other traitors appeared in the palace through a transport pool and reached the throne room," the guard related in a voice grown bored with repetition. "The emperor himself beat the attack off. The army still looks for traitors who may have escaped."

Laquatus nodded in thanks and continued on his way. An assault on the emperor might provide opportunities to explain his actions. He could explain fear of enemies intercepting his reports led to his silence regarding the orb. The palace grew closer, and he noted the observers peering from houses along the way.

The homes of nobles were closed up, few signs of the inhabitants visible. Years before the emperor and his wife had split, the cast-off empress had styled herself as queen in her own right. Many nobles, outraged by the emperor's arrogant and arbitrary manner, retired to the southern court. Aboshan became convinced that conspiracies must be in motion against him.

Laquatus had connections in both courts, and while no evidence existed against him, his exile to dry land soon followed the rift. Though the ambassador had no affection for the emperor, he had even less for his estranged wife. Llawan had become a champion of the displaced in Aboshan's rise to power. Laquatus had little use for those without the will or wiles to preserve their position.

His own exile he viewed as a purely temporary state. In addition, the queen opened dialogues with the air breathing races of the sea and the denizens of the deep ocean. Such species had their place, but it was subservient to the mer races and the upper ocean.

The ambassador swam directly to the palace, confident that his reception would be good. He concealed his fear. Revelation of any doubt might doom him if reported to the emperor. The guard recognized him and ushered him through the gates immediately. Laquatus was escorted through the entry halls, amazed at the high number of guards. He reasoned it merely a reaction to the earlier attacks. The interior of the palace hummed as counterspells resonated with the building's very fabric.

Laquatus was no longer as hopeful of his reception. He reminded himself that no mere amphibian could bring him down, Captain Satas be damned. The doorman failed to announce him, and briefly the ambassador wondered if an execution squad waited inside.

The emperor reclined in the nearly empty room with only a few courtiers present. Turg picked up the ambassador's nervousness and began to glower. His master sent him reeling back under a mental barrage. Though the mer ruler appeared unprotected, the hidden guardians were well known to those familiar with the court.

"Laquatus," Aboshan cried, rising and swimming closer. "How good to see you." The monarch had his trident in hand, and the ambassador decided boldness was in order.

"I am pleased and grateful to be here," Laquatus said and tried to appear concerned. "I was relieved to hear that you survived the attack."

"What do you know?" the emperor growled, raising the trident.

The ambassador reminded himself of the hidden guardians and the ruler's known powers.

"Only what I have heard on my way to the capital," Laquatus exclaimed, lowering his head in supplication. "I saw the bodies of the traitors and came immediately to see that you were well. I ask only how I may serve."

"They invaded our court through those very gates," Aboshan said angrily, pointing his trident. The walls seemed to move slightly as guardians almost revealed themselves at the violent gesture. "We were alone, our guards laid low by poison."

The ambassador nodded without fear, finding it unlikely that the monarch would kill his audience.

"We directed the waters to sweep our enemies away," the ruler said, his eyes lost in a refined memory. "Our guards finally came in, but a half-dozen of the scum still swam for us. We killed them in close combat despite receiving grievous wounds. We questioned the only survivor, but he took his own life before we could force the queen's involvement from him."

Laquatus nodded, sure that the enemies would become an even dozen before an official account of the event was set down. Perhaps they would be immortalized in a living mural on the palace walls.

"That brings us to you," Aboshan said with a pointed smile. "You have relationships with the queen's court. You might provide us invaluable service in proving her complicity." He swam back toward the throne, the ambassador following.

"I fear that my former acquaintances will not be forthcoming, sire," Laquatus said, careful to stay well away from the emperor's seat. "My banishment to the continent may have convinced them that I am no longer in your confidence or a position of power." A little of the bitterness at his exile leaked through despite the merman's best efforts to hide it.

"Easily remedied," Aboshan assured him. "We will give very public signs of our favor, concurring upon you suitable rewards and titles."

"Then I fear those in the queen's court will question my motives," Laquatus replied, drifting in front of his sovereign with his head bent in humility.

"Tell them that your long sojourn on land has made you more amenable to the southern court," Aboshan said as he reclined in the stinging tentacles. "We are confident in your abilities at deception."

Laquatus could only humbly nod.

* * * * *

The great windbag, the ambassador thought, looking back on the interview. The emperor recited hours of conspiracy theory, searching for enemies everywhere. He called in secret informers who gave the most bana reports, which Aboshan tried to turn into damnin indictments. Only the emperor's precarious hold on real ity prevented him from unleashing pogroms.

The monarch acted at once to rebuild Laquatus's politi cal stature, awarding him with a gold medallion and th appellation, Friend of the Emperor. The bauble was to heavy, and the friendship would last until Aboshan though him conspiring with others or of no more use. Finally, th ambassador was able to reclaim his jack and pursue his tru mission—locating Satas and the prize.

It was with some surprise that he learned the good captai was gone. He left for the coast before the ambassador eve arrived at the capital. Laquatus, using his new status, foun the entry logs for the day in question. The guard who admi ted Satas to the palace vaguely remembered the little amphib ian. He recalled directing the tresias to the treasure room. Th ambassador called Turg to him from where the frog lurked an swam to the lower portions of the palace to find the sphere.

Laquatus stopped at the lowest entry way in shock. Instea of a valve or gate there was a soldier planted in front of a shim mering sphere. The guard had a humanoid torso, but instea of legs or a tail, the rest of his body was a long stalk. The lowe portion of the column flared out and merged with an out cropping of the palace. The soldier swayed idly, his hands grip ping a short spear. He saw the aristocrat and his jack an straightened, his lower body altering color as if drawing forc from the structure surrounding him. Inside the sphere, o more properly hemisphere for it met the ground, was dry roc and a trapdoor.

"Greetings, Your Excellency," the guard said, tilting hi body down. "How may I be of service?"

The ambassador still looked at the sight of dry land under the sea.

"Yes, it is something of a surprise," the warrior said, "but it was necessary for the workers from the continent." His body bobbed as he looked at the merman.

"What workers?" Laquatus asked, crowding closer.

"Why the workers the Cabal sent in response to the emperor's order several days ago," the guard said in puzzlement. "The care of the treasure room needed specialized services that the caretaker could not provide. They became absolutely necessary when the previous holder died during the traitors' attack."

"Drylanders, here?" Laquatus questioned, his tone alerting the guard to his displeasure.

"Do not worry," the guard said. "I keep close watch, and none of them can breathe water. The captain of the guard inspected them for signs of the queen's magic, and they all were clean. They are as trapped as surely as a meal in a shark's belly."

"I would inspect the treasure rooms. What should I do?" the ambassador said as Turg tried to slip around to the guard's back. His master warned him off, knowing that those serving in the palace would be inspected for signs of tampering. The waxboard showed Satas's sigil. The amphibian had arrived and left within a half-hour, days before.

Laquatus chuckled at the quick exit. There was every chance that the captain never reported to the emperor or anyone except the caretaker. The merman made his mark and prepared to transform. Turg was already in the bubble and standing up, preparing to pull open the trapdoor. The guard returned his attention to the outside passage. At least Laquatus was spared the indignity of being observed as he grew legs.

The ambassador emptied his lungs of water as the frog opened the trapdoor. Stairs led down the bowed timber from ships' hulls. The floor was covered in muck and sand, and the smell of rotting seaweed rose through the door. Then the merman saw some of the workers inside and included rotting flesh as a source of the stench. The servants were, after all, from the Cabal.

"Ambassador Laquatus," a voice hailed him. A woman separated herself from the crowd of living and dead workers and hurried over. The underground room extended for yards in every direction. Groups of zombies and black-clad Cabal servitors piled garbage into baskets and dug down to rock. More timber waited, and Laquatus realized that they were putting up shelves instead of the matrix of pigeonholes and sealed pillars that sea people usually employed.

"I remember you from your marvelous party. I see you also brought my playmate." With a sinking heart he recognized Fulla, her braids plastered with mud against her head. "I would apologize for the mess, but I did not make it. Besides, I remember the condition of your embassy when I left."

Why did it have to be the dementia caster? Any ordinary servant or mage could be manipulated by false memories, but a despairing Laquatus remembered her resistance to his spells.

"Have I offended you somehow?" he heard her ask and brought himself back to reality.

"Not at all, my dear," he gushed, trying to match her enthusiasm. "I was just thinking what chance brought you here," he finished through gritted teeth.

"Well, I will be here for quite some time," she laughed gaily. She waved to the muck and mire. "I and my staff are retained by your gracious emperor to catalog and repair the treasures. Wonders that are rescued, only to be buried here under your palace."

A sucking roar developed as zombies pulled at a chest, uncovering an opening to levels below. Water and mud cascaded down.

"Your previous caretaker placed items randomly in a series of chambers, of which this is only one," she explained as she walked to the hole, looking down into the water. Laquatus could feel a spell engaging, and the water slowly began to subside. More mounds of muck were revealed with a few gleaming pieces of metal. The debris glittered slightly in the light pumped from the palace above.

"One of your ministers was bright enough to realize that we needed air to work. He also discovered that some of the pieces were damaged by water," Fulla said.

Zombies splashed into the lower chambers and began filling baskets the servants handed to them.

"He failed to realize that withdrawing the water would settle everything to the deeper rooms and bury them. To be honest, I do not approve of the former caregiver. There is an unholy lode of mud to be cleared away."

The ambassador nodded dumbly, accepting that a servant of the Cabal would be the best judge of unholy. He realized with a sinking liver that tracking down the orb might still be a formidable task.

"Are there no records of where materials were stored?" he asked hopefully. She shook her head in amusement.

"No. Just a record of what the caretaker received," she said. "For example, the last entry is of a sphere that gave an impression of tremendous power."

The ambassador nodded with excitement. The prize was here.

"The logs show what came in and what went out, but the actual locations are a complete mystery. And that was before nearly everything sunk into different rooms when the water was forced out.

"Surely the other workers have some idea?" he questioned her, hoping there might be someone else to interrogate.

"What other workers?" Fulla replied with exasperation. "From the logs, almost everything was handled by the previous caretaker. I am informed that the servants who did work here cannot function in the open air." Baskets of gunk were thrown out of the entry hole to splat into the mud. "If you can call this open air."

She retreated to a stack of shelves with wax boards and paper books open.

"I and my colleagues are cataloging what we find and entering a reference to the original logs and a current position."

She appeared busy, but Laquatus could not equate her new position as chief curator with her career as a jack in the pits.

"How did you end up here?" he asked with a raised eyebrow. She glanced back, and her face filled with the demons that drove her.

"By the same process that cast you to the Cabal's far shore," she replied. Her features calmed, and she spoke without intonation. "What truly brings you here ambassador? I doubt it was a quest for close friends."

Laquatus considered his answer for several seconds. Just for variety he essayed the truth.

"The final object received here," the merman said. "I want it. What will it cost for me to have it my possession, no questions asked?"

The novelty of a straight answer seemed to disarm the dementia caster, and she fumbled for a response.

"A great many pieces were damaged," she finally said, turning to the shelves. "Some of them beyond repair. But even ruined, they might be of interest the Cabal for research purposes." Her face turned sly, destroying any attempt at disguising her greed.

"Done," Laquatus said simply. "Hold the piece for me when you find it. In return I will aid you in smuggling your loot back to the continent." He looked her deep in the eyes. "Cross me, and I will prick this bubble of air. Your bones can be catalogued by the next curator."

She started running her hands over the pieces already gleaned, like a shopper handling fruit in the market. Laquatus turned and walked to the stairs, soiled at the crassness of the deal and having legs once again.

He mounted the stair and dived through the bubble, transforming even as he swam away, ignoring the guard who recorded his exit. He surged up into the palace. He might have been within yards of the orb, but he could not detect its power. It was hidden from his magical senses. Rumor spoke of perhaps a dozen chambers under the palace, and who knew where the fool of a curator might have put it. The ambassador also worried about his monarch. Fulla was a wild card, who knew what she might say if questioned.

Aboshan emptied troves cared for by the empire's mercenaries and selkies, dumping them to decay in his palace. Only the ruler's love of control and hunger for power had brought the relics to the palace. Now the distraction of a simple assassination attempt washed them from his mind.

"Well," vowed Laquatus, "if it is conspiracies that truly engage him, then conspiracies he will have." The ambassador laughed in the bowels of the palace. He would bring new treacheries before Aboshan to conceal his own. Turg followed his masters, grinning as new plans spawned in the merman's mind.

CHAPTER 20

Kamahl rode Emerald east, watching for signs of the ambassador's caravan. The gecko's sinuous gait lulled the barbarian as he remembered his escape from the town.

The mountain mage had climbed the rubble ramp to the keep's upper stories looking for signs of another exit as the cries from Order reinforcements sounded below. Through the dust laid down by his destruction, he could see tracks that led him to the postern gate. The mountain warrior skirted the crystal effect, seeing its rate of advance slowing as it continued to fill the castle. The taste of the orb's magic faded as the growth slowed.

The postern gate led down a hidden path outside the

city walls. The tumult inside the town died down as Kamahl rejoined the flow of refugees. A golden coin secured him a spare great cloak from an elen bird warrior. The garment was sized for someone nine feet tall and even after a few alterations with a dagger, it was still all-enveloping. It was a measure of the people's unrest that he did not attract more notice. He moved into the old city, listening for news. But rumor ruled the crowded streets, not the Order. He headed for the Citadel road once more, hoping to find out what had occurred.

Kamahl remembered the swell of power as he felt the orb change only minutes after he saw Turg following after the lieutenant. The mer must hold the prize by now. The barbarian wondered if Kirtar survived. Somehow he doubted it.

His leg began to pulse with fresh pain from the wounds inflicted by the frog. He moved down an alley, ready for any attacker, but it was a dead end. Despite the city's overcrowding, a momentary break in the traffic gave him privacy and allowed him to seek shelter. He drew an axe and knife and jumped, his leg screaming in protest as he rose. As he started to fall back, he sank his tools into the wood facing of the building's corner. Rot and lack of care allowed his blades to bite deeply, sending sawdust to the alley below. He crawled up the structure's side, his arms burning as he finally reached the roof.

This building was shorter than the others backing the alley. He crawled behind a storage shed and concealed himself from observation. Momentarily safe, he ate what food he had. Thirst led him to raid a rainwater cistern, and he gulped the cool water down. Weary, for even his endurance had its limits, he lay down to rest.

He awoke that night. The city was quieter, the sun set some hours before. He wrapped the cloak tighter around him and drank more of the water. He had no more food. Kamahl squatted to test his leg. Finding himself fit he decided to brave the city once more.

He dropped into the alley, his lower limbs hurting at the strain but healed enough for full use. There was still traffic on the street despite the hour but not like Cabal City, whose denizens never seemed to sleep. There was a different feel to these pedestrians. They were more afraid and more furtive, even as they stayed close to the lights. Kamahl remembered his friend Chainer who seemed to know most of his city's secrets. The barbarian decided the best source of information might be one of the night birds flitting through the streets.

The first lone walkers proved almost useless. His cloaked form emerged from the darkness provoking two responses. They collapsed in panic or attacked with suicidal bravado. One man continued to fight even after Kamahl slapped his weapons aside several times with his bare hands. Finally he knocked the man out in disgust. Perhaps a more predatory type would be more amenable to conversation.

A group of youths moved in concert through a street. The avenue was barely lit by damp wood burning in a metal basket. A copper hood reflected light to the ground.

The boys split up, settling into positions outside the flow of traffic. Their actions reminding Kamahl of feral cats choosing their prey. The gang looked into the street and not toward each other. The barbarian picked a member off silently, covering the young man's mouth. They disappeared into the night, Kamahl's cloak wrapped around his catch.

The boy was ragged and smelled, a rusty blade thrust through his belt. The dirty pallor of his skin and the color of his clothes hid him from those without Kamahl's night-sight. The barbarian watched him struggle to exude confidence as he stood an arm's length away.

"My friends will come looking for me," the city dweller said, staring hard at Kamahl. The gang member's hand was on his blade, but the weapon was left undrawn.

"Better for them if they do not," the barbarian said and stepped a little closer, forcing his captive against a wall. "All I desire from you is a little information. Do you know what happened in the castle today?"

The impromptu informant relaxed slightly.

"They say that western barbarian and a group of conspirators broke into the Citadel. They were the ones behind the animal attacks. The swine forced refugees into the city, so they could strike from the cover of the crowd." Kamahl wondered how good his information could be with these falsehoods cast as truth. "The traitors managed to kill the captain and the lieutenant despite all efforts to stop them. The entire Order might have been crippled if not for the mer ambassador's warnings."

"Tell me about Laquatus and his jack, Turg," Kamahl ordered, wondering if he should waylay an Order patrol. Perhaps they might have more accurate information.

"The merman and the pit frog were heroes," the young thug said excitedly. "They would have been feted for days if not called back to the ocean on urgent business." The city dweller paused. "How could you know nothing of what happened? The town has been abuzz for hours." He started forward, and Kamahl shoved him back.

"Why should I believe you know anything at all about the ambassador?" the mountain warrior asked, showing his teeth. "All you seem to know is rumor and innuendo."

"Because I watched them leave the city for the east!" came the hot reply, the injustice of being called a liar seeming to raise the boy's courage. Kamahl's snort of disbelief further inflamed the informant.

"I saw them leave this afternoon," he insisted, drawing his knife. "I watched the ambassador ride out the eastern gate." He waited for an attack, but there was only silence as the barbarian melted away.

Kamahl drifted through the streets, heading for the city walls. The thug's affronted pride convinced the barbarian that the boy had seen the ambassador withdrawing to the east. Moreover, if the orb fell to Laquatus, he would have set out for the sea. Kamahl knew that it might be a false trail, but whom could he question? The merman was as likely to lie to the powerful as mislead the masses. He would trust the word of a direct witness for now.

The walls were low with ramps and ladders leading to the upper walkway. Like most defenses, the guards were more interested in keeping invaders out than townspeople in. He appropriated a coil of rope from a storeroom and wrapped it around a stone. In less than a minute he rapelled down. With a practiced twist he pulled the strand down, leaving no sign that any had left the city. He doubted his informant would share his description. The boy seemed one who avoided the guards whenever possible. Kamahl set off to see if Emerald still waited out in the plains.

* * * * *

Kamahl crept through the long grass, threading between the sentries. Avoiding contact felt strange. However, the barbarian imagined it as a challenge to see how close he could approach the Order camp without being detected. It took nearly a day to find Emerald, and knowing the Order believed him a bloody murderer, he kept his distance from the road and other travelers. Only the gecko's incredible endurance and speed allowed Kamahl to finally catch up to the ambassador's party despite the rough country and avoiding enemy patrols.

The Order guards and mer hirelings flew the empire's standard. Kamahl's sharp eyes had caught sight of it as he paralleled them on the highway. He infiltrated the camp to see if Laquatus and Turg truly rode with the group. He had no time to waste on meaningless fights. If the orb was in camp, then he would declare himself and win the prize in honorable combat.

Circumstances demanded he fight tonight if he would fight at all. Some distance ahead of the party an empire caravan camped at a crossroads against a set of bluffs. As night fell, he took Emerald on a run, covering the miles in minutes. A large procession of wagons had left deep ruts along the merging road. Dozens of captive animals sent up cries of distress as they moved in their cages and strained at their hobbles. These guards were more aware. Dogs as well as warriors patrolled the camp perimeter, preventing the barbarian from sneaking in. There were signs of nervousness, the mercenaries reacting to every rustle as an imminent attack.

Kamahl heard the men talking. When would the next attack come? How bad would it be with such a long pause between them? The barbarian realized with surprise there were no fresh signs of rampaging forest animals or destruction along the road. True, they were much farther from the great trees and the animals that sheltered there. However, he understood the problem to be continent wide. Why had an uneasy peace fallen across the two traveling parties and, for all Kamahl knew, the rest of the plains?

Such questions would have to wait until he first completed his quest. The ambassador, if he were traveling with the party, would find reinforcements on the morrow. The barbarian decided to confront the pair tonight.

The tent below the standard was dark with no guards standing before it. Kamahl moved in. Wrapped in his cloak, he avoided the light of the campfires. He made sure that he could reach the weapons on his belt. His sword was secured to Emerald, its length difficult to conceal on the approach. He could detect no life within the tent, but he must be sure. He had watched the caravan settling for the night without any sign of the ambassador or his jack. If they were anywhere in the camp, they must be here. He opened the flap, the rustling canvas seeming very loud.

No one was inside. He saw only a mound of baggage piled on the floor. There was no sign it had even been opened. Each piece was secured with wax, imprinted with the ambassador's sigil, binding the bags' drawcords. However the merman traveled, Kamahl saw it was not with this detachment. However, the seals on the bags suggested he would eventually meet his luggage. The barbarian reached to his belt and pulled out the rope he used in his escape from the city. He was no thief, however stealthy he might be. The barbarian placed it on the baggage, returning it to the Order. The camp guards never saw him withdraw through their pickets on his way back to Emerald.

"They were not there," he said in response to the gecko's quizzical look. "We will have to meet them at the coast." The lizard seemed sluggish as Kamahl secured his gear. The mountain warrior seethed at missing Laquatus and especially Turg. Though the night was chilly he removed the elen robe, letting the cold flow over his skin.

"However they traveled I have lost them," the barbarian muttered as he hauled himself up into the saddle. Knowing that the cool air might slow his mount he sent a small surge of power to the gecko. The lizard blinked in surprise at the warm air but did seem sprightlier as he absorbed the magic. Kamahl directed Emerald down the road to the bluffs, planning to use the lizard's ability to handle any terrain. The steed would take them past the pickets over the bare rock faces, riding above the caravan guards' eyes.

The lizard slowed as they neared the large camp, Kamahl vainly trying to direct the gecko's path. The lizard looked through the night at the stacks of cages and hobbled animals. Its body seemed to vibrate in sympathy with the miserable calls sounding from there. The barbarian realized he could not force Emerald to go anywhere.

The gecko stared at the captured creatures intensely. There were no large predators in the gathering but rather numerous cages of small animals. The barbarian undid his sword from the gecko's side, shifting it up to his back. He looked once more back to the Order camp in the distance with the empty ambassador's tent.

"We cannot spend too much time on this rescue," Kamahl said, pulling small axes from his baggage and slipping them into holsters hung from the saddle. The lizard's long tongue flickered back as if in agreement, then the beast set off for the camp.

The caravan was set by the road, sentry fires out and burning in an attempt to cover the perimeter. Guards stood their posts nervously, talking to each other to reassure themselves. Kamahl wondered how the nightblind chattering fools planned to see anyone. The only danger seemed a pair of dogs that a guard escorted around the perimeter. The barbarian wondered what he would do if discovered but found himself unable to feel concern. The camp looked as deadly as a carnival and easier to move in and out of.

The gecko followed Kamahl, the mount nearly silent, with only its tail sometimes touching the ground. The outer pickets saw nothing as the pair worked through the line, using the terrain. The lizard lowered itself nearly to the ground to decrease its height. The dogs made no alarm, and the barbarian wondered if Emerald somehow stifled their senses. The cages grew closer, the smell assaulting the barbarian as the guards had not. Moving into the circle of cages was challenging, but without the threat of the dog it was only a matter of timing. He crouched by the cages after a slow roll from the darkness. Emerald followed, and the barbarian could scarcely believe his mount had crept into the camp as well. Hunters walked slowly among the captive animals in the cages and pens, lost in their own thoughts. Suddenly the joke fell flat to the mountain warrior. Loosing the animals silently would take far too long, and he was not inclined to waste the time. Kamahl was tired of stealth.

He drew his sword from a sheath on Emerald's saddle. He mounted, and a guard turned to behold him, a mounted intruder in the heart of the camp. The flat of his blade sent the mercenary crashing down unconscious. The first real warning the caravan had was the long whip of flame arcing down to blaze through locks and bars. The animals were maddened by the fire's closeness. The beasts battered at their prisons as they had done so often, but now the bars fell to the ground.

Mercenaries closed from all points with shouts of alarm, but Kamahl's sword streamed flame over the other enclosures, melting away iron. He ignored the guards as beneath contempt as he shouted and roused the imprisoned beasts to escape. One caravan hunter came at the lizard's side only to be met by the long tongue. The muscle wrapped around his head and yanked him into crushing jaws. Kamahl's steed spat out the corpse as his rider freed more of the captured. A chain holding a group of satyrs parted as he swayed to the side, his sword severing several links.

The humanoids rose on their goatlike legs and fell upon the guards coming to recapture them. Heads down, they charged, their horns impacting the guards' armor. The forest fighters caused no serious injury but knocked their oppressors down. Heavy nailed hands dug into throats and joints as the prisoners fell as groups on single guards.

Freeing the captured is useless, Kamahl thought as he turned Emerald to attack, if they are caught again by these mercenaries. Now he used the sword's edge but with no passion. There was little honor in such easy slaughter, and he looked for another means of diversion.

Wagons were parked opposite the animals, their contents hidden under secured tarps. There were no signs of live prizes. The guards protecting them still waited as the bar barian tore through the cage area. Such valuable cargo mus be more important to the caravan than small woodlan creatures, Kamahl thought and sent Emerald through th camp's heart.

A creature rose up in the night, its nebulous form becoming a winged dragon. The gecko showed no hesita tion, striding straight for the horned beast as it prepare to take to the air. The barbarian threw a charged axe tha spun through the enemy. Emerald followed the projectil into the illusion. There was a mage of some power comin against him. The barbarian looked around in interest a his missile discharged into the ground in an explosion c flame.

The gecko paused in its flight, its tongue flickerin uncertainly as its eyes followed nothing. The mountai mage felt the hum of hostile magic and sent showers c sparks and embers over the tents to flush out the enem Fabric ignited, and the restraining spell on the lizard fal tered as the other mage was surrounded by fire.

The barbarian swung his sword, the steel birthing a cir clet of flame that cut through the air and the enemy spell caster's neck, decapitating Kamahl's only worthy oppositio in the camp. The gecko started toward the wagons parke away from the cages. The guards massed to stop the barbar ian. The mountain mage simply bypassed them, hurling tw axes high over the crowd to detonate among the freigh wagons. A twisting pyre of energy and flame lit the sky, sec ondary explosions spreading destruction through the cargo The guards were blown down—those not blown up.

The caravan had been transporting excavated treasure to the sea. There were numerous rumors of the Mer Empir acquiring relics and fetishes from past battlefields. Items of true power must have been concealed among the wagons. Fires grew, and most of those still alive in the camp closed to extinguish the conflagration. Kamahl withdrew, ignoring the calls of his enemies.

The satyrs were gone, along with most of the animals. A few hunters looked through the wreckage, but the barbarian wasted no time on them. One stooped to peer into a cage, and a stream of weasels flowed over the man, biting everywhere. The mercenary tried to run as the animals swarmed up his legs and onto his head. His flight ended as the disoriented man plowed into another cage, falling down to die under the small teeth.

Calls sounded from the perimeter. Golden globes soared into the sky illuminating what the fires did not. Guards from the false camp down the road had come to investigate the disturbance. These were worthy opponents but too serious for tonight's light diversion. The barbarian left the camp to the newcomers, Emerald running out of the light and into the darkness. Kamahl's mount surged up the rocky bluff as the more intelligent investigators from the other camp fanned out to catch the raider. The barbarian leaned forward as the gecko went vertical, pulling away from any possible pursuit. The mountain mage signaled the lizard to halt at the cliff top. He crouched down and peered over the hunters' wrecked bivouac.

The fires began to die down, the knights of the Order using their magic against the flames. Magic flowed as a golden sheet over the burning wagons and tents, smothering the flames. The light died down as blazes were extinguished. The barbarian saw no signs of animals and hoped all of them were gone.

"I hope that satisfies you," he said to Emerald who seemed to nod in agreement. His mount's bloody jowls smiled though Kamahl was unsure if the fighting or the rescue pleased the gecko most. Below, the flames were dead except for the campfires, but more bad luck struck the hunters' camp.

Irritated at being forced to come investigate because of the mercenaries' obvious incompetence, the knights looked through the camp. The angry would-be rescuers tore into the last sealed wagons and suddenly treated the hapless hunters as criminals. The soldiers cut through leather and canvas to display the mounds of forbidden mechanisms. Mercenaries moved to reclaim what remained of their treasure. They were pushed away to sprawl on the ground. A few started angrily forward but stopped as golden maces lifted in warning.

The knights struck at wagons carrying recovered booty. Wheels exploded in showers of splinters as the Order guaranteed through blows that the fetishes would not leave the camp. A mercenary waved documents before a knight only to be ignored.

The mountain mage turned the gecko toward the sea and nudged it into motion. Perhaps the Order was right in their distrust of the debris of past battles. Kamahl knew his journey to reclaim the orb might be barely begun. Why did he chase after it? Merely for the power it held? Perhaps, but more importantly it was his by right. He would not let it be stolen away. Honor demanded he reclaim his lost prize.

CHAPTER 21

The manor was some distance from the capital, its buildings in deeper water. In the world above, the sun was just rising, the beams starting to filter to the undersea world. Turg held onto a harpoon fish's fin as the attack force surged ahead. The fish weighed thousands of pounds, its lumpy flesh rock hard under the frog's hands. The mouth gaped open and a fish fleeing before the detachment swam too close to the monster. A long tongue darted forth, spearing through its target. The pinned morsel was pulled into the mouth as the predator accelerated. Turg felt a brief burning sensation as they moved through a cloud of digestive enzymes. The harpoon fish forced the caustic liquid into its prey whenever it attacked.

The attack force closed on the target, the estate of a rich noble with ties to the air breathers of the ocean. Whales began to rise from structures on the seabed. Vast hemispheres of coral and stone held pockets of air, allowing the lord's allies to stay beneath indefinitely.

The whales began to call, the sonic pulse of their cries beating against the amphibian's skull. The whales were pale blue and almost invisible in the water. Only their motion drew the eye. The animals were several times the size of the harpoon fish, but Turg felt only contempt for them. The air breathers rose over their ally's home, preparing to meet the surprise attack. The mammals vibrated with magic to the frog's mystic senses. Power was gathering among the attackers as they raced to slay the whales, driven by the ambassador's overseeing spirit.

Magically summoned schools of barracuda surged away from the attack force. Like living projectiles, the school swept toward their warm-blooded targets. Defensive whale songs sounded, the waves of noise playing havoc among the predatory fish. Barracuda went in all directions, hopelessly confused by the air breathers' magic. Some of the toothy fish were in their death throes, their organs destroy by the powerful whale song.

Now the singers' voices swept the leading edge of the imperial attackers. Multiple whales, converge on individual harpoon fish, the rocky attackers' nerves burning out in novas of pain. A few imperial soldier, accompanying the attack tried to lead the whales astray with illusions, to no avail.

Turg let go of his fish as it finally reached an opponent.

The barbed tongue snapped into the whale's body, swelling as a prodigious load of digestive fluid surged into its victim. The air breather cried out, its call soaring beyond hearing. Several cephalids swimming past blurred, their skin rupturing and blood streaming into the water. The feeding fish drew its tongue back and slammed it again into the smooth hide. The whale expired as water filled its lungs. The harpoon fish looked for something else to kill.

The whales coalesced into groups, their cries sounding in all directions, unconcerned with killing their allies as long as the attack failed. On the outskirts of the fight, sharks began to appear, ripping apart the dead and the dying as the blood spoor drew them from miles around. The harpoon fish closed for the final battle with the air breathers, but Turg was surging ahead, leading a column of infantry now that the whales were engaged.

The frog swam forward as the fighting moved over the estate. Tritons and mermen followed him down as crab forces sprinted across the sandy bottom for the house. The defenders were like mollusks, trying to withdraw into the protection of their shell. The valves of the living structure closed, the tough armor resisting the frog's blows. He called down harpoon fish, the monsters leaving their bloody feast. Tongues lanced into the door, gallons of digestive fluids pumping into the fabric of the manor. The valve ripped free as the fish pulled. They loosed it to drift away.

Spears flew from the gap, sinking into imperial warriors who charged in too soon. The jack cast a spell, and eels swam down the hole. Their bodies were living batteries that discharged as they reached the defenders. Now Turg swam into the house. He ignored the twitching bodies of the slain. The crabs piling through the entrance began to corral the stunned. The house was dark, the defender's trying to use the lack of light to their advantage.

The frog loosed streams of light-emitting plankton that carried in the currents still moving through the house. A triton was a hulking humanoid, its finned limbs sending it around the frog as they advanced. A spindly crab joined them, as they penetrated the house.

The porpoises emerged suddenly, diving from the upper floor in ramming attacks. The frog's hands glowed, and he stabbed into his opponent. The triton's barbed fins sank into its foe, and malign energy poisoned its system. Mermen defenders thrust tridents at the engaged invaders only to be met by the crab. Though not tall, its claws snipped through weapons and amputated a hand as the crab closed. More porpoises came toward the frog, and Laquatus struck through his amphibious minion.

The counterspell attacked the magic allowing the cetaceans to stay underwater. Tissues suddenly starved for oxygen. Muscles flooded the blood stream with toxins. The defenders started to race for the surface, knowing themselves doomed but helpless against their instincts. Soldiers ignored the retreating cetaceans to fall upon the remaining defenders.

The frog and his companions moved ahead of the fighting, the inner rooms of the manor clearing as the manor guards rushed to the perimeter. A sigil spelled out in the living flesh of the wall told Turg they had reached the noble's private rooms. The crab scuttled forward, its claws making short work of the interior partition.

The quarters were almost stark in their simplicity. Only the huge number of pigeonholes and storage pillars showed the noble's wealth. The frog swam over, a spell whispering gainst the valves closing off the writing supplies. The container irised open, and the jack leaned over. Turg spat the seals and rings he had carried in his mouth throughout the battle. The planted objects were issued by the southern court, the queen showing on the crest instead of the emperor. The frog's spell ceased, and the container snapped shut, barring itself to one not attuned to its nature.

The crab scuttled over, several cruciform sheets of wax in its claws. Another spell provided by the ambassador's spirit whispered over the old letters, altering some of the strokes as the organic material responded to his will. The crab dipped them into the bottom of a storage column. Turg bled power as he touched the furniture. Growth accelerated, and he could taste the flow of byproducts as the living structure ged, sealing the damning letters under a layer of coral.

The green triton gave a grunt of warning, sending the trio across the room. Living cases lay stacked against the corner, the containers holding eggs and plankton of exceptional quality. The crab cut them open like lightning as the frog and triton grabbed up and devoured fistfuls of the delicacy. When the titular head of the attack force arrived seconds later, he found the group busy enjoying their loot. A snarl of disgust showed, but he dared not discipline the ambassador's jack.

The command staff arrived and began opening the sealed pigeonholes and chests in the room. A pair of soldiers came and searched through the food crates the trio had opened, their contempt plain as the triton growled and the crab clacked its claws.

"Sir," called an orderly, opening up a pigeonhole. A major swam over and inspected the contents. He tensed in excitement, diving in to examine the rings and seals Turg had planted. The sound of a struggle was heard from the hallway. A huge crab eased his way through the door pulling a tether. A merman came through, his flukes beating to escape as he was reeled in. Another line leading out slackened as a nearly identical crustacean followed, the aristocrat suspended between the two soldiers.

"What is the meaning of this?" the prisoner roared, his muscles straining in vain against the pair of armored monsters. "You have no right to invade my home! I am a loyal servant to the emperor!" The leader swam over and struck him with one of the seals clenched in his fist, the metal edge tearing the noble's skin.

"Traitors have no rights!" the officer snarled. He gestured to the writing implements and letters being impounded. "You are in service to the southern queen and will die for your treachery. Your alliance with the air breathers always inflamed suspicions. But for the actions documented here you shall die!"

The noble went goggle-eyed with incredulity. "Lies!" he cried, surging against his tether. "It is all lies!" He looked to his luxuries stored in the back and recognized Turg. "Everything is a lie spread by his master! He planted these forgeries."

The major looked at the frog whose face was smeared with stolen booty. The officer's laughter filled the room as the frog swam closer, his face showing no signs of intelligence.

"His master is a beast and a bigot," the prisoner snarled. "So superior to those who breathe though he spent years on the land. Even his chief lackey is an amphibian." The merman twisted on the line attempting to smash the frog with his flukes.

The jack dodged the blow, and electricity surged through

he champion's hands into the tail. The attack reduced the
noble to a glassy eyed wreck, small globes of blood drifting
rom an open mouth and breaking up in the water. The
najor looked at the amphibian in anger but remembered
vhose patronage the frog enjoyed.

"We do not need his confession anyway," the attack
eader groused. "We have enough to convince any that he
onspired against the crown. The dungeons will soon drag
he truth out of him."

He called for the incriminating evidence to be sealed for
mmediate transport and left his orderlies searching through
he rest of the archives. Turg swam back to his cronies and
njoyed the fruits of the noble's larder.

* * * * *

Laquatus came out of the trance pleased with all he had
een. Riding the jack during the attack allowed him to
rame the moderate aristocrat. He laughed at how close the
nerman's raving came to the truth. The drive to find con-
piracies was producing spectacular results. Every day
rought new arrests and revelations of treachery. The
mbassador admired the unrelenting torturers in their
fforts to gain confessions. Perhaps they even extracted the
ruth from someone, but the aristocrat doubted it.

The emperor, feeling more besieged than ever, granted
Laquatus more and more authority to pursue his inquiries.
Today's raid was the culmination of his attempts to stir up
rouble, and he could not be happier with its success. Even
he imperial officers started to believe the propaganda he
pread. Laquatus had expected them to be much more cyn-
cal and jaded. The sprawling chaos was a work of joy.

Sometimes, he even forgot it was only a cover for his thievery

Fulla had excavated five rooms without locating Kirtar's prize. Several loads of "damaged" goods had gone to the Cabal, and Laquatus was obliged to search all of them. He found no sign of the orb and wondered if perhaps she had no plans to betray him. Finding that conclusion highly unlikely, he was careful to document her thievery through exact manifests. Minus, of course, items of power interesting enough for him to steal.

The dementia caster had no contact with the Cabal and was unlikely to complain of thefts from her own looting operation. The emperor engaged himself in touring the army and moving against signs of discontent. The real bonus from his violent flailing against conspiracy was his actions were undoubtedly creating real plots against him. The cycle of violence was increasing, and the ambassador swam at the center, still untouched. He readied himself for court, putting on his finest jewelry.

He swam through the palace corridors, the building pumping light from above to the halls. Aboshan had called a meeting of nobles to go over the reports Laquatus gave him the day before. In the name of preserving theoretical contacts with the queen's court, he was spared from attending except occasionally. The door to the throne room was closed, but the emperor's shouting bled through in a wordless howl.

The ambassador ignored it, waiting for the end of the audience. Aboshan's rants had become distressingly predictable, often ending with a wild accusation that took a noble away to be investigated. Only the identity of the prisoner changed, and Laquatus thought it best to be absent when the sacrificial lamb was selected. Danger could add

pice, but maintaining a fictitious wave of conspiracies pro-
ided enough entertainment.

While the ambassador waited, he saw another merman
urtively hovering down the corridor. Thinking he recog-
ized the courtier, Laquatus swam toward him. The
merman remembered the other with a start. It was Petod, a
ower noble who had withdrawn to the southern court years
efore. He was dressed in palace livery, but Laquatus was
ure of his identity.

The noble realized himself recognized and swam into a
ide room, gesturing for company. Laquatus cast a spell,
ending an image of himself down the corridor to his
uarters. He vanished into the other room as well,
making sure that no one saw him. The door closed behind
im as soon as he went through.

"Thank goodness I found you," said Petod in a panicked
oice. The merman nervously twisted rings on his finger as
e swam to check the door. "I did not know who to turn
o." He reached as if to pat the ambassador's shoulder only
o stop at a forbidding gaze.

"The court felt too dangerous for me to declare
myself," Petod said wretchedly, seeming to collapse inter-
nally. Laquatus remembered him as weak willed. "I came
s an unofficial representative from the queen. Her
majesty is understandably upset at the attempt to kill her
usband and wished to reassure him that she was not
nvolved. I hope to serve as a private courier between the
wo monarchs."

"Llawan sent you?" Laquatus asked in disbelief. Petod was
poor choice from his memory, given to rash judgements
nd poor decisions. Laquatus thought her a better leader
han that.

"Of course not," the self-selected emissary said. "Th
nobles who fled south would view such a move on her pa
as unacceptable. I took it upon myself to offer my services
he finished smugly.

The ambassador nodded. Petod was a fool, but he coul
be quite congenial in social situations. Perhaps he wa
familiar in the southern court. Llawan would never use
back channel because her integrity would force her t
inform her allies.

"Why the disguise?" he asked.

"If I declared myself, I feared being called a spy or assas
sin," Petod confessed. Laquatus said nothing though sneak
ing into the palace under false pretense made such a fat
inevitable. "I hoped to find an ally that might help me mee
secretly with the emperor. I heard of your return from exil
and knew you could help."

Two thoughts surged through the ambassador's mind
First, such an action was suicidal with the emperor in h
current mood. Second, Aboshan's ridiculous pretense o
clemency to a returned exile had indeed enabled him t
contact a member of Llawan's court. He soon shook off th
surprise. He could not afford any knowledge of the souther
plans reaching the emperor. Already he had taken over th
emperor's spies who reported from the south. The ambass
dor recast Llawan's actions to make her appear more hostil
to the emperor. Petod must not meet Aboshan.

"I am astounded at your actions, my lord," Laquatu
said, his voice filled with warm regard. "Your clos
knowledge of Llawan's policies and private feeling
could alter the history of the seas." The ambassado
clapped the young noble on the back, a jeweled ring cut
ting into the flesh on the shoulder.

"A thousand apologies, Petod," the merman said stripping the ring from his finger. "It is a new piece and far too clumsy on my hand. Allow me to present it to you as a token of my esteem. No, I insist." Laquatus put the ring on Petod's hand, ignoring the young mer's stumbling refusal. The ambassador exercised great caution as he placed and released the ring.

The self-appointed emissary rubbed at the puncture high on his shoulder, trying to accept the gift graciously even as his flesh went numb. Laquatus was in full court regalia and that included poison for his jewelry. The southern noble gasped, water moving fitfully through his gills. He choked and gasped as he realized himself attacked.

The ambassador decided his poison was not quite virulent enough. Too much time away from court had made his venom weak. He used his magic and called a stream of tiny jellyfish into being. The fragile cloud was hardly more substantial than the water in which it swam. He guided Petod to it, and his gills sucked the tiny bags of poison down. Toxins poured directly into his bloodstream, and Laquatus held him steady as his body locked. The torn flesh plugged the organs, and they ceased to supply oxygen. The ambassador banished the summoning as soon as he knew the courier was dead.

He swam back to the throne room, towing his dead victim behind him. He put on a burst of speed wanting to arrive with maximum effect. The valve doors were open, the assembled nobles withdrawing as fast as they dared. The ambassador swam past them as gasps of shock echoed behind him. He swam to where the emperor reclined with a cluster of officers waiting around him. Aboshan looked exhausted, his rage having consumed him during the audience. Guards surged from the walls and stopped, uncertain what threat a corpse might pose.

"Laquatus," the monarch said, looking at the dead Petod. "What is the meaning of your companion?" He waved a moray eel closer, and it snared the body hauling it away from the monarch.

"An assassin from the southern court, your imperial majesty," Laquatus said boldly. "I spotted him outside your very throne room, and when I went to investigate he attacked me."

"Look," the merman said dramatically, pointing to the corpse being pushed back by the moray ell. "Slain by the very ring he plotted to use on others in the palace. Dare I say, including your royal majesty." Aboshan gestured with a tentacle.

"Show me the ring," he commanded. The eel was perhaps too literal, and his jaws snipped Petod's hand off and brought it near. The monarch regarded the offending appendage and threw it to the side.

"Is there no end to this infamy? The rumors you reported are true! Raids on some of our greatest nobles have revealed links to our shark of a wife. Now an assassin outside our very throne room? Why do they plot against me?" he cried, no longer using the royal plural. He collapsed back into the throne, and the ambassador could feel energy pulsing back into the monarch from the palace.

"Perhaps war is the only answer," a hesitant officer said, looking for support from his fellows. "The queen's forces are not so superior. Surely a surprise attack would put an end to these conspiracies."

The emperor looked up wanly. Laquatus spoke quickly to squash the idea. Open warfare would bring the emperor's interest back to the martial devices buried beneath his palace.

CHAPTER 22

Kamahl peered down at the sea. The wooded hillside overlooked the coastal town of Borben on the continent's edge. The town sat at the end of a major trade road, the last habitation before the open ocean. A long peninsula jogged out for the mainland creating a protected bay. Like a single finger of hills, it beckoned to ships searching for port. Waterfowl and a few seals sunning themselves populated the last spit of land.

The barbarian walked to the hilltop along an overgrown trail, soaring above the main road. The joint caravans of the Cabal and the Mer Empire broke apart many miles behind him. The animals went south, and a few of the wagons continued on to Borben. Kamahl had parted ways with Emerald some days before, leaving the barbarian alone to walk into the town.

A few small ships lay anchored in the bay, with only one pier stretching out into the water for the transfer of freight from small vessels. Out on the water, a single lighter accepted a net of cargo from a larger ship. Oars started to row the boat back to the docks and warehouses.

Well back from town, nearly in the surrounding hills, sat a small arena. Nearly oval in shape, it was constructed out of wood, the large logs and rough-cut timbers whitewashed in the sun. It pressed against an outcropping of rock, the interior looking muddy from a distance. Sand was piled outside the fighting ring. The color told the barbarian it was hauled up from the shore.

The arena stood deserted now, but the mountain mage knew it would be crowded during market days and festivals. The best source of information regarding the ambassador and his stolen prize would undoubtedly be the bars around the docks and the arena. He was no seaman, and he resolved to try the inns close to the fighting ring, knowing he could mix with the jacks.

The town looked still now, but when the fishermen returned to port the docks would teem. He wondered when the bouts would start in the arena, so he could interact with familiar types of people. He considered his own appearance as he thought about poking around for information regarding the troubles in the east. The Order would distribute descriptions, and the ambassador might have left word of him as well.

He wore a gray cloak now, the elen garment gradually shrinking to fit him as he plied needle and dagger. The metal-hued races were uncommon but by no means unknown on the continent. Only two things were uniquely his own: his name and his sword. He drew the weapon, holding it in his open palms as he considered it. Long as he was tall, the massive blade showed little sign of wear. Rings rattled softly on the blade as he rotated it. Ever since procuring it during his quests as a young man, he had carried it. The steel and fire evoked from the mystic metal had cut many an enemy low. But in the mountains, the sword had gained its own reputation, as fulsome as Kamahl's, and was more unique in appearance. Regretfully, he decided that the weapon must rest here, above the town, to await his return.

He walked to a tree, its roots wrapping around a boulder, as if holding it to the ground. He looked at his sword and called power. It flowed into the steel, the energy streaming fluidly throughout the weapon. He set the nearly flat point against the rock, the shallow edge still cutting the stone. His muscles ached as he pushed. Gradually the metal burrowed its way through the rock. Kamahl strained until the hilt began to disappear. He exhausted more of his strength as he picked up a stone and set it against the hilt. The weapon's advance continued as his hands held rock rather than the familiar leather wrapped hilt. Stone touched stone, and he closed the final inches. The smell of hot metal ceased as his granite pad disappeared into the rocky anvil.

Kamahl walked to his gear. Looking at the pack and several bags, he realized he had grown too dependent on steeds. He separated out the essential from the merely convenient and laid out tarps to encase the saddle and gear too heavy to carry into town. He opened a bag he intended to cache by the boulder holding his sword. Arms picked up during his travels rattled as he searched. Near the bottom he withdrew a weapon found just days before.

Roving bands of Order knights swept the roads looking for signs of Kamahl and the animals whose attacks had been so disruptive. The soldiers also inspected wagons for forbidden objects. News of the disastrous spell in the Citadel drove the knights to new heights in destroying past evils. The mercenaries driving caravans of excavated treasures lacked the will to fight the Order. During his trek here, the barbarian had come across a few of their abandoned wagons.

He drew forth a massive hammer. The head was black iron. Magic reinforced the metal and the haft. The long handle was white ivory, perhaps from some fallen mammoth or other such beast. The dense grip and over-sized head made it a weapon for a giant rather than someone the size of a man. His muscles bunched as he hefted it. He remembered Emerald's look of momentary outrage when he loaded the hammer. He had found it lying in the open near another cache of weapons. Knowing it abandoned, he had still dropped most of his money in the resting place. Whoever came looking for it would be disappointed but surprised at the consideration of the person who rescued it from destruction by the Order. Perhaps the Cabal or a corrupt bird warrior had his money even now, but it would have felt wrong to take it without any attempt at compensation.

He stuffed his sword scabbard in his bags and hid them and the saddle. He held the hammer in his hands and felt the weight. Only his constant practice with his own massive sword allowed him to swing it with assurance. He took one last look and started through the trees to the road.

It took sometime to reach the highway, even with the barbarian's rapid pace and sure feet. It drew toward evening as Kamahl came into the town. The streets led down to the docks, but he took a switchback trail to the arena. On the bay, the last of the fishing vessels were coming in, the catch being transferred to the packinghouses. Lights came up around the arena as street musicians began to play. Reeds and strings dueled in melody, as fighters soon would inside. A local inn competed with men selling food on the street, and clusters of fisherman up from the docks drifted toward the bars. Kamahl shouldered patrons aside as he came into the inn.

"What might I do for you?" a barman called, drawing drinks for the house. The light was dim and the room close and crowded. The smell of food cooking in the kitchen and the proprietor's face both seemed pleasant enough.

"I need a room and meals for the next several days," Kamahl said, resting his hammer on the bar. The fighting weapon drew only a few glances. Perhaps they were used to jacks from the arena. The coins he threw down attracted substantially more attention. The barbarian recalled how much he spent at the inns at the tourney in Cabal City. From the respectful glances, the cost of room and board in Borben was substantially less.

"We can accommodate you, sir," the bartender cried, grabbing up a set of keys. He came around the bar, ignoring the empty tankards waved in his direction. The proprietor's bald head sweated from exertion and the heat in the crowded room. He picked up the barbarian's saddlebags and tried to pick up the hammer as well. The unexpected weight left him standing still for a moment before Kamahl lifted the heavy weapon to his shoulder.

"I want a room with a view of the harbor," the mountain mage said as he followed the owner up the stairs. The steps were narrow, and the light peeked over the solid barrister. A single lamp lit the hall. The keys rattled briefly as the innkeeper unlocked the door. The room was small and the window sealed off. Kamahl's guide dropped the bags and threw the shutters open, letting a salty breeze carry over the sash to the barbarian.

"Best view in the house," the owner said. The makings for a fire were laid in a fireplace, and the linens looked clean. "There are chops and roast for dinner tonight and rabbits tomorrow. We always prepare food for the arena crowd. After that, the kitchen shuts down for the week unless a guest makes private arrangements. I'll send a girl with a coal to start a blaze and bring you whatever you want from the kitchen."

Kamahl waved, and a glowing ember seemed to float through the air to land on the prepared wood. The logs burst into flames, instantly pouring out heat with no showers of sparks.

"I will take my own meals tonight," the barbarian said, laying the hammer on the bed, which sagged. "I prefer my privacy and will have no trouble tending my own fire. If you would give me the key to this room and any spares."

The owner hesitated as the mountain mage approached. He laid the brass in the jack's hand and bowed his way out, eyes flickering from the fire to the weapon on the bed.

Kamahl closed the door and went to the window. The town folk flowed up from the sea's edge toward the entertainment offered behind him at the arena. A few heavy wagons were left on the pier, a luckless sentry standing guard as his friends climbed the hill. The wagons had the look of long-haul freight, and the barbarian resolved to make inquires about them tomorrow.

The crowds in the street and bars drained away as he left the inn. The arena was small, and Kamahl was immediately conducted to a box seat with a small tray of refreshments as he entered. Someone from the inn had obviously informed the arena operators of his presence. This was not the reception the barbarian—now a known outlaw—expected.

A porter waited to the side, ready to speak as the entertainment commenced. First was the light and easy comedy of blood sports. Two groups of men, fishermen from their gait, came into the arena. Kamahl looked for an emblem for the fight, and the porter swept forward.

"Just two crews who had a disagreement over boundaries, sir," the servitor explained. "The winner of the bout fixes the new fishing boundaries over the disputed area."

Kamahl turned to see if anyone else received such specialized service, but the layout of the boxes prevented him from observing others.

A piercing whistle sounded, and the crews rushed each other. Men were clad in padded jerkins, and their clubs were wrapped in cloth. They fell to like madmen, flailing at heads and joints. The fishers only disengaged when armed guards dragged away the wounded. Within minutes only one staggering figure remained through most of the others appeared to be recovering off on the sidelines. The winner left with arms held high though attendants came out to guide him to the exit. The next acts were simple acrobats and tumblers, their antics entertaining the crowd as the next bill readied themselves.

"Here we are too short of fighters and beasts to have more than a few matches during any night," the servant said nervously as he watched the barbarian eat.

Kamahl cast only occasional glances toward the exhibition. Finally the signal was given, and the acrobats somersaulted free, leaving the floor clear.

The servant left as two fighters emerged, each wearing colors of arena staff. One was tall and scarred, wearing a steel mask and leather armor. A short flail with two spiked heads swung slowly at his side.

The other opponent leaned on a staff of black wood, a brazier producing smoke in different colors that swept over him. He was short and spindly, dressed only in tattered clothes that ruffled slightly as a gust of wind swept the arena. The servant glanced in from his rounds of the other boxes.

"Does your staff fight or is it just the fishermen?" Kamahl asked, as hoots began to rise up from the audience.

"We are very small compared to the inland arenas, my lord," the servitor said, projecting obsequiousness in the face of perceived disappointment. "The large gladiatorial companies avoid us, the crowds being too small and the gambling syndicates unable to handle serious betting. We must rely on house fighters for the majority of the bouts."

The signal to begin the bout rang, and the waiting dementia caster dug his staff into the soil. The shaft cast a long shadow, though no bright light existed to throw such a pall. From the depths of the shadow came laughter. Then several twisted monsters exited the darkness. Their flesh appeared parched, their hands showing bone as they shuffled about in a gruesome dance.

The masked fighter swung his flail as the tall mage called more creatures from his mind and raised the bones of the dead from the ground. The race of the corpses was impossible to determine because the flesh was in such poor condition.

The dementia caster sawed his staff back and forth, the shadow racing over the ground. The black wave coated the flesh of the risen, drawing the moisture out. Their flesh shriveled as tendons and muscles grew too tenuous to keep the bodies together.

The field cleared as laughing corpses fell on each other and dragged food back to the darkness from which they sprang. Some of the horrific creatures called forth from the dementia caster's mind ignored everything and staggered around the arena. Cries sounded from the gate guards as the dead beat on the barriers keeping them inside. Others turned on the masked fighter who began to fall back. The flail smashed bones, but the twisted dead continued snapping at his heels, their bodies coiling and rebuilding into even more twisted fragments of the short mage's imagination.

A few of the creatures even turned on their creator, advancing on the staff. The shadow it cast began to sweep back and forth, the pall forming a cone in front of the mage. The rebelling monsters fell as their limbs spilled to the ground, their frames melting like frost on a skillet. The masked jack fought harder as more of the laughing closed on him.

Acknowledging defeat the fighter knelt in submission, his mask dipping to the ground. The dementia caster withdrew his staff from the ground and knocked the brazier over. The summoned vanished like nightmares at dawn as the short victor bowed to the applause of the crowd.

* * * * *

The crowd roared in the stands above as workers tried to reassemble the dead. The arena operator and two assistants laid out the bodies of the slain. Some had been dead a very long time, and the smell smashed against the barbarian. Kamahl had left his private box before the next bout to talk to the owners about fighting in their establishment. He found the master hard at work preparing for the next night.

"Make sure you find as many body parts as you can," the promoter told the groundskeeper. The arena owner's pale skin contrasted with the dirt and leather smock he wore. Splotches of blood and caustic burns covered his apron and sections of revealed skin. "There are rumors sweeping the docks, and the sailors are asking for burial at sea again instead of in port." He shooed the servant away and regarded the jack.

"So you wish to join our little family?" The pit boss asked, searching through a pile of limbs for an arm to complete a dead dwarf, preservative fluid dripping from the torn flesh. Kamahl shook his head.

"I wish to compete in the arena against your fighters," he corrected. He looked at the dead being reconstructed for later battles. "Your family appears quite big enough," he said with distaste. The promoter ignored the tone.

"You would be surprised how difficult it is to keep a large enough supply for Enoch and Apel, our necromancers," he said, surrendering in his quest and throwing a random arm in the dwarf's case. "We'll have to bury these tonight in the arena. Apel's zombies always cart off the dead despite how short we are. We used to get sailors, but my brother forgot to alter one's looks. Now it is almost impossible to get them after they die." He moved to the next casket whose contents the barbarian avoided looking at. "The crowds are growing very tired of the same old faces week after week.

"I am offering something new," Kamahl said, stepping around to peer in the mild eyes. "Someone whom your clients have not seen before."

The proprietor waved to his assistants and walked to the back with the barbarian following.

"You understand that we rarely fight to the death here," the official said, hanging his splattered apron on a hook before stepping into an office. "Also, the deal is contingent on my brother's agreement when he comes back from meeting with the bet-mongers."

"I'll not put on a show," Kamahl said, his eyes growing hard. "When I fight, it will be for real. However, I need not kill if your fighters understand that they can surrender when they are overwhelmed."

The owner waved the demand away.

"A jack in a small arena has no use for a champion's airs," he said, drawing forth a piece of paper. "Now, I will need your name for the criers circulating tonight if you plan to fight tomorrow."

The barbarian paused before answering. It would be easiest to give a false name, but an outright lie stuck in his throat.

"Call me the Hammer," he said, sparking the proprietor's interest. "Only by defeating me will someone learn my true name."

The fat man nodded, seeing the possibilities. "You will need to clean your armor, and we must design a suitable emblem . . . " the owner continued as he led the barbarian away. A host of functionaries followed, all trying to mold Kamahl to their own idea of what a fighter should be. He was brusque in refusing their offers of advice on how to fight and the proper attire to wear. He did allow the armorer to work on his protective gear, which had suffered during his travels.

It seemed only minutes, and he was standing in the center of the arena, the noise of the crowd merging into an unintelligible muttering. The gray cloak was thrown back, his iron shirt dark against his brass skin.

Kamahl swung his hammer, stretching out the kinks in his muscles. His first opponent was Apel, a short dementia caster. Knowing the reputation of such mages, Kamahl wondered if the house fighter would follow the rules. The barbarian believed the short summoner would soon be surrendering, but he must be prepared for a battle to the death. The crowd began to chant as Apel strode into the arena and lowered his equipment to the ground.

The dementia caster stood on the sand, a burning brazier at his side. Apel threw power onto the glowing coals and a heavy cloud of smoke rose, making his features waver and change. The dark mage dug his staff into the ground, and a thin shadow stretched out from the shaft, advancing toward the light behind Kamahl's head rather than away. The familiar shuffling figures of the mirthful dead began to appear, cackling perhaps at the joke of life itself. Kamahl wondered how predictable his opponent would be.

The barbarian called forth his own magic, a field of possibility forming over the sand. He would experiment, use the arena to teach himself new methods of attack and defense. Several cougars surged out of nothingness onto the arena floor, their roars stilling the cries of the crowd. The zombies came on, their laughter continuing even as many were pulled down and savaged by the great cats. If any of the dead were reconstructed corpses, the mountain mage did not envy the morticians' tasks in repairing the bodies.

The dementia caster seemed oblivious to the failure of his forces. Ignoring the feasting cats, Apel sent more undead onto the arena floor. A tattered wave threatening to overwhelm Kamahl's spell by choking his beasts under a wave of cold flesh. The barbarian concentrated again, the cloud of his summoning stretching wider as he played a little to the crowd.

A flock of mountain sheep stormed onto the sand. They milled for a moment, their waist-high bodies losing themselves in a blur as the fierce rams fought for position. Kamahl nudged them into action with a mental command, and the beasts lowered their tightly curled horns and stormed forward. The rams struck hard, shattering bone and bringing the dead down. Clawed hands and fangs struck at Kamahl's creatures but could not penetrate the dense wool that defeated the cold wind of the mountains and the hot breath of timber wolves.

Apel lifted his staff into the air, his face now agitated as his forces fell to mere sheep. In frustration he speared the oak into the sand. Power poured into the soil. Like cobras rising to strike, dark spears rose from the ground. The shadowy weapons bobbed and weaved before falling on the animals that ground up the dead. The wool that resisted the strength of zombies sundered as the beasts were transfixed. The few remaining cougars expired in yowling pain. The rams fell as mutton, the undead rising up as Apel poured new strength to their shattered bones. The bodies tottered toward the barbarian more twisted and cackling than before, but the upright spears of night were straight as they drifted toward the mountain mage.

Kamahl stepped forward, his brow wrinkling as his will

contested once more with the universe. Now hulking figures came onto the arena sands, their roars of displeasure shaking the crowd until the mighty monsters choked off their cries with dead flesh. Their white fur grew stained with blood and gore as they tore apart those coming too close to their master. The yetis discarded limbs as they worked their way back to the dementia caster. The enemy mage's black spears dived to spill life to the ground. But despite the humanoids' bulk, they dodged the dark weapons with ease, their agility honed by the mountain cliffs their kind regularly traveled. They wrung their way up the line of zombies, and Kamahl raised his hammer, waiting for the next attack.

The crowd cried out as the yetis approached the enemy, their bloody hands reaching for the weedy mage. The dementia caster dropped, and his body heaved. Kamahl paused, holding his minions in case his opponent was surrendering, uncertain with all the particulars of this arena.

A wave of corrupting flesh seemed to spew from the underworld. The zombies Apel called forth vanished, disappearing or devoured by his newest creation. The mass lunged for the approaching yetis, lifting itself into the air and spreading out in a great sheet of corruption. The mountain apes disappeared under the dark spell as the mound fell with a thunderous retort. The impact ruptured coffins buried in the dirt. Bodies lolled on the ground and were swallowed by the spreading wave.

The crowd called for Kamahl's defeat, cheering for their favorite. The barbarian was done with calling monster and readied his hammer. The iron head fell as the first tendrils reached him. The maul struck the ground, a shattering concussion setting the sand rolling, flinging back the formless flesh. The jack took a step forward as his hammer thundered again. The magic concussion splattered the corruption back, the waves of power shaking the stands. The strength of his attack diminished as Kamahl controlled his power.

He cleaved a path with reverberating blows, working his way across the arena until he stood before Apel. The power assaulted the mage's bones, and he leaned on his staff, too unsteady to remain upright without the support. The barbarian raised his hammer and paused to allow the dementia caster to forfeit. The necromancer bowed his head in defeat.

Cheers sounded as Kamahl nodded magnanimously and offered his hand in a show of sportsmanship. The barbarian turned and bowed to the proprietors in their box and the crowd in the stands. The fighter started for the exit and the alehouse, anxious to wash the stench of the dead from his frame.

* * * * *

The serving girl scooped meat onto the barbarian's trencher, and the gravy started to sink into the bread. Kamahl took a bite, and the juices tasted delicious as he washed the meal down with ale.

The other customers regarded him warmly, despite his defeat of the local fighter. The novelty of a new opponent gave him a popularity he had not received in Cabal City. The hill tavern was full, as new patron came to view the stranger. His deliberate air of mystery was another draw. So far, Kamahl had given no name except that of his new weapon. The ivory and iron creation lay across the table as enthusiasts walked slowly by, caressing it with their eyes.

The dementia caster's defeat and the adulation of the crowd pleased the barbarian. His battle had been the climax of the night. It had been a short bill with only the duel between an unknown and the local champion bringing an crowd. The enthusiasm and respect was heady, but Kamahl remembered this was only single step in his quest for the orb

A group crowded closer to his table, and he looked up Three young men dressed in armor and carrying brand-new weapons coughed for his attention. None of their gear showed wear, and most appeared of indifferent quality.

Two of them were dark, their skins rough from exposure to the weather. They were fit but were uncomfortable with their weapons. The middle boy was tall and thin, with muscle showing but lacking the calluses of his companions. He wore his clothes and elegant boots well enough. However, he seemed no more at ease with the sword at his hip than his companions.

The barbarian wondered if they were working up the nerve to challenge him or pick a fight to show their own bravery. Many jacks reveled in such fights but not Kamahl.

"You have a question?" he growled, his irritation deepening his voice. They jumped back, then two pushed the center of their trio forward.

"If you please, sir," the blond said hesitantly, his hands falling to his belt, "we wondered if you might be available for students seeking instruction."

Kamahl laughed shortly, the boys' faces reddening. His mirth was more at his own expense than the youngsters', but the adolescents were wound too tightly for any hint of humor. They started to withdraw, but the barbarian called them back.

"Your pardon, sirs," Kamahl apologized. "I expected a different question. Please join me." The three drew up stools and sat down. The serving wench brought more tankards at the barbarian's wave.

"I am Girter, son of a chandler," the blond boy said, giving a seated bow. "These are my friends Wasel and Birten. Their father owns two fishing boats. We hope to learn magic from you," he added bluntly

"Why me?" the mountain mage asked. "Surely there are others willing to teach, fighters from the arena perhaps." He took a sip as he thought. To be a fighting master was a serious relationship in the mountains. He had spent years working with his mentor and could not see himself in such a role for now. But he remembered his own stumbling steps in search of magic. Perhaps he could help the boys.

"We want you to teach us because there are few willing to teach. Apel and Enoch will both take students, but we feel uneasy with calling on the dead. Besides, you are the first in quite some time to beat either of them," Girter said, his friends nodding in agreement.

"I do not know my own plans," Kamahl said, playing for time. "I will offer my opinions on the available teachers. I have skill, but you need a master rather than a fighter. I leave soon, in any case. It depends on what I learn about the trade caravans."

"My father is completely familiar with them," Girter exclaimed, flushing with pleasure now, rather than rage.

"Our father sometimes hauls out cargo from the caravans to the freight ships waiting in the bay," one of the brothers chimed in. "Though there isn't much call for his services anymore."

"Yes," said Girter with a frown, reclaiming the conversation. "The number of wagons hauling cargo to the coast plummeted when the Order became more active. Th caravans across the continent, searching for a stole

"They say that an agent for the Cabal stole belonging to the head of the Order. She h in her sleep." One of the dark-haired boys—the barbarian thought it Wasel—spoke with a certain amount of relish.

"I heard an ambassador from the emperor's court and his fighting frog stole it during an animal attack on the captain," his brother Birten said, determined to speak at least once.

"They even say a metal-skinned barbarian killed the captain and her lieutenant and stole away a great treasure," Girter confessed, glancing toward Kamahl. His friends looked nervously at the mountain fighter, who smiled back.

"I never had the pleasure of meeting the captain.,"

The three youths laughed uproariously as if Kamahl told a great jest.

"I am, however, interested in occurrences inland. Perhaps I will return that way. I also might travel by ship, so I would appreciate any news of the empire. Please join me, and we will talk more."

Kamahl watched them wave for the waitress and wondered how many rumors and false trails battled with the truth. Perhaps he would stay in Borben a while, finding news sources from the empire. One thing was certain—further travel was pointless without more information.

CHAPTER 23

"Shall we come to order?" Laquatus called as the generals gathered around the table. The delicate murals on the throne room walls twinkled like submerged stars, the emperor's image looming over his councilors and servants. In the continent's dead buildings, the ambassador could take the image down or cover it. However, in the sea, the palace itself would bleed the image through any barrier. Besides, Laquatus could not decide the fate of the emperor's face, not just yet.

Already he had turned the throne room into the command center. From here he directed the action against the supposed rebels and agents of the queen. Aboshan had retired to his rooms in disarray. There he spent his time in debauchery with occasional bouts when he planned paranoid purges. Increasingly, the court relied on Laquatus to deal with the day to day running of the palace. Many decisions, formerly the exclusive domain of the emperor, were decided by him. Best of all, he was able to blame the bolder and bloody moves on the now isolated ruler.

A general droned on, but the ambassador ignored him for now. Most members of the new ruling body were military for Laquatus had taken over the government's civilian functions. Ministers who were former rivals or could impede his decisions were already cleared away. The obstacles were removed by denunciation. Some died, and others fled to the southern courts, proving their treachery or at least their taste for living.

The valuable and respected ministers presented more of a problem. Too many traitors in the government's highest ranks might lead Aboshan to suspect Laquatus. Remembering the effect of his own exile in isolating him, the ambassador found compelling reasons for the highest officials to be sent abroad or to the empire's hinterlands. Embassies opened in dozens of cities, and the reluctant diplomats tried to remove the queen from her undersea allies.

Many of those courtiers remaining in the palace found themselves elevated due to Laquatus's influence and transferred their loyalty to him. Having the whip hand over the civilian administration, the ambassador was considering his next target—the army. It agitated constantly for additional funds, soldiers, and action. Even now, officers looked to him to implement their latest recommendations. He wondered what they were.

"I will hear the next report and inform you of the
mperor's decisions regarding your requests, General." He
ould glance at the wax-covered slate later. He might even
cure a decision if he thought the outcome personally
vorable.

Another officer began to report, and Laquatus wondered
ow to gain ascendancy over the army. The problem was
oving more resistant to his attempts to weed out leaders.
he military had a higher sense of duty and loyalty to its
vn institutions. Moreover, he could not steer his own can-
dates to empty positions. Any openings were still filled at
e pleasure of the commanding generals.

What he needed was an eviscerating purge of the army's
ficer corps. Laquatus needed his own armed force to
plement it in the emperor's name. A personal guard, he
ought, and his eyes drifted to the rear of the throne
om. Turg and his lackeys were gathered together, gam-
ing quietly. The killers and scoundrels his jack recruited
id led in the raids lacked the strict discipline demanded
the army. However, there were many castes and species
ocean society that could be played against each other.
he lower orders had their place, and if a bloodthirsty few
anaged to improve their lot to the ambassador's benefit,
e saw no harm. His jack could find more compatriots
hile he looked for an excuse for Aboshan to create
other army.

He thought of the emperor entombed in his rooms with
aquatus controlling access to the monarch. Expanding the
rrent system of spies and thugs in a serious military force
ould not be too difficult. He could use subtle innuendo about
e military's loyalty to the emperor. However, that course was
sky. Aboshan might take personal command of the army

leaving no forces loyal only to the ambassador. Perhaps it wa[s] time to find avenues to power beside manipulations in th[e] throne room.

"Thank you all for your time," Laquatus said suddenl[y] cutting another general off in mid-speech. "I believe thes[e] problems deserve an immediate response. I will go to ou[r] beloved ruler and urge him to act on these concerns a[s] soon as possible."

Many officers could not hide their irritation at the abrup[t] dismissal, but it was hard to complain of an advisor movin[g] promptly to convey their problems to the sovereign.

Turg, he commanded mentally, *ready to leave for th[e] vaults.*

The frog resisted, wanting to stay with his companion[s.] The ambassador swam over, wondering what could be s[o] engrossing. A huge glass cover from the imperial kitchens la[y] on a tabletop. The amphibian and a triton released fightin[g] fish under the glass, sealing them in. The fish, at first, swelle[d] until one appeared bigger than its opponent did. Laquatu[s] thought of Aboshan's swollen ego as one tried to drive th[e] other off. But the lesser was trapped and could not escap[e.] Both fish attacked, forced to combat because one could n[ot] leave. The noble dragged his jack away, sick of resistance t[o] his will. The other scum scattered at his show of wrath.

Laquatus led the sullen champion to a waiting room. H[e] could leave for the treasure rooms in a little while. He coul[d] afford a little time to adjust his servant's attitude. The frog[']s sounds of distress carried into the throne room as his maste[r] took pains to educate him.

* * * * *

"My enemies decay in the depths," Aboshan, Emperor of the Seas, chuckled as he reviewed the execution lists. The wax showed his enemies' names, and he rubbed them out in glee, imagining himself rubbing them out of existence. He *had* erased them. No one mentioned their names for fear of contamination, and the state already held their property, appropriated in his name.

The past weeks had been difficult. He constantly feared conspirators might break in despite the increased guards and secret police. He stopped allowing his attendants into his quarters because assassins might infiltrate them. He had been reduced to looking at the names of his dead enemies. Suddenly he was afraid, perhaps removing them from the death lists would bring them back to plague him.

He rolled in the water several times, trying to shake off the black thoughts oppressing him. His forces were stripping the empire of criminals every day. Arrest and execution warrants traveled with the army and the police. He was growing safer, he reminded himself.

The emperor needed to get out, to make sure something existed outside these rooms. But where could he go where his enemies might not find him. Aboshan suddenly remembered the vaults and the land walkers that he employed to service his treasures. Surely in the depths of the palace he would be safe. Yes, he would go and see what wonders had been reclaimed.

"Guards!" he screamed, wanting to leave but afraid to unless surrounded. The waters frothed with predatory fish seeking attackers as mermen sped from their posts at the doors.

"What is it, Your Majesty?" a guard asked, his fellows splitting to sweep the room for intruders.

"We wish to inspect the treasure rooms under the palace," he commanded, his voice stronger than it had been in some time. "Have them cleared of undesirables for our tour."

The guard stared slackly then retreated at Aboshan's angry expression.

Servants streamed in as the announcement spread of the emperor leaving his rooms. They brought his jewelry and worked to make him presentable. The uneasiness made him wonder if he should stay. But it had been so long. . . .

He must not allow his subjects to think him cowering in a corner. He was in control, not the rebels or his wife. Not even his loyal servant Laquatus directed the path of the empire. The realm was his to use as he saw fit. Aboshan resolutely swept out into the halls. Guards raced down side passages to clear a path for the monarch, unable to cut in front of the emperor.

The halls appeared deserted, the ruler knowing many feared to be in his presence while his moods were so unpredictable. They must learn to live with it, he decided. He would not be a pariah in his own house. The passage wound down to the sea floor. Light blazed from normally dark walls as the palace reacted to his presence.

Aboshan reached the bedrock. A shimmering bubble stretched across the room to a partition. He could see a squad of tresias chivying someone behind the screen. At least he would not have to soil himself by looking on the land-bound. The sentry bowed to the ground, his stalk pivoting to bring his torso flat to the rock. The emperor ignored him as he swam closer to the bubble of air. The monarch remembered his ministers creating the spell. The problems with item preservation dictated that Aboshan,

ho despised all above the sea, have a pocket of air and dry
and in his own house. Worse, he could not swim among his
treasures but must walk on legs.

"Avert your eyes as we inspect our treasures," the
mperor told the guards. He swam closer, then passed into
he bubble. He writhed with unexpected pain. He had
uried his ability to form legs at least as deep as the treas-
res below. He lay on the floor, gasping for air as his ten-
acles combined and formed legs. He laboriously expelled
vater cleared from his new lungs. He tried to stand, but
is muscles protested. The best he could manage was a
rawl as he neared the trapdoor. He sat at the top of the
tairs leading down, the air feeling as chill as the ocean
epths. At last he slid down the wooden steps. He gripped
he banister and laboriously pulled himself to his newly
reated feet.

The room was lit by unpleasantly flaring lamps. Crys-
al globes captured traces of fire and threw their harsh
ays from the chamber's corners. The shelves erected on
he floor were taller than his head, his treasures laid upon
hem and cataloged. He tottered toward the first set, grip-
ing the sides as his feet shuffled over the uneven floor.

Some of the wooden planks groaned under their loads.
The steel and glass heads of forgotten fighting machines
tared at him as he worked his way down the aisle. Mechan-
cal limbs threw threatening shadows. He passed a section
of knives, their wavy edges promising death to who ever
ouched the blade, the wielder as well as the victim. A pile
of jewels, separated by type, covered the wood at the end of
he aisle.

"Is this all?" he asked himself. Where were the magics to
weep away his enemies? He had no interest in baubles or

small devices. He could draw on an empire to build h
armies. These items were inconsequential compared to h
might under the sea. Perhaps the greater wonders wer
deeper under the palace?

Aboshan moved toward the hole leading down to th
next room. His stride improved as he went down the ladde
He was no weakling to be overwhelmed by walking. Th
shelves seemed more of the same. A projector lay groanin
on a set of tables. He could see the spears containe
through gaps in the mechanism. The weapon might make
single warrior or machine nigh unstoppable but was of n
use against the hordes a war must bring.

He strained to topple the trestles. He snarled at his impo
tence as he tried to move weights unsupported by water fo
the first time. Dry land oppressed him. All but a tiny frac
tion of his forces could not leave the water at all. The con
tinent's interior seemed remote as distant islands to the sav
ages inhabiting the world of air.

The real weapons must be hidden. He stretched out hi
senses, drifting between the shelves. He could smell th
water and mud down in the lower levels. His eyes saw littl
sign of hidden cases or rooms as he worked his way back. I
was only his meticulous attention to the walls that tippe
him off.

One section of rock changed slowly as the light bright
ened. The shift reminded him of the palace walls, but i
appeared bare rock. He approached and let his senses wasl
over it. The surface was a façade, and he felt the thrill o
discovering a secret trove. His will grated against the sur
face, and the covering slowly sloughed away. Water poure
out, murky and stinking of metal and rot. The cache mus
predate the Cabal's arrival, Aboshan realized. The forme

curator must have hidden the object before dying in the rebel attack.

A leather sack lay on the floor. The emperor knelt down, nearly falling as he performed the maneuver. He opened the bag, the material tearing like paper. He held the world in his hands.

The orb was brilliant blue, the globe's surface covered in places by chop, as waves and weather collided. The depths of the sphere called to him, speaking its name.

"Mirari," the emperor whispered.

He stared in wonder, his senses diving beneath the surface to explore the world he ruled. The abysmal depths called to him, and he raced to answer.

The orb spun out of his hands as he toppled, the ball rolling away to fetch up against a shelf. The emperor's legs split into tentacles. He thrashed in panic as his lungs tried to turn back to gills. His mind convinced he swam in the ocean, his body had attempted to adapt to the new reality. Aboshan shuddered as his magic slowly halted the transformation and forced himself to revert to his land-bound form.

He rolled upright, furious that his being could betray him so. He walked quickly to the orb, the sphere's glory feeling slightly less. He stooped to pick it up and rapped his head against the wood.

"Everything conspires against us!" Aboshan swore, closing his eyes against the pain. "Forced to walk on legs like a common animal. How I despise them all!" The ruler put his tentacles to his head as if to press the anger back in. The land assaulted his mind. Even for the care of treasures like the orb he depended on the Cabal. He wondered what trick they had prepared for him?

He held the Mirari before his eyes. The sphere's endless seas were swept by waves without land's interruption.

"That is what I want. For my kingdom to stretch on forever." Perhaps his wife might come back to him if he were more powerful. But the continents seemed forever beyond his reach.

"We will sweep you all away!" he said madly and thrust his magic into the sphere.

CHAPTER 24

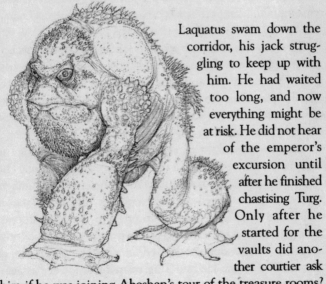

Laquatus swam down the corridor, his jack struggling to keep up with him. He had waited too long, and now everything might be at risk. He did not hear of the emperor's excursion until after he finished chastising Turg. Only after he started for the vaults did another courtier ask him if he was joining Aboshan's tour of the treasure rooms?

"What do you mean?" Laquatus bellowed, as he crowded the noble back. His champion took hold of the aristocrat's limbs. Outrage filled the minister's face as the amphibian laid hands on him.

"I demand you let me go," he hissed. The frog broke his

prisoner's collarbones at his master's surge of irritation.

"You might heal if you hurry to a doctor," the ambassador said intently, giving the broken bones a nudge with his hand. "Or you could suffer injuries leaving you with flippers instead of hands." Turg gave the noble a simple fracture in a lower arm. Guards and servants ignored the impromptu torture session. It was unhealthy of late to be interested in Laquatus's business.

"He is clearing the treasure rooms of workers and will inspect the rooms in person. He left while you talked with this animal." Turg broke his other arm in passing as Laquatus rushed to the vaults in the depths of the palace.

The way was clear, the servants keeping as much space as possible between themselves and their sovereign. The aristocrat passed guards and checkpoints, but they were never challenged. The ambassador was now the second most powerful person in the northern court, but he could be cast down at the emperor's whim.

Laquatus passed the interior banquet rooms, ignoring the delicacies that eternally awaited a courtier's dining. The hall changed shape and direction as he passed chambers that had been sealed at the emperor's pleasure. Rumors abounded of disloyal subjects interred in the finest rooms, lacking nothing but an exit. The swim was taking too long, and the ambassador accelerated, cursing the grand airs of the marine rulers. He and Turg neared the lower passages, leading to the vaults. There were few doors here, most of the space devoted to the organs which allowed the palace to live. Laquatus passed members of the imperial guard, posted to protect the emperor as he toured the bowels of the palace. A giant squid jetted back and forth through the narrow corridor. The ambassador wanted to force it aside.

However, he knew how aggressive the cephalopods were, so he slowed and gave it as wide a berth as possible. A huge eye looked him over as the ambassador continued on. It took seconds to pass the monster. The long whips stretched beyond the other tentacles. Laquatus dodged the long clubs with their oversized hooked suction cups.

The squid was one of Aboshan's proudest achievements, recruited from the queen's allies in the abyss. The emperor proved at least in his own mind that he could compete with his wife. The pair neared the entrance to the vaults.

The sessile warrior still floated on his stalk. He held a trident in his hands as he directed the guards in moving a partition. Laquatus was surprised to see Fulla and her companions penned in the bubble set over the trapdoor. The air was stretched until it resembled a loaf of bread. The spell seemed to be straining. The dementia caster poked her hand out through the water barrier, watching the boundary ripple with interest.

"Guard," the ambassador said, drawing the stationary fighter to attention. The arms on the rooted figure crossed as he drew himself upright. "I would speak with the emperor."

Laquatus wondered how he would deal with an outraged sovereign. He had no idea how obvious the Cabal's looting operation of the vaults was. Aboshan might have no idea anything untoward was happening.

The flare of powerful magic seemed to fill the room. A massive spell's presence set the magical field to vibrating. The air bubble shook violently as the palace spells interacted with the new force. With a sinking heart Laquatus realized Aboshan must have found the orb.

"I must see the emperor now," the aristocrat demanded, determined to find out what was happening. The guard

twisted his stalk, the trident no longer at attention but lo
ered for use.

"Absolutely not," the sessile warrior said flatly, coiling
his long stalk as if to lunge forward. "His imperial maje
did not wish to be disturbed, so none shall pass. Th
emperor allowed for no exceptions." The soldier waved f
reinforcements from the corridor.

These guards might move from where they were root
only a few times in their lives. As a result, Laquatus believe
they were the most stubborn and unyielding guards in
existence. Rigid obedience to all orders was their tradema

Another pulse shook the ether, but this time the co
cussion was also physical. The ambassador felt the wat
surging in sympathy to some spell perpetuated by Abosha
Laquatus remembered the disaster that had struck t
Order. Aboshan had no interest in what happened to t
Citadel, and Laquatus neglected to share the informatic
for fear of drawing the emperor's attention to the orb. Ev
now a spell might be encasing the vaults in impenetrab
crystal. The palace wall shivered as a new wave of ener
blasted through the living tissue.

"There is no time," Laquatus growled as his comman
leaped from his mind to the palace walls. His authori
unquestioned by any in the court, the building obeyed. Th
walls closed. Laquatus imagined the panic that must be fi
ing the upper floors of the building for he did not limit h
command. He wondered how many would die as the pa
sage pinched shut, sealing the troops away from th
emperor. The giant squid the ambassador had passed jett
down the corridor, it speed blinding as it tore into th
vaults' antechamber, getting through the door before la
tices of chitin and coral could crimp the passage shut.

and walked farther away from the building. He had never felt a spell of such strength. His prize must be close by, but there was no sign of anything strange. The town looked perfectly calm as the fisherman and wagon drivers went about their business. Then something dragged the barbarian's eyes back to the sea.

The boats along the pier lowered as water flowed out of the inlet. The bay continued to drop, and soon boats were hung up. The catch of fish fell to the exposed mud below.

Interested, people went toward the bay to see the unusual event. Here and there a few figures started running as hard as they could for the hills. More and more people fled, and he wondered why. A flicker of movement brought his eyes to the horizon. Something was coming toward all points of the coast. The line grew to a wave striking the beaches far in the distance. He realized the size of the disaster as he saw tall trees stripped away. He looked directly to the sea, the hilly peninsula shielding him from the closest view. A roar smothered screams as a wall of water carried over the hills and fell down the slope toward the town. Now everyone in sight ran for higher ground.

The hatred and spite of the spell were nauseating as Kamahl started higher into the hills, not knowing how high the water might carry. The sound of smashing houses and shops tore the day apart. The barbarian wondered if anyone would survive the disaster. He stumbled as a new note of magic, just as strong as the first, stung his senses. The orb's magic was what drove the wave he guessed, but the bitter emotions drained away as the wave sped toward him. The magic was changed, and Kamahl knew the orb no longer belonged to the sea. Then a blast of air pushed him over, and the water came down.

* * * * *

Laquatus saw the orb lose its beauty, the blue ocean fading away until only gleaming metal remained. The imperial bastard, Aboshan, had cost him everything. The orb still radiated tremendous power as he looked at it, but it no longer resonated with his soul. His spirits sank lower as he realized he might be trapped here with Fulla. Who knew what insane spell she would cast now that she held the orb in her hands?

The dementia caster held the orb absently as she kicked through the destruction, sending water high into the air. Another aftershock threw her off her feet, and Laquatus slowly sat up, hoping she would lose her grip on the orb. Instead she surfaced from the water spitting a stream of the filthy liquid into the air.

I need a spell to distract her while she played likes a lunatic, he thought. If he could just capture the orb maybe he could recall its glory. But he could not grip any magic with his mind. The wound inflicted by Turg's death was crippling. The gaping hole of his bond allowed his magic to flow uncontrolled. If he were more prepared, he might have avoided it, but for now his spells pushed power to one no longer alive. An infinite void swallowed his effort, and he could not force the mental focus to end the drain.

Fulla seated herself on the stairs, bored with her horseplay. She looked at the guard enveloped by her predatory plant. She began to throw debris at him. Laquatus stood up and started toward her. The body of his former sovereign floated past, and he shoved it aside, ignoring it like a forgotten toy. The room plunged into darkness as the palace light system failed. The merman tried to coax forth light, but the Cabal member called up a luminescent mold that coated the walls.

Fulla glance absently at the orb but turned to the rising water. The air was becoming stuffy. She tucked the powerful item under her legs and looked at the ambassador. He hid his disbelief at her dismissive attitude toward the orb.

Laquatus decided that her resistance to its attractions was related to her resilience to his own magical attacks on her mind. Dementia casters simply lived in a different world. Their perceptions of reality were so strange that perhaps the orb appeared mundane. Maybe it replicated some other effect they experienced often. Regardless, she showed little interest, and perhaps he could procure the sphere from her at a later date.

"We must escape," he told her, sitting down close to her but out of sword's reach. "This air bubble will disperse sooner or later. Unless you wish to die, you must flee to the surface."

"Why not swim away, little fish?" she asked, kicking the orb back and forth between her feet. "It is a big pond, and you are old enough to be on your own."

Laquatus curbed his first answer.

There was every chance some of the guards survived to report his treachery. At this very moment, his name might be added to the execution warrants that he signed this morning. The blanks concealed in his office with the emperor's seal already imprinted seemed a very bad idea now. The orb might be the only thing rescued from this debacle. If only he had brought his poison rings.

"You saved me, and I owe you a debt I can never repay," he said, curbing his nausea at the sentiment. "Perhaps

working together we can reach the surface." If she woul
just help him clear the way, she could drown. A corpse ha
no possessions.

Another shock collapsed the stairs, and they fell into th
water. The ambassador saw that she swam with difficul
though she still managed to find the orb. She struggled t
one of the few shelves still standing.

Next time she is in the water I'll pull her under, Laqua
tus promised himself.

*   *   *   *   *

Fulla looked down at the merman who stood smiling lik
a shark. The bodies, the threat of death, and the danger o
betrayal was comforting—just like home. If she returned t
the Cabal it would be a disaster. Her mission to the sea ha
failed. Despite her manic outer denial, she could feel depres
sion threatening to crush her. Returning as a failure was no
an option.

But perhaps she could return to the arena instead o
being bundled off to distant postings. She weighed the or
in her hand. She found it mildly interesting, but othe
seemed to covet it beyond all reason. Even now the ambas
sador waited for his chance to steal it. Only the chance tha
he might become interesting kept him alive.

It was dark and cold in the vault. Her ears started to hur
as the last remnants of the air supply spell failed. It was tim
to go home. Home, where a person could find a decen
graveyard and strangers could disappear without awkwar
questions.

Laquatus meant nothing to her. She needed no aid t
escape from something as simple as a collapsing underwate

building. The plant still held a pocket of air though the earthquake might rip it free any moment. She concentrated, calling into being a mount she had studied for a long time.

The travel fish faded into being. Its flesh was transparent, and the dementia caster could see the bones and organs pulsing inside its monstrous body. It flopped and wallowed in the shallow water, the wave it created reinforcing its gigantic size. She watched the ambassador jump for safety as the fish smashed whatever was in its way.

"Be still," she commanded, and it was. Laquatus was talking, but she ignored the words lost in her new creation. She stood before a blind eye, the monster unable to see except through her. The pressure was increasing, and she knew that the chamber must be moments away from catastrophic failure.

The fish turned, and its mouth gaped open, the toothless jaws stretching wide, inviting her in. She laughed, waved to the merman, and leaped into the monster's throat. She slid down the tube to the stomach still able to see the outside. It reminded her of her childhood, and she wished she could go again but time was running out. She knelt in the monster's belly, the chamber draining of the water that accompanied her on her entrance. The travel fish transported its passengers inside, and the room expanded as she stood up, her gigantic steed responding to her will.

She could see Laquatus hurling himself into the fish. She wondered if the monster should gulp him down in pieces, for the jaws were strong enough to shatter bone. No time for such rough horseplay she decided and turned her attention to the outside.

Fulla dispelled her plant, the rotting vines vanishing.

The cork holding the air pocket down ruptured. The corpses caught in its grip floated free as the travel fish wriggled through the hole to the first room and the trap door. The chamber was full of debris, but the fish blindly searched the murky water and surged out of the bedrock.

The palace gaped open above them, a direct path to the ocean torn through the structure. The travel fish surged up, its motion jostling the dementia caster against the ambassador. She half-drew her sword, hating his touch.

"Wait, good caster," Laquatus cried, throwing himself back against the stomach wall. "Remember our agreement on shipping treasures back to the Cabal. I can still be of use."

The travel fish shot out of the palace. Huge rents in the sea floor sent gas bubbling to the surface. There were few signs of other survivors. The Cabal operative imagined them swimming far away. The empire was decimated, and the noble who had overseen its fate sat beside her. She laughed and loosed the ball the fascinated Laquatus so.

Fulla looked at the sphere as the fish swam up through the depths. The orb called to her, entreating her to commune, telling her its name—Mirari—but she ignored it. Most of her attention went to directing her steed. The glassy fish swam away from the destruction and violence that even now reduced the mer capital. Fulla turned the beast to avoid the currents rising from the sea floor.

The dementia caster regarded her stolen prize. The Mirari had turned from liquid metal as she rescued it from the dead emperor's grasp. A ball of dirt lay in her hands, the black soil reminding her of a grave. She believed the change inconsequential as her senses often misled her. Still, something lay beneath the surface, and part of her ached to raise it up. Perhaps the orb really did promise power. She noticed Laquatus's trepidation as he regarded her in the dull light glowing from the fish's belly.

Fulla chuckled and tossed the sphere into the air, laughing harder as the ambassador barely restrained himself from diving for it. She opened a pouch and dropped it in, closing the leather bag without hesitation.

"It offers you what you want, not what you need," she crowed to Laquatus, thumping her purse. The call of the globe was lost and muted in the fractured horror of her mind, its visions overwhelmed by the dementia of her calling. Grim merriment filled the undead steed as she directed it to shore, leaving the corpse of a kingdom behind her.

Magic The Gathering®

Invasion Cycle J. Robert King

The struggle for the future of Dominaria has begun.

Book I
Invasion
After eons of plotting beyond time and space, the horrifying Phyrexians have come to reclaim the homeland that once was theirs.

Book II
Planeshift
The first wave is over, but the invasion rages on. The artificial plane of Rath overlays on Dominaria, covering the natural landscape with the unnatural horrors of Phyrexia.
February 2001

Book III
Apocalypse
Witness the conclusion of the world-shattering Phyrexian invasion!
June 2001

MAGIC: THE GATHERING is a registered trademark owned by Wizards of the Coast, Inc.
©2001 Wizards of the Coast, Inc.

MAGIC: The Gathering®

Legends Cycle Clayton Emery

Book I: Johan

Hazezon Tamar, merchant-mayor of the city of Bryce, had plenty of problems before he encountered Jaeger, a mysterious stranger that is half-man and half-tiger. Now Hazezon is caught up in a race against time to decipher the mysterious prophecy of None, One, and Two, while considering the significance of Jaeger's appearance. Only by understanding these elements can he save his people from the tyranny and enslavement of the evil wizard Johan, ruler of the dying city of Tirras.

April 2001

Book II: Jedit

Jedit Ojanen, the son of the legendary cat man Jaeger, sets out on a journey to find his father. Like his father, he collapses in the desert and is left for dead until he is rescued. But rescued by whom? And why? Only the prophecy of None, One, and Two holds the answers.

December 2001

MAGIC: THE GATHERING is a registered trademark owned by Wizards of the Coast, Inc.
©2001 Wizards of the Coast, Inc.

Tales from the world of Magic

Dragons of Magic
ED. J. ROBERT KING

From the time of the Primevals to the darkest hours of the Phyrexian Invasion, dragons have filled Dominaria. Few of their stories have been told—until now. Learn the secrets of the most powerful dragons in the multiverse!

August 2001

The Myths of Magic
ED. JESS LEBOW

Stories and legends, folktales and tall tales. These are the myths of Dominaria, stories captured on the cards of the original trading card game. Stories from J. Robert King, Francis Lebaron, and others.

The Colors of Magic
ED. JESS LEBOW

Argoth is decimated. Tidal waves have turned canyons into rivers. Earthquakes have leveled the cities. Dominaria is in ruins. Now the struggle is to survive. Tales from such authors as Jeff Grubb, J. Robert King, Paul Thompson, and Francis Lebaron.

Rath and Storm
ED. PETER ARCHER

The flying ship Weatherlight enters the dark, sinister plane of Rath to rescue its kidnapped captain. But, as the stories in this anthology show, more is at stake than Sisay's freedom.

MAGIC: THE GATHERING is a registered trademark owned by Wizards of the Coast, Inc.
©2001 Wizards of the Coast, Inc.